THE SAVAGE EARTH

THE VAMPIRE WORLD SAGA BOOK 1

P.T. HYLTON
JONATHAN BENECKE

1

ALEXANDRIA GODDARD HOPED there'd be trouble. She didn't say it out loud, of course; none of them did, but when you spent your life training to fight an enemy, it was only natural that you'd hope to meet them now and again, if only to bump chests and show them you meant business.

Her commanding officer, Captain Brickman—CB to the team—apparently had other ideas.

"This is a quick mission. We should be in and out in no more than a couple hours. We'll stay on the east side of the building, in the sunlight. Even still, I don't want you taking any chances in there."

Alex sighed. CB was a good commanding officer, but he was cautious to a fault.

They were standing in the hold of the Ground Mission Team's ship. Alex cast an anxious glance at the still-closed cargo door. She wanted to get this show on the road.

"Our Engineering department is in need of a certain kind of heating element," he continued. "Just so happens that this heating element was part of a common household appliance back in the day."

He held up a tablet and passed it down the line, so all five members of the Ground Mission Team got a good look. It showed a picture of a small, boxy appliance with a glass pitcher nestled inside it.

"It was used to make a hot, bitter drink called coffee. Apparently, they were all addicted to it, and nearly every kitchen had one of these things. Your goal is to go from apartment to apartment, grabbing as many of these as you can. Working together, we should be in and out in two hours."

Alex nudged Drew Layton, the man sitting beside her. "Wanna make a bet on who bags one of these things first?"

Drew chuckled. At thirty years old, he was five years older than Alex. He'd been on the team three years longer than her, and he never missed the opportunity to give her a hard time. "How about we go for total count? You might be quicker than me, but I'll bet I put you to shame long-term."

Alex grinned. "You're on. You'll be buying drinks tonight. Again."

"You got lucky last time. If it hadn't been for my shotgun jamming, I would have won."

"It's the poor carpenter who blames his tools, my man."

CB shot them a look, and they fell silent. "Drew, Firefly, and Alex, you'll be going down. Simmons and I will stay topside. Any questions?"

"No, sir," the team said in unison.

"Good. Let's go to work. If you would, Owl."

The pilot's voice came through their earpieces. "Roger that, Captain."

The cargo door began to open with a mechanical whir, and Alex stared out at the ruins of what had once been the city of São Paulo, Brazil.

Dorothy "Owl" Fowler's voice came through their

earpieces again. "São Paulo was the twelfth largest city in the world and the largest city in the western hemisphere."

"Do we have to do this now, Owl?" CB asked.

"It is sort of tradition, Captain," Simmons said.

Alex glanced at him. She knew Simmons well enough to be sure he wasn't happy to be staying behind on this mission, but he wasn't the type to complain. He'd do his job and hope for a better assignment the next time out. He was a true professional.

"Fine, get it over with," CB said.

"The city's population peaked around thirteen million before the infestation," Owl continued. "The official language of Brazil was Portuguese, and the city's official motto was *I am not led, I lead.*"

"Somebody take away her almanac," Drew joked.

The cargo door finished opening, and Alex leaned out and looked down at the city below. They were hovering one hundred feet above a skyscraper that seemed to be mostly intact. Even from up here, Alex could see that plant life had reclaimed most of the city. The streets were a patchwork of broken pavement with trees growing through the massive cracks, and ivy clung thickly to the face of most of the structures. The top section of the building directly below them was clear of ivy, which was part of the reason they'd selected it.

"There's no way for us to be sure of the structural integrity of the building," CB said, "so we'll hover here and lower you down. Ready to roll?"

Alex was more than ready. She clipped the rope to her vest and prepared to be lowered down.

Drew grabbed her arm. "Wait for me on the roof. It's not fair if you start working before I get down there."

"I know. You need every advantage you can get." She

stepped out the cargo door and hung suspended in the air, the decaying city of São Paulo stretched below her. The wind was brisk up here, and it whipped against her fatigues. Even still, there was something peaceful about hanging midair, neither on the ship nor the surface, but somewhere in between.

Her feet touched down on the concrete roof, and she unclipped the rope from her vest. As the other two were lowered down, she looked for a place to secure her rope. They'd be rappelling down the side of the building from here. By the time Firefly and Drew touched down, she was ready to begin her descent.

Her two teammates soon joined her on the building's edge.

"Ready?" Firefly asked.

Alex briefly considered whether she should have included Firefly in the wager, but she quickly dismissed the thought. He wasn't interested in such things. He was probably busy moping that he wasn't going to get to blow anything up on this trip.

"Ready," Alex said.

Drew and Firefly leaned back and began carefully rappelling their way down the structure.

Alex waited another moment, enjoying one last look at the city before going to work. She pulled out a pistol, took a deep breath, and leaped backward over the edge.

She'd gathered fifteen feet of slack in her rope before jumping, and she quickly dipped past Drew and Firefly. The rope went taut as she reached the bottom of her slack and swung like a pendulum toward the building. She raised her pistol and fired three quick shots into the window in front of her.

She crashed through the shattering window feet first

and swung into what had once been the living room of a luxury apartment. Her feet touched down lightly on the still-beautiful hardwood floor. Sunlight streamed in from the floor-to-ceiling hole that had until moments ago been a window.

Alex quickly located the kitchen. Sure enough, the appliance CB had shown them was sitting out on the counter, ready for the taking. She took the duffle bag off her back, unzipped it, and stuffed the appliance inside.

She touched the radio strapped to her chest and spoke into her headset microphone. "That's one. What's taking you guys so long?"

Over the next hour and a half, Alex, Drew, and Firefly worked their way down, apartment by apartment. They stayed on the east side of the building, where the morning sunlight shone strong. The layout of every apartment was nearly identical, so they were able to move quickly. Only a few kitchens didn't have the appliance, though occasionally, they had to go digging through the cabinets to find it.

Alex shoved another coffee maker into her duffle bag, twisting until it fit, and the zipper still closed. "Captain, I'm full. Sending my bag up."

"Roger that," CB said in her earpiece.

She reached out the shattered window and grabbed the rope dangling from the ship. For a woozy moment, she rested her weight on it and looked down twenty stories to the broken streets below. Then she attached her bag and gave it two quick tugs. The bag began its ascent toward the ship.

"Shame you have to wait for them to empty your bag, Alex," Drew said in her earpiece. "I'm on number forty-three."

Alex cursed softly. She was only one ahead of him now,

and this level was just about cleaned out. The sun was rising fast, which meant they were losing their direct sunlight into the building. CB wouldn't let them stay down here much longer.

She grabbed her rappelling rope and leaned out. A shadow from the next building fell across her face. Glancing down, she confirmed the next level was draped in shade.

Two gunshots split the air as Drew entered his next apartment. A moment later, he proudly proclaimed, "Forty-four. All tied up."

Screw it, she was done waiting. CB could lower the bag to her on the next level down. She checked her rope one more time, then leaned backward out the window and hopped down, out of the sunlight. It felt five degrees cooler in the shade, and goosebumps sprang out on her arms as the icy wind licked her skin.

She looked up and saw Firefly on the side of the building two floors above. He glanced down at her, a curious expression on his face, but he didn't say anything.

Alex shot the window and entered the apartment. It suddenly struck her that this might not be an altogether wise move. They'd been making one hell of a racket all morning, and now she was stepping out of the safety of the sunlight.

She raised her pistol, doing a quick visual scan of the living room. She appeared to be alone.

The appliance wasn't on the counter in the kitchen. Crap. Was she risking her life for nothing in here? She started digging through cabinets.

CB's voice came through her earpiece. "Alex, what's your twenty?"

She pushed aside pots and pans but came up empty and

moved on to the higher cabinets, keeping one eye on the living room for movement. "I dropped down a level, sir."

"Are you in the shade right now?" CB's voice betrayed his concern.

"A little. But I'll be back in the sun in a moment." She opened the cabinet next to the refrigerator and hit pay dirt. The cabinet was stuffed with a handful of appliances, and there, in the back, was the one she was after. She knocked the others out of the way to get to it.

"Don't be an idiot, Alex!" CB said.

"Captain, I'm sending up another bag," Firefly said.

"Okay, I'm calling it," CB said. "We've got enough. You three head back up."

"Forty-five," Alex said triumphantly.

"You've got to be kidding me!" Drew said with a moan.

Something in the living room moved, and Alex spun toward the motion, pistol raised.

The living room was empty now, and yet she was almost sure she'd seen something.

She backed toward the window, keeping her gun trained on the living room. "Where are you, you bastard?" she whispered.

As she reached the window and clipped herself in, a low, animalistic growl came from somewhere deep in the apartment.

"Alex, you coming?" CB said.

Alex's heart was racing. She stepped off the edge and hung in the air, never taking her eyes off the apartment's dark interior. "I'm all set, Captain. Let's go back to *New Haven*."

2

TWO HOURS after returning to *New Haven*, Alex headed to a bar called Tankards, out near the agricultural district. It was a long walk from the GMT headquarters, but it was worth it for the quiet and the anonymity. To get there, she had to pass through Sparrow's Ridge, the neighborhood with the densest population in the city, and through the Hub, the center of all things, where the most important members of society lived in more spacious quarters.

The bartender, Louie, gave her a friendly nod as she entered, but didn't say a word. That was part of what she loved about this place. Louie understood that people weren't coming here for lively conversations with him. People came to this inconveniently located bar because they either wanted to be alone or wanted to have a conversation away from the prying ears that were all too prevalent in the busier sections of town. Keeping secrets in *New Haven* was difficult.

Alex headed straight for a large table in the corner. She knew Drew, Firefly, Owl, and maybe even Simmons would be along shortly for a drink. The team needed to wind down after a dangerous mission like the one today, and they nearly always ended up here, in an unspoken, unplanned practice that was becoming a tradition.

The bar was nearly empty tonight, and it was quiet enough that Alex could hear two men at a nearby table talking in hushed tones.

"It's a pipe dream," the first man said. He was heavyset and spoke in a low, rumbly voice.

"Maybe it *was*," the other said. He was short, thin, and had a truly impressive mustache. "Now we've got Fleming on our side. Resettlement is a very real possibility. It could happen in the next few years."

The fat one scoffed.

"Mark my words," the one with the mustache said. "Councilman Fleming isn't like the others. He's gonna make things happen."

Alex did her best to ignore the conversation. The last thing she wanted to do when she was supposed to be unwinding was to think about politics. Still, it was always there in the background, whether she chose to think about it or not. The City Council was in charge of the GMT and approved everything, from their budget to their missions. She saw the direct impact of the decisions the Council made up close and personal. She and her teammates were weapons that the Council aimed to help achieve their ends. So maybe she should care a little more about politics.

Louie set a beer down in front of her, and she nodded her thanks before he turned and walked wordlessly back to his station behind the bar.

Alex took a long pull on her beer. There was something wonderful about these post-mission nights. She'd spent the day in the former country of Brazil, rappelling down a skyscraper, facing down the possibility of an attack at any moment. And the people of *New Haven* had no idea. The secrets, the things she and her team had been through, burned like a lantern in her heart. Very few people alive had experienced the things she had. That thought—the understanding of her lucky and unique position in life—kept her going, even when things got tough.

The bell above the entrance chimed, and Alex looked up to see if it was one of her teammates. A group of three women entered, all talking at once. She shook her head and went back to her beer.

A moment later, her radio chirped. She muttered a curse and grabbed it off of her belt. Members of the Ground Mission Team were required to carry a radio at all times. They were always on call—just another perk of the job.

"Goddard here," she said into the radio.

"Alex, I need you back at the hangar." It was CB.

Alex's heart sped up just a little. Could it be another mission already? "Sure thing, Captain. What's going on?"

"I just got word Councilman Stearns is swinging by in an hour. You ready to give him that little demonstration we've been talking about?"

A slow grin spread across her face. "Yes, sir, I believe I am." She signed off, finished her beer in one long drink, and headed out the door.

———

CAPTAIN ARNOLD BRICKMAN didn't often get nervous. Over the course of his twenty-five years with the GMT, he'd seen too much. He'd witnessed unbelievable feats of courage and watched as friends and colleagues died in the heat of battle. He was a careful man, especially when it came to planning his team's missions, so it would be easy for someone who didn't know him very well to mistake his caution for nervousness. He'd faced down things on his missions that had changed him. He liked to think they'd made him wiser. But nervous? No. That was something he felt very rarely these days.

Yet, he had to admit that the impending visit of Councilman Stearns put a strange tightness in his stomach that bore at least a passing resemblance to nerves.

CB and his commanding officer, General Isiah Craig, had been trying to get Stearns to visit the GMT headquarters for over a month now. The primary purpose of the visit was to demonstrate a new type of jet pack the GMT's Research and Development team had created, but the larger goal was to get the Council to increase funding for R&D all around. General Craig and CB hoped that if Councilman Stearns saw the jet pack that they'd been able to build with the shoestring budget they'd been working on, he might be more inclined to see what they could do with some real resources.

CB turned to Alex, who was standing next to him, dressed in a flight suit, the lightweight jet pack barely visible on her back. "You ready for this?"

"Yes, sir," Alex said.

"Good. We won't get a second chance. The key here is control. Stearns already knows this thing's expensive. We need to convince him it's worth the resources."

The plan was for Alex to demonstrate the jet pack by hovering fifteen feet in the air inside the hangar. CB wanted to show the ability of the jet pack to operate accurately in tight quarters. If they wanted to see more, Alex would zoom around the hangar, showing her control of the device. Alex was good with the jet pack, and he was confident the councilman would be impressed.

He stared out the glass wall of the hangar to the road

beyond. General Craig was already waiting out there. In the distance, an electric cart was approaching.

"That'll be him," CB said. "I better get out there."

CB trotted outside and arrived at the general's side just as the cart pulled up in front of him. CB was surprised to see it wasn't just Councilman Stearns. He'd brought Daniel Fleming, the newest and youngest member of the City Council. CB didn't know a lot about Fleming, other than the fact that he was the leader of the opposition party and had a passionate following, primarily among the people of Sparrow's Ridge. Fleming was maybe thirty-five years old, about half Stearns's age. They made quite the odd pair, especially because of their frequent political clashes during Fleming's recent campaign.

CB exchanged a quick glance with General Craig. This had to be a good thing. They were getting two councilmen for their demonstration instead of one.

The councilmen rolled their cart to a stop and got off. Councilman Stearns introduced Fleming to CB and the general.

"I know it doesn't look like much," Stearns said to Fleming, indicating the large building in front of them, "but nearly a tenth of the City Council's resources goes into this place."

CB had to admit that the councilman was right on his first point. The hangar that served as the center of the GMT's headquarters might have easily been mistaken for a warehouse, if you didn't notice the burly men with guns standing near each of the three entrances.

"Fleming wanted to see this place for himself," Stearns said.

"Excellent," General Craig said. "If you'll follow me

inside, we'll get started. We've prepared a little demonstration."

Stearns shook his head. "It's been a hell of a day, General. We spent most of it in the Agricultural section, listening to Director Williams drone on about corn. You can imagine how mind-numbing that was. Then we spent the afternoon in Engineering, which wasn't much better. Honestly, if Councilman Fleming hadn't insisted, I wouldn't be standing here."

CB did his best to keep the shock off of his face. After all this planning, they weren't even going to come into the hangar?

General Craig cleared his throat. "Of course. Totally understandable. If you would just come into the hangar for a moment, we have something to show you that I promise will wake you up a little."

"This isn't about the jet packs again, is it, General?" Stearns asked. He turned to Fleming and spoke again without waiting for an answer. "Their R&D department developed a lightweight jet pack that they'd like us to approve for field use. From what I hear, it's not very reliable, and its battery life is incredibly short. The resource cost just doesn't justify its usage."

"That's what we wanted to discuss," CB said. "We've made some huge improvements, and I can attest to just how useful they'd be in the field. Our mission today, for example—"

Stearns held up his hand, stopping CB. "Listen, if you want to give us the five-minute tour of the hangar, okay. Let's do it. But I don't want to hear any more about the jet pack today. I simply don't have the time. Call my office and set up an official visit to discuss it."

CB gritted his teeth. That was exactly what they'd done.

"I had another purpose in coming here," Fleming said. "It's the real reason I pressured Councilman Stearns into bringing me today, despite our time crunch." He looked at CB.

What the hell could this politician want with him?

"I understand you've been on more missions than any other member of the GMT," Fleming said.

General Craig jumped in before CB could answer. "That's right. He's been to more dangerous places than most of us have even heard of."

Fleming grinned at that. "Wonderful. I'm wondering if we could set up some time to chat, Captain. I'd love to hear some stories and pick your brain about what things are really like in the world beyond our little city."

CB didn't love that idea, but he didn't see how he could turn it down. "Of course, Councilman. I'm at your disposal."

"Indeed," General Craig said. "And you've picked the right man for the—"

A blaring siren split the air, cutting off the general's words. Both councilmen's hands went to their ears.

"CB!" the general yelled. "What the hell's going on?"

CB swallowed hard before answering. He knew exactly what was happening. *Damn it, Alex.* "Sir, it would appear someone's opened the hangar door."

———

ALEX COULDN'T HEAR what CB, General Craig, and the two councilmen were saying, but she could see them clearly through the glass wall. Their body language told her that things were not going well. The general had cocked a thumb toward the hangar, clearly inviting them inside. Councilman Stearns had shaken his head at that. Since then, they hadn't moved toward the door at all. If anything, Councilman Stearns was slowly inching his way back toward the cart, like a man trying to escape a conversation.

All this added up to one thing in Alex's mind: they weren't coming in here to see the demonstration.

She knew how important it was to CB and the general that the Council increase R&D funding. They'd planned this as a way to wow the Council into allotting more resources. But now the councilmen weren't even going to see the demonstration.

Without stopping to think, Alex moved toward the large hangar door. The one that was never to be opened except by explicit orders of the general. The one that led outside the city.

If the councilmen weren't going to come to her demonstration, she'd have to bring the demonstration to them.

She lifted the cover over the button that opened the hangar door, then pressed the button. The door behind her locked with an audible thud of bolts sliding into place, then the room depressurized.

As the hangar door began to open, Alex lowered her goggles over her eyes. The siren was blaring now, but she barely noticed. She was too focused on what she needed to do. The wind slapped her face as she stared at the vast blue sky beyond the opening door.

Maybe it was better that the councilman had refused to come into the hangar. The general wanted a demonstration of the device. He'd wanted to do it in the hangar, a safe trial in a controlled environment. In Alex's opinion, that was insanely stupid. If he wanted to show Stearns how cool their new toy was, they couldn't do it inside.

After all, what was the point of having a jet pack if you weren't going to fly it in open sky?

The hangar door finished opening, and Alex took a deep breath. This was it.

She ran forward, activated the jet pack, and leaped out of the door.

The jet pack propelled her upward faster than she'd expected. For a terrible moment, she couldn't stop her ascent. But after a bit of toying with the controls, she got the hang of them. She couldn't contain a delighted laugh as she engaged the thruster and shot upward, slowing as she reached a spot directly above General Craig and the City Councilmen, who all stared up at her, mouths agape.

For a moment, she considered descending until her feet touched the dome that surrounded the city, but she decided against it. Instead, she flew east, putting some distance between her and her home.

Finally, she turned around and looked at it. She'd never seen it like this, all at once. It was beautiful.

She stayed like that for a long time, looking back at the massive airship that was *New Haven*, the last human city, as it flew thousands of feet above the surface of the Earth.

3

ALEX SAT in the Strategic Planning room, trying to disappear into her chair. She was still in her flight suit, adrenaline from the evening's demonstration still coursing through her veins. General Craig sat across the table, leaning forward as he glared at her. CB sat to her left. She couldn't bring herself to look his direction, but she could feel his hot gaze as he, too, bore holes in her with his eyes.

General Craig's voice was a low snarl when he spoke. "I'm not going to ask what you were thinking, Lieutenant Goddard, because I don't care. What I *am* going to ask you is which of the five major violations you committed today I'm most angry about. Go ahead. Take a guess."

Alex squirmed in her seat but didn't reply. Maybe this was a rhetorical question. The less she said in this meeting, the better. She was in hot enough water already.

"I'm waiting, Lieutenant," the general growled.

So much for that theory.

She considered how to respond. "Sir, I believe you are most upset that I disobeyed Captain Brickman's direct order, sir."

"An interesting answer. You also could have gone with opening the hangar door without authorization, endangering your fellow officers, misuse of experimental equipment, or abandoning your post."

Alex felt her face redden as the anger rose up inside her. "Abandoning my post? General, I was—"

The stern look on the man's face convinced her that it would be wise to stop talking.

"You mentioned disobeying your captain's order, so let's talk about that one." The general turned his fiery gaze to CB. "What was that order, Captain?"

"Sir, I directed Lieutenant Goddard to wait in the hangar while you greeted the City Councilmen. Upon your return, she was to demonstrate the precision of the jet pack by hovering at an altitude of no more than fifteen feet above deck, sir." CB's voice was low and strong, like always, but Alex thought she could detect a quiver of anger in there as well.

"And did she follow this order?"

"No, sir, she did not."

Yep, there was definitely some anger in that voice.

"And, as her commanding officer, what could you have done differently to avoid this situation?"

CB's voice was ice when he spoke again. "I should have done what I'm going to do from now on, sir. I'm gonna watch her like she's a fresh recruit rather than a lieutenant in the goddamn *New Haven* Ground Mission Team."

The general nodded. "You're damn right you are. Goddard or any of your other people pull something like this again, I'm holding you personally responsible. Tend your field, CB, or I'll do some reaping of my own."

"Sir, yes, sir."

For the first time that day, Alex felt a twinge of guilt. She could take a dressing-down from the general. She'd disobeyed orders, even if it had been for the right reasons. She'd done the crime and she'd take the punishment. But she couldn't stomach CB taking heat for something she'd done.

She risked a glance at CB and saw his square jaw was set and two prominent veins stood out on his forehead.

"General, may I ask a question?" It was a risky maneuver, but Alex had to know.

"Don't test me, Goddard."

She decided to take that as a yes. "What did Stearns and Fleming think of the jet pack?"

He hesitated for only a moment before answering, but it was enough. Alex knew they'd loved the demonstration.

"That's hardly relevant, Goddard. You were given a direct order and you disobeyed it. Explain yourself."

Alex considered what her best approach would be here. The general was more pissed than she'd ever seen him. She'd seen him cuss men out, scream, and make grown men cry. But this gravely, smoldering anger was somehow worse. For the first time, Alex considered the possibility that she could lose her spot on the GMT. The thought sent a chill down her spine.

The majority of the badges in *New Haven* were designated law enforcement. Forty-thousand people crammed into an airship, even one as big as *Haven*, and there was bound to be some need for cops. Alex had started her career as a cop, but her superiors had quickly spotted her potential and recommended her for Officer Candidate School and then for the GMT.

The Ground Mission Team was the only section of the badge not dedicated to law enforcement. The only ones who ever left *New Haven*. The only people who set foot on the enemy territory that had once been humanity's home. Earth's surface.

Alex had been on two dozen missions to Earth. They'd all been terrifying, exciting, and brutal. She'd loved every moment of them.

Being part of the GMT was the only thing Alex had ever wanted, and it was the only thing she could ever imagine herself doing. Still, she wasn't going to mince words or beg for forgiveness. Not even from General Craig. She'd done what she'd done for a reason.

"I'm waiting, Lieutenant."

Alex met the general's eyes. "Sir, my orders were stupid."

The general's face went a shade darker. "Excuse me?"

"Sir, my *orders* were stupid. The *objective* was not. From what CB told me, the goal was to get Stearns and Fleming excited about the technology. To get them thinking about the military and non-military applications so they'd increase our R&D funding. No way that was going to happen by hovering fifteen feet off deck in the hangar. Even if they had agreed to come inside."

"Goddard, if you disregard orders, you are a liability to your team. And we cannot afford liabilities. Is that understood?"

Alex nodded sharply. "I screwed up, sir. I was wrong to disobey orders, and I apologize. But you asked what I was thinking, and that's what I'm telling you. If you wanted to inspire the Council to invest, they had to see it fly. Anyway, that's what I was thinking. Sir."

The general stared at her coldly for a long moment before speaking again. Then he said, "Insubordination will not be tolerated, Lieutenant Goddard. I could have you bumped off the GMT for this. I could have you walking night patrol in Sparrow's Ridge with the rookie badges for the next decade. Instead, I'm giving you latrine duty for a month."

Alex struggled mightily to keep the smile off her face. Thankfully, she succeeded. "Yes, sir."

"I'm also giving you a warning. You disobey another order, just one, and as God is my witness, you will not wear a GMT uniform again for as long as I have anything to say about it. Do you understand me, Goddard?"

"Yes, sir."

"Good."

The general stood up and a bit of the anger drained his face. Alex and CB quickly rose as well and stood at attention.

"As to your other question," the general said, "the Council has increased R&D funding fifty percent, and they want the entire team outfitted and trained for jet pack usage as quickly as possible."

This time, Alex had to look down to hide her smile.

"Captain, come with me." With that, the general turned and marched out of the room, CB close at his heels.

Alex barely had time to snap a salute before they were gone.

She sank back into her chair, relieved that the meeting was over and she was still a lieutenant in the GMT.

———

"SHE'S A GOOD KID, GENERAL," CB said. They were walking down a long hallway in a part of the GMT Headquarters that only a select few ever saw. CB was careful to pace himself exactly a half step behind General Craig.

Craig sighed. "I know. She just needs to learn some discipline."

"She'll learn. She's not that different than me, when I was her age."

The general barked out a harsh laugh. "Honestly, I think you were worse."

Now that they were out of the Strategic Planning room and alone, Craig was letting down his guard a little. As much as he'd blustered at Alex's little stunt, CB suspected the general was secretly amused by the whole situation. It certainly helped that the demonstration had been successful.

"Only question is, will she be ready when we really need her?" They came to a locked set of steel double doors, and the general swiped his ID over the key reader. The light above the doors turned green, and they pushed them open.

CB raised an eyebrow at the general's comment. "Something I should know, General? We got a ground mission coming up?"

The general shook his head. "This is something else."

CB waited. He'd worked with Craig long enough to understand that the best way to get something out of him was to shut up and let him talk.

"The intelligence spooks tell me there are some serious people throwing around the idea of landing the ship and trying to take back some ground on the surface."

CB stopped in his tracks. That idea was pure idiocy. "Resettlement? But it's just talk, right?"

The general shrugged. "For now. But apparently, they're organizing. It's becoming a bit of a movement."

"Jesus." As someone who'd been to the surface of Earth more than a hundred times in his career, CB knew survival was impossible. Forty thousand humans versus what was down there? The humans wouldn't last three days.

They came to another set of steel doors. This time, Craig

punched a ten-digit code into the number pad on the wall and again swiped his badge. The doors opened, and they stepped into the most restricted area in *New Haven*.

It was a large open room, mostly empty except for a fifteen-by-fifteen steel box. The walls on three sides of the room were glass, and sunlight streamed in, making CB blink against the brightness.

"How quickly they forget, right, CB?"

"Yes, sir."

"Humanity fights for its survival and somehow, against all odds, our ancestors are among the lucky few who escape on the *Haven*. And just a few generations later, people want to go back."

Steel rang out as the thing inside the cage slammed against the wall.

"In their defense, sir, they haven't seen what we have."

There was a hint of sadness in the general's voice when he replied, "No, they haven't."

Craig stepped toward a monitor mounted on the wall. It showed a live feed of the inside of the steel box. CB reluctantly walked to the general's side in front of the monitor.

The general gently tapped a fingernail on the screen. "You and I both know the only way we're going back to Earth is if old Frank here kicks the bucket."

CB forced himself to look at the screen.

He'd seen the creature hundreds of times, but it never failed to make him shudder. Huddled in the corner and looking directly into the camera, the creature looked more animal than human. Its ears, teeth, and fingers were longer than any man's, and its eyes were as red as the blood for which it hungered. The feral creature was *New Haven*'s sole vampire.

4

ALEX'S FEET slapped the concrete as she ran through the Hub. It was midmorning of the day after she'd been reprimanded by CB and the general. She'd spent the last hour cleaning latrines, and now she needed to sweat a little. Exercise always helped to clear her mind, too. Things that seemed complicated often clarified themselves after a few miles of running.

After a night of reflecting on the jet pack situation, she understood why the general had been upset. More than that, she knew that he was right. Her actions had been rash, and she'd put herself in danger with untested equipment. It had been the wrong move, even if it had achieved a positive result. But she also knew what had driven her to do it: she loved the Ground Mission Team more than anything, and she wanted the best possible equipment for her teammates.

Before she'd joined the GMT, she'd been a traditional badge—an officer of the law. While that had been rewarding in its own way, it had been a means to an end. She'd wanted to be a member of the GMT for as long as she could remember. She'd wanted to set foot on the surface of Earth, the place humans had lived for most of their history. The place humans belonged.

Here aboard *New Haven* everyone had a job to do, and all those jobs added up to keeping the massive airship in the sky. It hadn't been until the first time she'd stood on the surface of Earth that she realized how different things were there. It felt like home. Standing there had felt *right*. For the first time, she'd understood that humans didn't have to exist simply as tools to keep *New Haven* functional. On Earth, she'd felt free.

She'd tried to explain the feeling to a couple of non-GMT friends, but she couldn't properly put it into words. Her friends had looked at her like she was crazy. Maybe that was part of the reason she'd been spending less time with them over the past six months and more time with her teammates. There was a bond among those who'd been to the surface, a shared knowledge that others just couldn't understand.

The streets were quiet this morning, and the sun shone brightly through the windows of the ship. Alex wiped a forearm across her brow, sweeping away the sweat before it fell into her eyes. She pushed a little harder, increasing her pace.

Up ahead, she saw a familiar building. She'd spent twelve years there, learning history, math, and science. As she approached, she glanced through a window into a classroom of twenty or so children she guessed were about ten years old. She hoped they weren't giving their teacher as much trouble as she had given hers. It was strange to think these kids would live their entire lives aboard *New Haven* while the great big Earth sat below them, not a single human on its surface.

Seeing the children brought on another passing

thought: as a member of the GMT, she had the right to have up to three children. Births were highly regulated on *New Haven*; they had to be, if the proper population required for the safe operation of the ship was to be maintained. A baby boom would be a disaster, stretching the limited space, food, and other resources past the breaking point.

Couples on *New Haven* were allowed to have two children, no more. The GMT was the exception. Probably because so many of them didn't live long enough to start a family.

Alex wasn't in a rush to have kids, but having the option was nice. For now, she just wanted to be the most kick-ass GMT member CB and the general had ever seen. If she got lucky, maybe she'd have the chance to make a real difference in the future of the kids in that classroom and everyone else aboard.

It was a long shot, but on runs like this she often dreamed that she'd one day help humanity return home.

———

JESSICA BOWEN, Director of Engineering, stood in the center of the control room, surveying her team, hard at work all around her.

The Engineering control room was hidden away in the depths of the airship, and most residents of *New Haven* rarely gave it any thought. It wasn't like the Agricultural section, which covered a significant percentage of the ship's surface. Most residents didn't go more than a day or two without seeing the fields of corn, wheat, and vegetables covered by a glass dome that darkened to simulate night for twelve hours each day.

Jessica had to admit that there was something beautiful

about the fields, something that screamed *Earth*. Not that she'd ever actually been down to the surface. But the pictures and videos she'd seen resembled the fields more than anything else on the ship. It felt especially Earthy when the gentle, artificial mist fell on the crops, gathered by the ship from cloud vapors.

But just because people didn't think about Engineering didn't mean it was any less important. That was part of the reason Jessica loved her job. She was surrounded by the guts of the ship, the moving parts that kept humanity afloat and alive.

She cleared her throat and addressed her four-person monitoring crew. "All right, gang, hit me with the numbers. How we doing?"

She'd addressed the question to everyone, but Steven, the newest member of the crew, was monitoring the power levels, so he was expected to answer.

"Um, we're looking good, Jessica."

"Care to be a bit more specific?"

Jessica waited as the young man frantically scanned the monitors in front of him for the required information.

"Um, okay, here we are. Cruising altitude, holding steady at just over twenty-five thousand feet above sea level."

"Twenty-five thousand, one hundred sixty-two," another crew member interjected.

"Right," Steven said, clearly a little flummoxed. "Speed, four-hundred-two miles per hour. Current location, just off the tip of the land mass that was formerly known as the nation of Australia. Power levels holding steady."

Jessica nodded toward Steven. "Good."

The kid visibly relaxed now that his report was over.

On most days, Engineering did very little. The ship's auto-regulation systems kept things running smoothly the majority of the time. The computers flew the ship near the poles—the south pole for half the year, and the north for the other half—at the precise speed needed to keep them in sunlight. They traveled with the rotation of the Earth, maintaining speed and altitude through a combination of solar and nuclear power.

Jessica wasn't one to be complacent. The only reason things ran so well was because previous generations of engineers had worked hard to make it so. She intended to leave *New Haven* to her successor in better condition than she'd found it, so she was constantly looking for new, better ways to do things. Questioning was part of her nature.

She still remembered a conversation she'd had with her mother shortly after she'd toured the Engineering department as a teenager.

"Don't you think all the work we put into staying in sunlight is overkill?" she'd asked her mother.

Her mother had smiled. She'd always encouraged Jessica's questions. "You know what dentures and vampires have in common? They both come out at night."

Jessica had chuckled. "I know that. But do we even know if the vampires are still alive? They need blood to survive, right? And even if they are alive, we're at twenty-five thousand feet."

"It's a fair question. One of the reasons is that the ship is partially solar powered. *Haven* needs all the sunlight she can drink."

"What's the other reason?"

"We really don't know what the vampires are capable of. They've had the Earth to themselves for one hundred and fifty years. I'd like to think we're safe up here. On the other hand, we're the last of humanity. As far as we can tell, the vampires don't even know *New Haven* exists. Best to keep it that way."

"Ma'am, there's something you should see." Steven's voice brought her back from the memory.

She marched to his station and saw a red light flashing on one of the monitors. It was a motor in the temperature-regulation system. Not vital to keeping the ship in the sky, but things would get pretty cold in *New Haven* if that went out.

"Check the inventory for a backup unit," she said.

Steven's fingers danced on his keyboard. "Um, that is the backup unit, ma'am. Looks like the primary went out last year. We requested the Council send the GMT down for a replacement, but the request is still pending."

"After a year?" Jessica shook her head in disgust. She stormed back to her desk and radioed Councilman Stearns's office.

————

ALEX SHOWERED AFTER HER RUN, then headed toward the R&D room. She still needed to de-stress, and nothing calmed her like playing with experimental weapons that could blow up in her hands at any moment.

Besides, she owed the R&D department a report on how the jet pack operated.

To call Research and Development a department was a bit of an overstatement. It was really one man, Brian McElroy, and his dozen or so assistants. Brian was a certified genius, with a curious mind, a sleep disorder that let him work long into the night, and a major crush on Alex, one she wasn't above exploiting when it came time for him to select who would test his latest creations.

Today, like most days, she found him hunched over a circuit board in the corner of the lab. His assistant, Sarah, saw Alex approaching, but Alex put a finger to her lips.

She snuck up close behind Brian. Not that she had to sneak too carefully. He was oblivious to everything in his world when he was working. She looked over his shoulder to make sure there was nothing too breakable in front of him, then grabbed him from behind in a big hug.

He nearly jumped out of his skin and let out a decidedly unmanly squeal, but when he realized who was hugging him, he quickly relaxed.

"Brian, the jet pack was kick-ass!"

A broad smile broke out on his face. "Good! I'm glad it, you know, performed to your expectations."

She punched his arm playfully. "It did more than that. It was like the thing was obeying my every thought. I was corkscrewing, flipping—you name it."

"You were doing corkscrews in the hangar?"

"You didn't hear? I took it outside."

Brian's face grew pale. "Wait, seriously? It wasn't ready for that. The stabilizers aren't calibrated for that kind of wind."

"Relax, buddy. It worked great." She glanced a Sarah, who was watching the awkward interaction with a smile on her face.

"It must have gone well," Sarah said. "We just got the City Council's requisition. They want two dozen more of these things in three months. Between that and everything else our boy Brian is working on, we'll be pulling some long hours for the foreseeable future."

"You're welcome," Alex said. She leaned against Brian's desk. "So, you're working on other stuff?"

Brian glanced at Sarah. "Should we tell her?"

"Probably not."

Brian considered that for a moment, then said, "Okay, Alex, but you can't tell anyone."

Sarah groaned. "If you're not going to take my opinion into consideration, maybe don't ask."

"Seriously, Alex," Brian said. "I need to tell leadership about it when I'm ready. Can you keep it secret?"

That was part of the reason Alex pushed him on this kind of stuff. If it were up to him, he'd keep tweaking things until they were perfect. If it hadn't been for her "accidentally" letting something slip to CB, the jet pack would probably still be sitting in this room, untested. "Yeah, of course I'll keep a secret."

"Good." Brian scurried across the room and pulled something out of a drawer. He tossed it to Alex, but the throw was off target and she had to lunge to catch the small object. "Look familiar?"

She weighed it in her hand. "It's a bullet."

"Yes!" Brian smiled like she'd just solved a tough math equation. "But it's a better bullet. Think of it as a hollow-point round taken to the next level."

It felt pretty ordinary to Alex. "You have my attention."

Brian was talking faster now, getting excited. All his shyness and awkwardness disappeared when he started talking about his work. "This thing explodes just after impact. It was difficult to get the timing down, but I think we've finally nailed it. You shoot a vampire in the neck with this thing, it'll take its head off."

"That's fantastic." Alex was tempted to hug Brian again, but she didn't want to overdo the flirting. "Can I take some with me? Test them on the shooting range?"

The smile disappeared from Brian's face. "I wish that

were possible, but you know it isn't. General Craig needs to approve the design before we can test it."

Alex sighed. "Okay. You can't blame a girl for trying." She headed toward the door. "Stay brilliant, you two."

————

AFTER ALEX LEFT, Sarah waited ten minutes, then slipped away. She hopped in her cart and left GMT headquarters. After taking a few unnecessary turns to assure herself she wasn't being followed, she cut through Sparrow's Ridge and headed for the Hub.

She parked her cart a block away from the City Council Building and approached the rest of the way on foot. Once she was inside, she headed toward a service elevator in toward the back of the building. Using the key card she'd been given, she let herself into the restricted area and made her way to an unmarked door. She knocked three times, then waited.

After nearly twenty seconds, a voice said, "It's safe. Come in."

She opened the door and slipped through the back entrance to the office of Councilman Fleming.

"Were you followed?" Fleming asked.

Sarah shook her head. "I doubled back twice like you said."

"Good." Fleming leaned forward and smiled. "Now tell me what the GMT R&D department is working on."

5

ALEX ARRIVED at the GMT workout facility just after lunch. The place was more crowded than usual. Her teammates Drew, Firefly, and Owl were working out with free weights, and two non-GMT members, Wesley and Thomas, were sparring on one of the mats.

CB had identified and trained five candidates for the team just in case the need for a replacement arose. Wesley and Thomas were the best of these candidates. Both were employed as badges, and they spent as much time as possible here, working out with the team. It was clear that they both badly wanted a spot on the GMT. Alex could relate. She'd been in their position, not so long ago.

Alex walked toward the climbing rope. She pushed her body hard on her daily workouts, and it showed. Her peak conditioning was the product of long hours in this gym. She paused next to the sparring match, allowing herself a moment of fun before she went to work.

The two men circled each other like animals. Alex knew they were fast friends, but that didn't matter here. Every moment in this gym was another chance to impress the real members of the GMT, and neither of them was going to waste it. Thomas was the bigger of the two, but Wesley was quicker. Thomas threw his head to the right in an obvious feign, then lunged at Wesley, swinging his right arm in a roundhouse punch. The smaller man didn't fall for it, and he easily stepped aside. As Thomas reached him, Wesley spun, slamming into the taller man's back and driving him to the mat.

Alex couldn't help but smile. "Nice move!"

Wesley smiled back at her sheepishly. "Thanks."

"Alex is easily impressed." The voice was Firefly's. Alex hadn't noticed that he was watching too. "Councilman Sterns could have dodged that punch."

Alex frowned. "Give the kid a break, man."

"A break?" Firefly laughed. "This *kid* could be watching your back someday." He turned to Wesley. "Want me to teach you how to dodge a real punch?"

Wesley and Thomas exchanged nervous glances. Then Wesley looked up at Firefly. "Yeah, of course."

Firefly smiled. "Good."

Wesley started to stand, but before he could get all the way to his feet, Firefly dashed forward and drove his fist into Wesley's stomach. Wesley crumpled to the ground.

Firefly shook his head. "See what I'm saying? It ain't so easy when it's for real. Stand up."

This time Firefly allowed Wesley to finish standing before he attacked again. Wesley moved to his right, but not quickly enough. Firefly's fist connected with his ribcage.

"Firefly, that's enough!" Alex was surprised at the fury in her own voice.

Firefly looked at her with surprise. "Enough? It's not nearly enough. You think there's any vampire on Earth as slow as me? If he can't handle a little sparring, what's he going to do down there? He needs to learn a lesson."

Alex stepped onto the mat. "Okay, let's show them something. Why don't you throw a punch at me? We'll see how that goes for you."

Firefly smiled. "Yeah, okay. I think I'll just—"

He swung his left fist toward Alex's jaw in a tight hook, but Alex slid right, easily dodging it. She could have struck back and ended it there, but she wasn't ready for it to be over.

She took a step back and smiled. "Well, you're right about one thing. There aren't any vampires as slow as you."

Firefly shot her a cocky smile, then lunged forward. His body uncoiled as he attempted to punch her in the stomach. This time, she didn't just dodge. Mirroring Wesley's move against Thomas, she spun, driving her elbow into Firefly's back as his momentum carried him past her. He landed face first on the mat with an *oomph*.

Alex turned to Wesley and Thomas. "There's always somebody faster than you. If you want to be on this team, you gotta learn that right now. Vampires are quicker than any of us. You rely on your own speed, your own strength, your own skill, whatever, you're dead." She reached out a hand to Firefly. "The one thing you need to rely on if you're gonna survive is your teammate."

Firefly took her hand, and she pulled him to his feet. He clapped her on the back. "That was a hell of a move, Goddard. Glad you're on our side."

Alex smiled at him. "Back at ya." She looked toward the weights and saw Drew and Owl staring at her. "You know, those weights work better if you lift them."

Owl grinned. "Drew was just thinking he's glad that wasn't *him* facing you on the mat."

"Damn right about that." Drew went back to his weights. He knew better than to face Alex, even though he outweighed her by sixty pounds and had four inches on her.

Alex noticed CB standing in the corner, his arms crossed. How long had he been watching?

"What's up, CB?" Alex asked. "Miss us so much you had to come visit?"

"Not exactly." CB's face was a mask of seriousness. He was here on business.

"Don't keep us in suspense, Captain," Drew said.

CB nodded. "I hope you don't have any big plans tomorrow. We're going down to the surface. It's not going to be an easy mission. There's a good possibility of contact."

Alex's pulse instantly increased, and she couldn't hide her smile. Contact on the surface meant only one thing: vampires.

———

THE ENTIRE GROUND Mission Team met in CB's quarters that evening for dinner.

There were only six active members of them on the team, and all of them were there tonight: CB, Alex, Drew, Owl, Lincoln Simmons, and Garrett "Firefly" Eldred.

Firefly was in the kitchen, preparing the food. He was the second oldest member of the team after CB, in his late 30s. He was also the team's demolitions expert. Sometimes Alex thought maybe he liked blowing things up a little too much, but he mostly kept to himself. He was also a surprisingly good cook. Tonight's menu included Pad Thai, a lovely soup, and some beautiful cupcakes for dessert. The cupcakes were adorned with crudely formed frosting vampires, their faces stained red with what Alex imagined was supposed to be blood.

CB, Alex, Drew, Owl, and Simmons sat at the table playing an overly complicated card game called Wishing Well. Alex still wasn't sure she fully understood the rules, and she was struggling to keep up with the conversation and the game at the same time.

"The thing that makes this job tricky is the lack of good intel," CB said. "Based on military records, we believe the motors we're looking for are inside an old factory."

Simmons looked up from his cards and raised an eyebrow. "Inside?"

CB nodded.

Simmons whistled softly. Alex could tell he was trying to look concerned, but she could see it in his eyes that he was as excited as the rest of them at the prospect of entering an old building. Buildings provided shelter from the sun. Which meant vampires.

A wide smile broke out across Drew's face. "It's about time. I haven't gotten to decapitate one of those undead bastards in what, six months?"

Simmons ran a hand through his perfect hair. "Don't get your hopes up, buddy. By the time you get there, I'll have the place as clean as the latrines Alex has been scrubbing." He was in charge of recon for the GMT, which meant he'd be the first one sent in to scout out any dangerous situation. He was also stealthy enough that he'd made it out of every one of them, so far.

"You ask me, you all are crazy," Owl said. "You fools actually want to face vampires?"

Drew laughed. "Why else join the GMT?" He looked at the table and frowned. "Your play, Alex."

Alex flipped through the dozen cards in her hand, trying

to make sense of the eight suites. "Sorry, one sec." Finally, she plucked out a card almost at random, the six of keys, and tossed it on the pile on the table.

Everyone groaned.

"Seriously, Alex?" CB said. "Why the hell would you play a key?"

Alex kept her face blank, hoping they'd believe the play was part of some grand strategy. Simmons shot her a quick smile that said he was onto her.

Owl shook her head in mock pity. "All I know is I'm going to be sitting in the rover, feet up on the dashboard tomorrow, while you fools are getting killed."

"Spoken like a true pilot," Alex said. "So, what do we need these motors for anyway, CB?"

The captain chuckled. "Something about the heating system. Hell if I know. Ours is not to question why—"

"Just to be prepared to die," the rest of the team finished.

The tongue-in-cheek mantra was the closest the GMT had to an unofficial motto.

"Yeah, yeah," Alex said. "Might be nice if they told us the actual need. We might find something else down there that would solve the problem."

"Keep dreaming," Owl said.

CB laid down a nine of clouds, and Drew, Simmons, and Owl groaned again. "And that, my friends, is how the game is won," he said.

"See, Alex, that's why you never play a key when the next player is showing a staggered straight," Owl said.

"Right. Guess I forgot."

CB slapped Alex on the shoulder. "Admit it, you have no idea what Owl's talking about."

"Let's just hope she's quicker with her gun than she is with her cards," Drew said.

"Quicker than you," Alex said.

Firefly appeared in the doorway, four bowls of soup precariously balanced in his hands. "It won't matter. This mission isn't going to be any different than the others we've had lately. We won't see any vampires."

Drew cleared the cards off the table to make room for the food. "He's probably right. We'll be on the surface, inside dark buildings that haven't been entered in over a hundred years. What could go wrong?"

———

AFTER THEY'D FINISHED the last surprisingly light and fluffy cupcake, the team decided to call it an early night. They needed to reconvene at oh five hundred hours, so everyone was anxious to get some shuteye.

Alex found herself taking the long way back to her room. She was doing everything she could to not get her hopes up. The last few missions had all held the possibility of a vampire encounter, but each had turned out to be a disappointment.

Not that it hadn't been exciting. There was something strange and alien about standing on solid ground, of not feeling the familiar rumble of the ship beneath her feet. The smell of earth and vegetation. The way the air itself seemed to hum with life.

And the quiet. *Haven* was generally a loud place, with people always clambering around. But the Earth in daytime... It felt dead. As dead at the creatures that now ruled it.

Even though she'd only ever encountered three vampires, Alex studied them obsessively, first in her GMT training and then on her own. She'd learned about their anatomy and their weaknesses—silver and sunlight. She'd learned how to kill them. Decapitation was the surest and most highly recommended method, but destroying the heart with silver worked, too. She'd watched videos and seen pictures. But she'd never killed one herself. The few she'd seen had been at a distance. Drew had taken out one of them, Simmons took the second, and CB killed the third.

Tomorrow, if everything happened as she hoped, that would change. It wasn't that she wanted to be in a life-and-death fight, exactly. She had no desire to die. But she'd trained for the past two years for one purpose: to kill vampires. She wanted to put her hard-won skill set to use.

She wasn't entirely surprised when she found herself standing in front of a door three floors up from her quarters. It was as if her feet had brought her here without her consent. Maybe that meant that this was where she was supposed to be. She paused only a moment before knocking.

Simmons opened the door, dressed in boxers and a tee shirt, apparently ready for bed. "Hey."

"Hey. I was just out walking and—"

"You found yourself in my neighborhood." There was no reason for her to be on this floor except to visit him, and they both knew it."

"Listen, there's no way I'm getting to sleep tonight unless I blow off a little steam." She tried on a coy smile. "Think you could help me with that?"

Simmons broke out in a grin. "I'm always ready to help out a teammate, Lieutenant Goddard. Get in here."

Alex slipped inside, shutting the door behind her.

———

SARAH SAT in Fleming's living room, a glass tumbler containing a splash of whiskey in her hand. Whiskey was precious, a rarity and a status symbol, and Fleming must have been especially pleased to offer it to her.

He sat across from her, drinking from his substantially fuller glass.

Sarah followed suit, taking a small sip. She enjoyed the way it burned as it ran down her throat.

"They'll be leaving in the morning," she said. "Roll call's at oh five hundred. Then they'll gear up and head down."

Fleming scratched his chin. "You checked the gear yourself?"

Sarah had already told him she had, but she didn't take offense to the question. He was under a lot of pressure. "Yes. The gear's ready."

"Good."

Sarah's lips curled in a sly smile. "Be honest. How much did you have to do with making this mission happen?"

"That motor has been failing for months. Our man in Engineering just helped bring it to the attention of the right people." He took another sip of whiskey before continuing. "We're at a crucial point here, Sarah. The people are starting to realize the Council lives in fear. They're out-of-touch fools, too afraid of the old legends to fight for what's ours. I've seen it up close. Anytime I bring up any proposal that challenges the idea that we should avoid contact with the surface, they immediately shoot me down. But if I have the people in my corner…"

Sarah leaned forward and gave Fleming a supportive smile. "You do. The people want to return to Earth. They just need a strong leader to show them it's possible."

"Not enough of them believe. Not yet. That's why this mission is so critical. If something goes wrong, it could set us back years. But if it's successful? If we're able to demonstrate that the technology we have now is enough to keep people safe on Earth? We could win a lot of support."

"Then what happens?" Sarah asked.

"The City Council will bend to the will of the people. They have to. Then we'll resettle the Earth."

6

ALEX ARRIVED in the hangar to find her locker stocked with the gear she'd need for the mission. Brian and his crew in R&D had been busy. Firefly was standing in front of the locker next to hers, quietly slipping into his chainmail suit. She saw that his locker was stocked with explosives.

Simmons was three lockers down. Alex exchanged a glance with him, then quickly looked away. She couldn't afford to be distracted. Not today.

Alex pulled her own chainmail suit out of the locker and stepped into it. She had to admit that the suit was one of Brian's greatest creations. It was lightweight, formfitting, and, most importantly, made of silver composite. It went on under all the other gear and fit tight all the way to the top of the neck. The suit served a dual purpose. Any vampire who tried to bite a member of the GMT team would be in for a nasty surprise. The second purpose was one that they didn't talk about much but they all understood: if one of them were turned into a vampire, the silver would kill them before the transformation even had a chance to complete.

Alex wouldn't have called the suit comfortable, but the peace of mind it provided was well worth the discomfort.

Then she put on the rest of her fatigues, her combat boots, her belt, and her vest. R&D had already loaded her vest with two knives and a pair of pistols.

She strapped the last piece of gear to her back—her favorite. A laser-etched composite steel sword, perfectly balanced. Alex spent as much time practicing with the sword as she did on the shooting range. Some of the others laughed at her for it. CB always said, "If you let the vampires get close enough to use a sword, you've already lost."

Alex didn't see it that way. Besides, even if it was a waste of time, the swordplay calmed her. The finely sharpened sword felt like an extension of her more than her other weapons.

She glanced around at the others gearing up. Just as Alex had her pistols, each of her teammates had their weapons of choice. Drew carried a shotgun modified to carry one hundred rounds and to fire spiraling slugs made of silver.

Simmons preferred to do his killing from a distance when possible. He carried a sniper rifle that could punch a two-foot hole in a brick wall.

CB was outfitted much like Alex—dual automatic pistols with one-hundred-round clips of silver bullets that fragmented on impact.

Owl was nowhere to be seen. She was probably in the ship running her diagnostics. She'd modified much of the ship herself, and she did as much of the maintenance on it as she could get away with. Owl seemed to have bonded emotionally with the ship in the way most people bonded with other humans. She'd taken it as an insult when CB had ordered her to train Simmons on how to operate the quirky vehicle in case something happened to her.

CB walked down the line of lockers, checking the status of his team. They each gave him a thumbs up to indicate their readiness. Except for Firefly, who gave him a middle finger. CB just chuckled. Alex knew the captain would allow such shenanigans here, but once they hit the surface, it was all business. Fooling around would not be tolerated. Nor would questioning orders.

When he'd checked the readiness of every team member, CB cleared his throat. "All right, GMT, let's go down."

———

THE AWAY SHIP raced across the sky, away from the sun and to the edge of dawn. The ride was quite different than the slow, steady rumble the citizens of *New Haven* were used to. This one was turbulent, loud, and anything but peaceful. To add to the cacophony, Owl insisted on narrating into their earpieces.

"We are now approaching the western coast of the area that was once the country of Argentina. We will be landing shortly in the city of Buenos Aires. The name translates as 'good wind.'"

"You read a geography book," Drew growled into his headset. "We get it."

Owl ignored the jab. "Buenos Aires was once a major tourist destination, and it was the heart of a thriving economy. Notable residents included writer Jorge Luis Borges, Pope Francis, and composer Gustavo Cerati."

"I guarantee she doesn't know who any of those people are," Alex said.

Simmons and Drew both laughed. CB remained stoic, and Firefly was overly interested in the detonator in his hand.

Alex frowned. "Should he be playing with that on the ship?"

Firefly grinned at her from across the aisle. "Probably not."

Alex tugged at the restraints securing her to the seat, trying to get comfortable. After a lifetime spent walking freely around an airship, she'd never get used to being strapped to a chair.

The seats on the ship were lined along either side, two rows facing each other. There was seating for up to ten, though the GMT had never had that many members.

After a brief respite, Owl resumed talking in their headsets. "We'll be setting down in what was once the barrio of Parque Patricios, in the south part of the city. This neighborhood once housed the city government. If you have time for any sightseeing, I recommend The Monument to the Victim of the 1871 Yellow Fever Epidemic, which is surprisingly intact."

"That's enough, Lieutenant Fowler." CB's voice was calm but firm. He'd shifted into business mode. "Just set us down in the right spot."

"Roger, Captain," Owl said, her voice still filled with cheeriness.

Drew elbowed Alex and pointed out the window. "You see that?"

To the east, the sky was alive with color. Reds, oranges, purples. Sunrise. It was truly a sight to behold. The constant blue sky that *New Haven* flew under was pretty too, in its way. But this was one of the true pleasures of being part of the GMT. They were the only residents of *New Haven* who ever saw the sunrise.

Alex glanced at Drew. He'd been on the GMT for ten years, and he'd been on many times more missions than she had. "You ever get used to seeing that?"

Drew shook his head slowly, his gaze fixed out the window. "Not yet."

Owl's voice crackled again in their headsets. "Lady and gentlemen, we are on track to touch down in three minutes. Prepare for landing."

Alex took a deep breath and caressed her sword.

———

OWL SET the ship down in a clearing twenty yards from the factory. As they exited the ship, CB glanced at his watch. It was 6:12 a.m. *New Haven* time. Technically they had about thirteen hours until sunset, but the goal here was to complete this job in four hours or less, then reconvene as *New Haven* passed over their location. If they were running a little behind, it wouldn't be the end of the world. Owl's ship was faster and could catch up, but it also had limited range. If they got more than an hour or two behind *New Haven*, they'd have to hide out down on the surface and wait for the ship to pass again the following day.

A night spent on Earth? CB shuddered at the thought.

But there was really no reason to worry. This should be a fairly simple salvage job. Assuming everything went well.

Outside the ship, CB held up a hand to stop the team. He scanned the area with his eyes, taking in the streets and buildings around him. He tried to imagine what it must have been like one hundred and fifty years ago, before the vampires. The streets would have been bustling with people, just like the streets of *New Haven* were today. Now the buildings were dilapidated, and the city had been reclaimed by nature. Trees grew up through the busted pavement. The vines and moss covered the buildings like a web; nothing in his sightline was free of plant life. City locations like this always made him a little edgy.

He shook off the thought and tried to focus.

"We're going to take this nice and slow," he said. "If there are any vamps in that factory, they're probably spending the day in dreamland, but we're not going to take any chances."

Simmons cocked his head to the side. "Wait, do vampires dream?"

Drew grinned, gripping his shotgun. "They have nightmares. About me."

CB shot them both a look. "Stay on your toes. Remember where we are. Things can get real bad real quick down here. Let's find a way into the building."

They split into two groups. CB and Firefly headed left, while Alex, Simmons, and Drew headed right. The building looked to be pretty secure. The doors were solid steel, and every one of them was locked. Two sets of sixteen-foot bay doors stood at the front of the building, but they were locked too.

"I don't like it," CB said. "One-hundred and fifty years, and not so much as a broken window?"

Firefly grinned. "I can fix that."

CB shook his head. "We're not blowing anything up. Not yet."

"Aw, come on, Captain. I'll have you in there in two minutes flat."

"Yeah, and any vamp sleeping inside will be on high alert."

"You ask me, those bay doors out front are our best way in."

"The locking mechanism looked pretty sturdy," CB said. "Maybe we could cut our way through. Blowtorch?"

The rumble of a familiar engine sounded from the front of the building.

"You gotta be kidding me," CB said. He took off running toward the sound. He rounded the corner just in time to see Alex in front of the one of the bay doors, sitting in the driver's seat of the eight-wheel rover the team used to haul equipment. The vehicle's front-end loader was jammed under the door. She pulled a lever, and CB heard the locking mechanism break. The bay door went up with a clang.

Alex turned off the vehicle and hopped off.

CB stormed toward her. "What the hell was that, Lieutenant?"

Alex looked genuinely perplexed. "Sir, you said you wanted to find a way in."

"Finding a silent way in can mean the difference between the whole team making it back or not. Running in without thinking is never the play."

Drew cleared his throat. "Uh, Captain?"

CB ignored him, keeping all his rage focused on Alex. "We have to work as a team, especially down here."

"Seriously, Captain," Simmons said. "You need to see this."

CB and Alex both turned in the direction the others were facing and looked through the open bay door.

Inside, there were a dozen mounds of dirt on the factory floor. CB knew those mounds could only be one thing: vampire graves.

———

ALEX SWALLOWED hard as CB gave her one last angry glare. Clearly, he wanted to continue this conversation, but there were more important things to focus on now. Alex was glad. She was beginning to think facing a vampire would be far preferable to facing a pissed-off CB.

He turned to face the others. "Okay, we move quickly and quietly. You know your jobs. Do them well and do them efficiently."

Drew raised an eyebrow. "We're still going in? With those things?"

Alex stared at the mounds of dirt. There was likely a vampire under each one of them.

"If they haven't woken up yet, we should be okay," CB said. "Vampires are groggy in the daytime. It takes a lot to wake them."

"Could be these mounds are abandoned," Firefly said.

CB shook his head. "Let's assume they aren't. Proceed with caution, people. Move out."

Owl hopped into her customary place in the rover's driver's seat and eased the vehicle forward. Alex carefully followed, pistol in hand. She gave the mounds of dirt a wide birth as she passed.

They found the motors quickly enough. The things were mammoth, and every member of the GMT groaned softly at the sight of them—even CB. Trying to finagle these beasts out of here was going to be no easy task.

The group went to work. They did their jobs in near silence, each doing their best not to think about the numerous mounds of dirt between them and the exit, and in forty-five minutes, they had the first motor out, loaded on the rover, and headed back toward the ship.

The second motor was a bit more tricky. It was wedged further back, and the crew didn't have as much space to work. Still, with the knowledge gained from removing the first motor, they were able to get this one out even faster than the first.

As they were loading it onto the vehicle, Drew let out a soft cry of pain.

"What's up?" Alex said.

"Nothing. I'm good."

Alex trained her flashlight on his hand and saw dark liquid seeping through his glove.

"Holy shit. You're bleeding, Drew."

"It's nothing," Drew snapped.

"We need to get out of here. Now."

Owl backed up the rover and started toward the door. The team flanked the vehicle, weapons drawn, as they trotted toward the exit.

Alex jogged next to Drew. She saw his left glove was soaked with blood now, about to drip.

"Drew..." she said.

"I'm fine!" he snapped.

As he said it, a single drop of blood began to fall, and dirt exploded into the air as a vampire erupted from the ground.

7

THE VAMPIRE LANDED on all fours and hissed.

For a terrible moment, Alex froze. All the pictures and videos she'd seen, all the mornings of practice and afternoons of study, none was like facing the real thing. She'd never been this close to a vampire.

Its leathery skin was stretched taut across its body, and it was the color of old, yellowed parchment. Webs of skin connected its upper arms to its torso, forming wings that Alex knew would allow it to glide, giving it the ability to jump absurdly long distances. Its eyes were a solid gray. Alex didn't know if that color had a name, but it should be called *death*.

Looking at it, smelling its rotting odor, it was difficult to imagine this creature had ever been human.

The vampire leaped into the air, heading for Drew, probably drawn by the scent of his blood. Drew raised his shotgun, but he was moving too slow.

Whatever temporary paralysis had gripped Alex was gone now. She took a step away from Drew and swung her sword.

The weapon cut cleanly through the vampire's neck, and its head separated from its body, continued on its trajectory, and landed at Drew's feet with a thud.

"Holy shit," Drew said, pushing the decapitated head away with his boot. "Thanks, Alex."

Alex brought her sword back to the ready position and steadied her breathing. She barely noticed the black, gooey substance that clung to her blade, the vampire's thick, coagulated excuse for blood.

How many times had she dreamed of this moment? How long had she waited? But, to her surprise, she felt no joy. Instead, she felt the hyper-alertness that came with combat and the thrill of adrenaline coursing through her.

Alex looked at the exit, then at Drew's hand. There were a dozen mounds of dirt between them and sunlight.

"We gotta move—"

Before she could finish, two more vampires burst from the ground. Unlike the first one, these didn't take a moment to get their bearings. They both charged Drew, their long fangs bared.

The one on the left suddenly jerked as its head exploded. The report of Simmons's rifle echoed in the distance.

Drew had his shotgun up now, and he fired at the vampire on the right. The creature moved more quickly than Alex would have thought possible, spinning to the side, and the slug hit it in the arm. The creature squealed in pain and tendrils of smoke rose from the wound. Its arm was barely attached now, held on by only a flap of skin and exposed muscle, but the creature didn't slow.

Alex stepped forward, sword raised, ready to meet the attack. But, before the creature got to her, two gunshots rang out, and a gaping hole appeared in the middle of its chest. The creature let out an unholy scream and fell dead.

CB sprinted toward them, his twin pistols still in his hands. Firefly was close behind, rifle at the ready.

"They're blood crazy," CB said. "They'll all be zeroing in on Drew. Firefly, Alex, flank him. Anything coming at him from his six is your responsibility."

Another two vampires burst from the ground ahead.

"Drew, you and me take the ones in front," CB said.

One of the vampires fell as Simmons's rifle sang out again.

"Along with a little help from Simmons. Let's move."

They headed toward the bay door and the safety of the light, seemingly progressing by inches. Vampire after vampire leaped from the darkness. They all seemed to be attacking mindlessly, operating by pure instinct as they honed in on Drew's blood.

A vampire glided toward them, its webbed wings stretched, and Alex dropped to one knee and thrust her sword upward as it reached her, stabbing it directly in the heart. A pool of inky, thick black goo bubbled from the creature's chest as she removed her weapon from its body.

Another vampire quickly followed, and Drew fired. The slug removed half the thing's neck, but still it staggered forward. Drew's second shot finished the job of decapitating it.

They team worked wordlessly. CB's pistols bit at the creatures with uncanny precision, dropping vampires with a barrage of silver bullets to the heart. Drew was less precise, but no less effective. His shotgun maimed vampire after vampire, slowing them down enough for the others to finish them. Firefly worked his rifle like a mechanic, cold and efficient with his shots. Simmons struck with his sniper rifle from the safety of the light.

Alex stuck to her sword.

Time felt like it was both moving at a snail's pace and happening so fast she could barely keep up. She had no idea how long they'd been fighting or how many they'd killed.

Finally, they were almost at the bay door. Firefly stepped through, and CB grabbed Drew and pulled him into the light. Alex had somehow fallen a few steps behind. From across the field, she heard Simmons's voice.

"Alex, look out! Three o'clock!"

She spun to her right and saw the vampire gliding toward her. She quickly stepped aside and, as the vampire soared past, she drove her sword into its back, slammed it down, and pinned it to the floor.

Drew tore away from CB's grasp, ran back into the shadows, and blew the creature's head off. Then he grabbed Alex and pulled her through the bay door.

Alex stumbled into the light. She let her sword fall to the grass and put her hands on her knees as she tried to catch her breath.

"Everybody okay?" CB asked. "Check yourselves for bites, scratches, anything."

Alex peeled off her gloves and checked her hands. No damage. Her clothing didn't appear to have been ripped. It looked like she'd made it out intact.

She breathed a sigh of relief and closed her eyes as the heat of the sun fell on her face.

———

AFTER TAKING a minute to gather themselves, the crew got

back to work. CB whispered something to Firefly, who nodded vigorously, his eyes suddenly alive with excitement. The short man ran around the other side of the building.

While Drew, Simmons, and Owl worked on securing the salvaged motors in the cargo hold, CB pulled Alex aside.

"Alex, you wanna tell me what happened in there?"

She couldn't keep the smile off her face as she answered. "I know. It was amazing. The way the team worked together? It was just like you drilled us."

"That's not what I'm talking about." CB's face transformed in a scowl of barely restrained anger. "Your lack of caution was the reason we had to fight in the first place."

Alex took a step back, shocked. "Hang on, what are you talking about?"

"First there was that stunt with the doors."

"Captain, that was the only way we were getting in. The place was locked down tight. You said it yourself."

"Maybe yes, maybe no, but that's not your call. It's mine. You can't keep running off and making your own decisions. That's not how this team works."

Alex concentrated on not showing her emotions. No way was she going to let CB know how much he was pissing her off. The worst part was that she knew he was right. "That was stupid of me, Captain. I should have waited for orders. Anything else, sir?"

CB's scowl deepened. "Yeah, if I might have another moment of your time. You knew Drew cut himself, and you didn't say anything."

This assertion genuinely surprised her. How did he even know? "It all happened really fast."

"Too fast for you to alert your commanding officer?"

She drew a deep breath. She was losing the fight to

remain calm. "I made some rookie mistakes. No doubt. But have you considered that maybe this wasn't such a bad thing, sir?"

"What are you talking about?"

"We've been training for this. Exactly this. And now we've put our skills to use. We've proven we're better than the vampires."

CB barked out a strained laugh. "Are you kidding me right now?"

She spoke softly, struggling to keep the shock out of her voice. "Sir, I don't understand. We annihilated those things. We were surgeons in there."

"Okay, Dr. Goddard, then tell me this. How many vampires did we kill?"

Alex blinked hard, surprised by the question. "I think I killed four."

"That wasn't the question. How many did the team take out?"

"I... Sir, I don't know. I was focused on keeping myself and my teammates alive."

"We killed fourteen, total. And you killed three, not four. You missed the heart of that second one. The fight lasted one minute and thirty-four seconds."

"How do you know that?"

CB stepped close, approaching until he was up in her face, and he spoke softly but firmly. "Because I'm a goddamn soldier, who is aware of his surroundings. I keep tabs on what my team is doing. I don't get caught up in bloodlust, like a damn vampire."

Alex couldn't believe this. It was her first vampire encounter, and she'd taken out four—okay, three—of the creatures. What more did he want from her? "Captain, you're right. I could have paid more attention to the team. But with all due respect, didn't we perform well? It was fourteen to five, and we won. Without a single injury. Doesn't this prove we're better than them, sir?"

"If you believe that, you're a fool." The anger in CB's voice was gone now, replaced with a weary disappointment. "The vampires we fought were half asleep, disoriented, and day sick. The vampires that come out at night? They are a whole different animal. After sunset, the team wouldn't have been able to take out fourteen of them. We would be lucky to survive a fight with one." He gave her one more disappointed look and shook his head sadly. "Go rejoin your teammates. Get to work."

Firefly ran up to CB. "Now, Captain?"

"Not yet."

The crew finished securing the motors and stowed the rover.

Owl glanced at her watch as she stepped out of the ship and into the sunlight. "We're right on schedule. *Haven* should be passing overhead in twenty-one minutes. What do you say we join up with her?"

As the ship lifted off, Firefly tapped CB on the shoulder. "Now, Captain?"

CB nodded, smiling slightly. "Light 'em up."

If he hadn't been wearing his safety harness, Firefly would have leaped for joy. "Eyes on the factory, everybody."

He only gave them two seconds to comply before pressing the detonator in his hand.

The explosives he'd placed around the foundation of the factory went off in a thunderous series of bangs.

As they rose into the air, Alex watched the factory collapse. Any vampires still in there might not be killed by the falling debris, but they certainly would be killed by the sunlight.

Firefly giggled as the dust cloud around the factory grew. "That's how we do it in the GMT."

8

THE CREW ARRIVED BACK at *New Haven* just before noon. Owl timed the rendezvous perfectly, meeting the airship as it was almost directly over Buenos Aires. They docked in the hangar and waited for the all-clear to debark the away ship. After a five-minute wait, Owl spoke into their headsets.

"Lady and gentleman, we've been given permission to debark. Please remember to follow standard procedures. Wait for your handler to call you, and do not exit the biohazard containment room until you have been cleared to do so. I hope you enjoyed the flight."

The team left the ship one by one as their names were called. Alex waited as Drew, Simmons, and Firefly left. She was alone with CB.

"Hey," she said. "About before. I want to apologize."

CB sighed, not meeting her gaze. "Look, Alex, I have high expectations for you. You could be a key contributor to this team. Maybe even lead it someday. But the mistakes you've been making are because you don't look at the whole picture. Making a show of the jet packs and rushing into a vampire-invested building might work out sometimes, but things like that have just as much of a chance of getting you killed. Or worse, getting your teammates killed. The general won't stand for that kind of short-term thinking on his team. And neither will I."

A voice came up through the open door of the ship. "Captain Brickman!"

CB stood up. "They're playing my song. We'll talk later."

Alex sat on her seat, safety harness still buckled, feeling shell-shocked. When they'd recruited her, they'd said they were looking for people who could think for themselves. People who could improvise successfully in extremely stressful situations. Hadn't that been exactly what she'd done? Now CB was talking about benching her?

"Lieutenant Goddard!"

Alex unfastened her harness and shuffled out of the ship.

She was met at the bottom of the ramp by a woman in a full biohazard suit.

"Hey, Shirley, how you doing?"

The woman's voice sounded a bit crackly as it came through the speaker in the suit. "Not bad, Alex. You ready to go?"

"You know I love getting naked for you."

Shirley had been Alex's handler since her first trip to the surface, and in that time, Alex had worked hard to build up a rapport. No matter what she tried, though, the woman was all business.

Shirley led her through the hangar and into the biohazard containment room. As they were leaving the hangar, Alex saw a team of five people in identical suits to Shirley's board the ship. They'd scrub it bow to stern, then scrub the hangar. Even after all these years, doctors still didn't understand how much vampire blood it took to turn someone, or really much about the process at all. They weren't taking any chances that a stray drop might infect someone and set a vampire loose on *New Haven*.

When they reached the biohazard containment room, medical techs took Alex's weapons from her. These would be cleaned and decontaminated before Alex saw them again. The techs took special care handling her sword, which was still smeared with the sticky residue of vampire blood.

Alex stripped, handing each piece of clothing to a tech as she removed it. Some of these, like the silver mail suit, would be cleaned and returned to her. All the exterior clothing would be burned as a cautionary measure.

"Any breaks in the skin you're aware of?" Shirley asked.

"Nope, I'm fully intact."

After she'd toweled off, Shirley took out a flashlight and inspected every inch of her skin, looking for any cuts. When she was cleared, Alex was given a fresh set of clothes and dismissed.

"Always a pleasure, Shirley," Alex said as she left. "Maybe next time we'll mix it up, and *you'll* get naked for *me*."

"So long, dear," Shirley said.

Alex shook her head. Some people just didn't know how to bust balls.

As she was leaving the hangar, someone stopped her. It took Alex a moment to place the woman, but she finally did. Alex had never seen her outside the R&D lab.

"Hey, Sarah."

Sarah smiled warmly. "Welcome home! I heard it was quite the mission."

"I won't argue with you there."

"Do you have anything going on right now?"

Alex glanced at the clock. "I've got a debrief in two hours. Why?"

"There's someone who wants to meet you."

———

ALEX HAD BEEN to the Hub plenty of times, and she'd even been to the City Council building once. It may have been on a field trip when she was in third grade, but it counted. However, she'd never been in a City Councilman's office before. She had to admit this was far more intimidating than a few sleepy vampires.

They were in Councilman Fleming's office, sitting on couches near a window that looked down on the city. Sarah and Alex sat on one couch, and Fleming sat on the other. The councilman was leaning forward, seemingly transfixed by Alex's story.

She was giving him the blow-by-blow rundown of every-thing that had happened that morning. She told the tale coldly, matter-of-factly, careful not to make herself the hero of the story.

Fleming shook his head in disbelief as she finished. "Incredible."

Sarah had told Alex on the way over that Fleming was extremely interested in the GMT and that he felt they were being underutilized. He wanted to get the GMT more fund-ing, get more aggressive with how often they were sent down to the surface.

Even as she started telling Fleming the story, Alex knew she was once again breaking protocol. This kind of thing should be passed up through the chain of command, not delivered straight from grunt to politician. Hell, they hadn't even debriefed yet, and here she was telling the raw story, warts and all.

On the other hand, wasn't the City Council ultimately her employer? If her boss's boss's boss wanted details on the mission, who was she to deny him? And if her telling the story somehow resulted in more funding for the GMT, all the better.

"Incredible," Fleming repeated. "So, there were only six of you? And one was injured?"

"Drew cut his hand, sir. I don't know if I'd call that an injury. But, sure."

Fleming stared out the window for a long moment, apparently lost in thought. Then he said, "What're your feelings on Resettlement, Lieutenant?"

The question surprised her. "As in, resettling Earth?"

He turned and once again settled his intense gaze on her. "Yes."

Alex considered carefully before answering. She knew some members of Fleming's party were in favor of Resettlement, and that the movement was growing. But she didn't pay a whole lot of attention to politics, and she didn't know Fleming's stance on the issue.

"That's above my pay grade, sir. I go where General Craig points, and I fight who he tells me to fight."

Fleming waved the answer away with a flick of his hand. "I'm not asking General Craig. Nor am I asking Captain Brickman. Nor am I asking for the Ground Mission Team's official stance on the issue. I'm asking you, Alexandria Goddard, citizen on *New Haven*, for your opinion. There is no wrong answer."

Alex nodded slowly. She was in dangerous waters here, no matter what the man said, and she was going to proceed with caution. "I expect Resettlement is inevitable. We can't stay up here forever. Question is, whether now is the right time. I haven't seen anything to convince me it is."

Fleming grinned at Sarah. "I believe she just told me Resettlement is both foolish and necessary. Is she always this smart?"

"Not at all," Sarah said with a laugh.

Fleming turned back to Alex. "This period of living in the skies, this is a blip in our timeline. It's an odd, tragic moment in our history, but it's only a moment. The Earth is ours, not theirs. You know how I know that?"

"How?" Alex said.

"Because sunlight is deadly to them. Killing fire falls from the sky every day. Nature itself is designed to burn them from existence. They are an occupying force in hostile territory. They hide from the sun, in the shadows, under the dirt, whatever, but the sunlight still falls, waiting to kill them. The time is coming very soon when we'll fall on them like fire from the heavens, and the dirt won't save them from us."

Alex shifted in her seat, not used to the plush upholstery of this couch. "Forgive me, Councilman, but that seems a tad bit optimistic."

"Perhaps. But I believe it. Six of you were surprised by fourteen vampires, and you took care of them. You didn't lose a single man. Now, imagine if you had six hundred soldiers." He held up a hand before Alex could object. "I'm not talking about wiping every vampire off the face of the Earth, not right away. I'm talking about setting up a stronghold, a real city. Something we could defend. And over time, we'd begin to spread out, like humanity always has."

"And if a vampire manages to get into this city of yours?" Alex asked.

"I'm not saying I have all the answers. There will be challenges we need to overcome, but it's doable."

Alex couldn't help but get caught up in the man's excitement, his vision. Maybe he was naive, but his idea was certainly alluring.

"I'm sure you've heard that the Resettlement movement is gaining momentum?"

"I have," Alex said.

"The Council won't vote for Resettlement. They're too set in their ways. But the idea has enough support to force a popular vote."

Alex raised an eyebrow. She knew the idea was gaining popularity, but enough for a vote? Maybe this was less of a pipe dream than she'd assumed.

"When people hear about your mission this morning, that you took on fourteen vampires without a single loss, it will inspire them. Your actions on the GMT are making a real difference for the future of humanity, Alex. The time is coming, and it's coming soon. If the vote goes the way I hope it will, can I count on your support?"

"Like I said, I go where the general points me. If the vote passes, I'll fight until my last breath to make Resettlement happen."

Fleming smiled. "That's what I wanted to hear. This is real, Alex. We're going to take back the Earth."

———

"So, what's your final assessment?" General Craig asked.

Captain Brickman had just finished giving him the rundown of the day's events. Craig always asked this question after every mission. He was the type of leader who preferred to make those under his command uncover their strengths and weaknesses rather than pointing them out for them. It was a solid approach, but CB still hated the question.

"Well, sir, we accomplished our objectives, brought both motors home, and didn't lose any soldiers. And as much as I tried to avoid it, the vampire encounter was probably a net positive for the team. A minute and a half of real combat experience is worth more than a hundred hours of drills."

The general nodded, acknowledging the point. "How about negatives?"

CB shifted in his seat. He knew Craig well enough to know he wouldn't accept *nothing* as the answer to his question. "I'm nervous that the fight with the vampires went a little *too* well. I don't need them any cockier than they already are."

"And what are we going to do about Goddard?"

CB had been mulling that question over ever since they'd boarded the away ship to return to *New Haven*. "She's good, sir. She proved that this morning. Drew would be dead if not for her. The problem is, she's unpredictable. She acts independently of the team."

"Agreed. You, of all people, know how bad it can get down there. In those situations, we need team players, not heroes." The general sighed. "She's earned her place on the team, but it's time for her to grow up."

"I think I know how to make that happen, sir. With your permission, I'd like to introduce her to Frank."

9

ALEX FELL BACK into Simmons's arms.

"Well, that was certainly energetic," he said.

Alex laughed. "That's one way to describe it."

After leaving Fleming's office, she'd found herself wandering here again. It was becoming a habit. Before the mission. After the mysterious talk with Fleming. She'd have to watch herself, before she became attached.

"So, CB chewed you out pretty good?"

"How could you tell?" she asked.

"Well, you were certainly angry about something."

She rested her head on his chest. "Am I really that easy to read?"

"It took a little practice, but I'm a dedicated student of the material," he said.

She laid her head back on the pillow. "Seems like you only read in bed."

"I'd be open to reading in other places, too. Anywhere, really."

She turned and gazed at him, wondering if he was kidding. He wore an easy, but sincere smile.

It was all she could do not to laugh. "What, you want to be my boyfriend now? I'm sure that would go over great with CB and the general. We could hold hands on away missions."

"Come on, Alex. Don't be like that."

"Look, I'm not saying it wouldn't be nice. It's just there's a lot of risk. Would CB even let us both stay on the team? What we have going right now is pretty nice. Let's not screw it up."

He smiled again. Clearly, he'd expected nothing less than this response. "I agree."

It wasn't that she didn't want a relationship with Simmons. Or, at least she didn't *not* want it. But things were so complicated right now. Especially since her meeting with Fleming.

"Hey, let me ask you something," she said. "I've been seeing all these Resettlement flyers around."

"Yeah, no kidding. Those idiots are everywhere."

"So, you think Resettlement's a dumb idea?"

"Not dumb exactly. More like naive." He thought for a minute before continuing. "I mean, think about it. All those people who died one hundred and fifty years ago? It must have been, what, ninety-nine point nine-nine-nine percent of the people?"

"Add a few nines at the end there."

"Exactly! The people who got on this ship, the people who thought to launch this ship, they were the smart ones. Of all the people on Earth, they survived."

"What's that have to do with Resettlement?" she asked.

"It means the people running this place are pretty damn smart, even if it doesn't always seem that way. Will we return to the surface someday? Yeah, probably. But when it's time, they'll know. Until then, I ain't rocking the boat."

Alex's radio chirped. "Damn it."

"Probably just one of your other boyfriends hoping for a booty call."

"Whatever." She grabbed the radio and said, "Goddard."

"Alex." It was CB, and he sounded serious.

She exchanged a glance with Simmons. "What's up, Captain?"

"I need you to meet me in the hangar. Be there in five minutes."

"Roger that, CB. See you there."

She stood up and started to gather her clothes, which Simmons has distributed rather wildly around the room.

"Wonder what that's about," Simmons said.

"I don't know," Alex said, picking up her shirt. "But I can't imagine it's good."

―――――

CB WAS WAITING in the hangar when Alex arrived. The look on his face was pure business.

She greeted him with a sharp salute. "Captain."

He returned it. "Lieutenant."

They stood in silence for a moment, until Alex wasn't able to take it anymore. "Care to tell me what I'm doing here in the middle of the night, sir?"

CB rubbed his chin. It was a nervous habit, something he did when he was deciding how to proceed. She'd seen him do it dozens of times, but it had never bothered her as much as it did now. She wanted to scream at him to just say it, to rip off the bandage, to reveal her fate.

"General Craig and I had a long discussion about how best to address your recent lapses in judgment. We've come to a conclusion."

Alex waited, counting the seconds, willing herself not to speak.

"I'm going to show you something, Alex. Something no one else on the team has seen. But I need you to keep it in the strictest confidence. The security of *New Haven* depends on this remaining confidential."

She struggled to keep her surprise off her face. "Of course, sir. You know I can keep a secret."

CB nodded. "Indeed. Whatever your other failings, you've never had a problem there. Come with me."

He led her to an unmarked door on the north side of the hangar. Alex had never seen anyone enter or exit through that door. In fact, she'd never given it more than a passing glance. CB used his key card to open it, and they entered a long hallway. One entire wall was made of glass, and Alex could look straight past the left edge of the walkway and down at the clouds far below. Even for someone used to living aboard *New Haven*, it was a dizzying view.

"There are things you weren't told about the Remnants," CB said as they walked.

That gave Alex pause. She'd learned about the Remnants in school, of course, just like everybody else. They'd been the survivors of the three waves of vampire infestation—each more deadly than the last—who had come together to build and launch *New Haven*. She thought back to what Simmons had said earlier about how they'd been the only humans smart enough to know when the battle was lost and to take flight.

"The Remnants knew a fair amount about what caused the vampire outbreak by that point," CB said, "but they didn't understand vampires themselves. Not really. So, being scientists, they decided to study the problem."

"How'd they manage that, sir?"

"You've got to remember that their experiences were quite different than ours. They remembered a time before the vampires, when life on the surface was easy. A time when people slept peacefully at night. When they didn't dread sunset. It's difficult for us to imagine such a thing, but that's how humans lived for most of our history."

Alex let her fingers graze the glass wall as they walked. What was CB leading up to here? He'd said he had something to show her. Surely this would be more than a history lesson.

"Then the outbreak happened, and they lost their friends and families. We've got to imagine that every one of the Remnants lost almost everyone they knew. The vampire threat was urgent, and they were willing to go to extreme lengths to fight it."

"Clearly," Alex said, tapping a finger on the glass.

"There was a guy named Frank among the Remnants. He wasn't an engineer, or a farmer, or a soldier. He didn't have any skills that were especially suited for life in *New Haven*. His family had died in the third wave. So, when the scientists put out the call for a volunteer, he stepped forward."

"A volunteer for what?"

CB paused before answering. It was clear that this was a story he wasn't comfortable telling. "The scientists knew that vampires thrived on human blood, but they didn't understand what would happen to the creatures if they didn't have it. Would they die? Would it affect them at all? They didn't know."

They came to another door. This one had a key pad as well as a card reader. CB stopped in front of it. "They needed to find out, so they infected Frank."

Alex's eyes widened. She suddenly forgot to be worried

about what punishment she'd soon be facing. "Wait, they turned him into a vampire?"

CB nodded. He held his key card up to the reader.

"There was a vampire aboard *New Haven*?"

CB typed a long series of numbers into the key pad and the door beeped. He pushed it open. "Not was. Is."

Alex followed him into a large room with glass walls and a fifteen-by-fifteen metal box in the corner. "No way."

She wandered toward the monitor on the other side of the room. The screen clearly showed a vampire. It was a bit scrawnier than the ones she'd seen in Buenos Aires, but it was no less animalistic.

"Meet Frank," CB said. He sauntered over and rapped on the box with his knuckles, causing a metallic clang. The vampire on the monitor looked up sharply like an animal that had caught an interesting scent.

Alex stared at the screen, transfixed. She'd known all her life the vampires were people. Or, had been people. But to see one who'd been a citizen of *New Haven*, one who'd chosen to infect himself voluntarily for the greater good of humanity, made the whole concept more real to her somehow.

"The Remnants didn't know what would happen to vampires without human blood," CB said, "so Frank was used as sort of a canary in the coal mine. Like in the old stories. They fed Frank animal blood, just like the vampires on Earth would have access to, but he remained ravenously hungry. Apparently, only human blood can sustain the creatures. The idea was that if Frank eventually starved to death, they'd know it was safe to return to the surface."

"But that didn't happen." Alex watched, fascinated as the vampire raised up on its haunches, head tilted, as if it were listening to them.

"No, it did not. Truth is, we never learned all that much from old Frank, here. He deteriorated, becoming less human and more like an animal. He lost the ability to speak and his body slowly transformed into the state you see today. It's tracked pretty well with the vampires we've seen on Earth. Trouble is, we don't know if that's from lack of human blood or just the natural aging process of a vampire."

"So why not kill him? Put the poor bastard out of his misery."

CB shook his head. "This man gave his life for us, and we're going to learn as much as possible from his sacrifice. We still haven't observed the entire vampire lifecycle. What will he look like one hundred fifty years from today? Will he eventually die of old age? If he does, that could be our cue to head back down. There are no humans down there for the vampires to infect, and we know they can't reproduce—"

"Do we?" Alex asked. "Do we know that for sure?"

CB thought for a moment. "Fair enough. We strongly believe that they can't reproduce. So, we wait for Frank to die."

On the screen, Frank was settling back down. He raked one clawed hand across his elongated ear, as if scratching it.

"You ever think maybe we shouldn't just keep waiting, Captain?"

He looked at her, his eyes alive with surprise. "Don't tell me you're a Resettler, Goddard."

"No, it's just...the vampires in the Remnants' day were smart. They were just people with enhanced senses, a hunger for blood, and a strong aversion to sunlight. It's no wonder the Remnant couldn't stand up to them. But now? They're animals. I'll take our brains, versus their brawn, anytime."

CB's eyes narrowed. "You don't know what you're talking about. You haven't seen them at night."

"So, we don't face them at night. They surprised us today, and you saw what we did to them. What if we led a series of carefully planned assaults during the daytime? Find a defensible area. Clear it out. Move some people in there and spend every day securing the surrounding area. I'm not saying we move everyone down there right away, but we could set up a small colony. It could work, CB."

"The vampires would tear through the colony in hours, Alex. They wouldn't last a single night."

"You don't know that."

CB sighed. "That's enough for now. Besides, it's not our call. You think the City Council doesn't want Resettlement? Of course, they do. When it's safe, when there's a way to make it work, they'll move on it."

"Seems to me the City Council has it pretty good now. Maybe they don't want things to change. And maybe Frank's not the only one in a cage."

"Alex, I brought you here because I trust you. I brought you here because I need you focused. Like it or not, you're a big part of the future of this team. Frank made the ultimate sacrifice for humanity, because he knew it was important. What we do, what I'm asking you to do, is no less important. But I have to be able to trust that you're not going to run off and do your own thing, like you did this morning. That you're going to follow orders. I need your commitment that you can do that. Do I have it?"

Frank sat back down on the floor of his box, his arms huddled around his shoulders.

"Yes, Captain," Alex said. "You have my commitment."

10

BRIAN SAT HUNCHED over his microscope, staring into its magnified world. Even though it was five thirty in the morning, his eyes were already tired. Maybe it was more accurate to say his eyes were *still* tired. He'd worked so late the previous night that he hadn't even had the energy to walk back to his quarters, and he'd crashed on the couch in the R&D department for a few hours before waking up and getting back to it.

He didn't have the luxury of wasting time on sleep. Every moment spent resting was another moment that he wasn't growing closer to his breakthrough.

He was so close. He'd almost keyed in on the correct wavelength, he was sure of it. After years of work, he was only days, maybe hours, from completing it. He needed to get as much time in as possible before his employees showed up and started asking him questions and distracting him with pleasantries. Because this was too important. If he got this right, it could change everything.

He punched a number into the key pad, making an incremental adjustment to the frequency of the light. He hit enter and...something happened. The specimen under his microscope sizzled, and, a moment later, burned.

With a shaky hand, he placed another specimen under the microscope and once again activated the light. When the second specimen reacted the same way, Brian let out a high-pitched sound, half gasp, half giggle. He couldn't believe it.

He pushed himself to his feet, threw his hands in the air, and let out a whoop of joy.

———

ALEX WAS the first one in the gym that morning.

She picked up a jump rope and began her warm up, but her mind kept returning to what she'd seen the previous night. All her life, there'd been a vampire aboard *New Haven*, and she hadn't known it. What other secrets were the City Council and General Craig keeping from the citizens?

And then there was the matter of Resettlement. The more she thought about it, the more foolish it seemed to not at least try to reclaim the Earth. Wasn't there an isolated mountaintop they could hold? An island? A remote location that had been sparsely populated before the outbreak? They could set up a new city in one of those locations and start the process of recolonizing the Earth. Maybe it would work, and maybe it wouldn't, but why not try?

CB had been trying to teach her dedication by showing her Frank, but what he'd taught her instead was that sometimes, in extreme circumstances, extreme measures were necessary. Frank had known that. Alex didn't know what measures she'd be called on to take, but she vowed that when the opportunity arose, she'd be ready.

She was just starting to break a sweat when the gym door banged open and Brian stumbled in. Of all the people she expected to see in here, Brian was just about the least likely. He wasn't exactly one for physical fitness. In fact, as he came in, he blinked hard and looked around, disoriented, as if he'd never seen this place. It wouldn't have surprised Alex to learn that he hadn't.

Finally, his eyes settled on her and he smiled. "Ah, excellent, I was hoping you'd be here."

"Morning, Brian. A little early, isn't it?"

He blinked hard again. "Is it? I mean, yes, I suppose it is. Guess we're just more dedicated than the rest of them, huh?"

He chuckled awkwardly and Alex managed a polite smile.

"Anyway, I need you to come with me."

"Um, I'm a little busy here, man. This is kinda part of my job. Want me to stop by later?"

His smile didn't waver as he shook his head. "You're gonna have to trust me, Alex. You want to see this."

———

THE NEXT DAY, Alex stood in the corner of the R&D lab, trying not to draw any attention. She still wasn't entirely sure how she'd managed to score an invite to this demonstration. She supposed maybe it was because she'd been the one to bring news of the breakthrough to Captain Brickman and General Craig, a favor Brian had allowed her to help get her out of the doghouse. Or maybe Brian had insisted on her being here.

Either way, here she was, standing in the background while CB, General Craig, and Councilman Stearns waited for the R&D team's demonstration. Brian stood in front of them, his hair a disheveled mess and dark circles under his eyes. The table next to him held a clipboard and a lantern. He was flanked by Sarah on one side and an assistant Alex didn't know on the other.

Brian cleared his throat, somehow managing to make even that small action seem awkward. "Okay, well, thanks for coming, everyone. I'm Brian McElroy. But I guess you know that. Except you, Councilman...or did you know that? I'm sure you didn't. You have to meet a lot of people. Why would you remember me?"

Alex subtly motioned for him to move it along. He responded with an easily noticeable nod.

"Right. Let's get to it. Before I show you the device, I should preface it by saying it does still have its limitations. It's currently only effective at a distance of five meters or less. We may be able to increase that range with time, but I'm not entirely convinced—"

"Get on with it, man," General Craig growled.

"Right. For years we've struggled with the problem of vampires' reactions to artificial light. We have lights that plants respond to in the same way as sunlight; however, when we tried those on vampires, the results were lackluster. The best we've managed to accomplish is momentarily stunning the vampires, and even that didn't seem to work consistently. We were focusing on full-spectrum solar distribution levels, but not on the elements of non-visible light. I've been working on a theory that the proper levels of gamma, x-rays, inferred, micro, and ultraviolet waves are the key. It's not just the visible light that kills the vamps, but a proper recreation of all elements of the sun's rays. Sarah, if you would?"

Sarah clicked a device in her hand and the overhead lights dimmed. At the same moment an image was projected on the wall in front of them. It was a strangely shaped object that Alex couldn't identify.

Brian cleared his throat again. "Okay, so this is a sample of muscle tissue from a vampire. It's incredibly resilient and heals quickly from any form of damage. Except, of course, sunlight. Watch what happens."

A bright light shone on the lump of muscle. It quickly shriveled and, a moment later, caught fire.

"Brilliant," CB said dryly. "Sunlight kills vampires."

"I'm sorry, but I'm a little confused," Councilman Stearns said. "What did you bring us here to see?"

A mischievous smile grew on Brian's face. "Actually, sir. You just saw it. That wasn't sunlight."

He flipped on the lantern on the table next to him and light filled the room.

———

IT WAS a long moment before anyone spoke. Alex understood. She'd been speechless, too, when Brian had demonstrated the light for her the day before.

Finally, Councilman Stearns said, "Just to make certain I understand, are you telling us you've developed an artificial light that can kill vampires?"

Brian's head bobbed up and down in a frantic nod. "Obviously, we haven't tested it on a live vampire, but it perfectly synthesizes the aspects of sunlight that damage vampires, so I'm confident that it will work in the field."

"Jesus!" CB said. He walked over and clapped Brian on the shoulder. "This is amazing!"

Even the general let out a delighted laugh. "Imagine arming our GMT with these."

"Even better," Brian said. "Imagine setting these up on motion sensors. Any vampire gets within five meters? Zap!"

The group laughed, and Alex joined them. Her mind had been reeling with possibilities ever since she saw this thing. Suddenly, Resettlement wasn't some distant dream. This light made it a real possibility. She imagined city walls lined with the lights, perpetually protected from vampires. She imagined what it would be like to see night, real night, for the first time. To see the stars. The nighttime moon!

Councilman Stearns spoke, interrupting her thoughts. "This is wonderful work, son. It's going to save a lot of lives. But we have to be careful with this technology. People might get the wrong idea."

Alex felt a chill, her joy suddenly dampened by what she knew they would say next.

"You think people will assume this means we're ready for Resettlement?" General Craig asked.

"Perhaps." The councilman held his hand up to the light.

"With all the people coming in and out of this lab, we might not be able to keep it a secret."

"If word gets out, it gets out," the councilman said. "We'll just have to remind people that the future of humanity is at stake. We're safe up here. Will we resettle someday? Perhaps. But that's many years in the future. A light isn't going to change all that."

The group fawned over the light and discussed its possibilities for ten more minutes, but Alex had stopped listening. If the Council wasn't going to respond to Brian's discovering how to manufacture artificial sunlight, what *would* they respond to?

They'd never approve Resettlement. They liked running things up here too much. Something had to be done.

After CB, the general, and the councilman had left, Alex grabbed Sarah's arm and leaned in close. "You know that *one last straw* Fleming's been waiting for? Tell him we've found it."

Within a few days, the lights were public knowledge.

11

"IT'S ABOUT DAMN TIME," Drew said. His mouth was full of eggs, but he never seemed to let a little thing like that stop him from speaking his mind.

They were having breakfast in Firefly's quarters. The whole GMT was there except for CB, who was with the general. Depending on how things went with the vote, GMT leadership wanted to be ready for action.

"Of course, you like it," Owl said with a smile. "You've been going down to the surface for what, ten years? You're a hard case. But imagine how the average *New Haven* citizen will react to seeing their first vampire. Even if it is over a wall, or something."

Drew shoveled in another mouthful of eggs before answering. "That's why I want it to pass. Maybe they'll finally appreciate us."

It seemed everyone was in fine spirits this morning. There was an energy in the air that Alex couldn't remember having felt before. It took her a while to identify it, but when she did, it was unmistakable: the possibility of change.

For her part, Alex was unusually quiet at breakfast.

She'd played a role in making today happen, no matter how small.

The day after Brian's demonstration of the light to Councilman Stearns, Fleming had publicly announced the invention, made his case for how it made Resettlement possible, and called for a popular vote to decide the matter. The idea had enough support that the rest of the City Council had been powerless to stop it.

Today, that popular vote would take place. Every adult in *New Haven* would vote electronically from the communicator stations in their living quarters and throughout the city. The results would be available in real time, which meant less than half an hour from now, life aboard *New Haven* could change forever.

The Ground Mission Team had gathered this morning to enjoy some of Firefly's famous omelets and watch history unfold. The team was overwhelmingly in favor of Resettlement, with only Simmons voicing any dissent.

"Sure, they'd appreciate us," Simmons said. "They'd come to appreciate the good old days aboard the ship, too."

Owl punched him on the arm. "You telling me you seriously don't want to be down there, fighting vamps full time? I thought you loved that stuff."

"Just because it's fun doesn't mean it's healthy long-term, you know?" He glanced at Alex. "All I'm saying is, nobody knows what it's like down there at night. Not even us. Not even Drew."

"I know plenty!" Drew said, managing to send only a few small bits of egg shooting from his mouth across the table.

"We've heard CB say it a thousand times. Things are different at night. You want to risk the future of humanity?"

Firefly set down his fork and spoke for the first time. Normally at these gatherings, he stuck to cooking. He was quicker with a grenade than he was with words. "You ask me, you're being a wuss, Simmons. Everything in our arsenal and you're telling me we can't keep one city safe?"

"You'd like that, wouldn't you?" Simmons said. "Free rein to light the Earth on fire?"

A smile crossed Firefly's face. "Wouldn't you?"

Before Simmons could respond, the screen mounted in the corner turned on and Councilman Stearns's face appeared.

"Here we go," Alex said.

The councilman was standing in front of a crowd gathered in the Hub, outside the City Council building. Voting stations were set up along the edges of the crowd. Many of them held homemade signs. One read, "Earth belongs to the humans!" The sign next to it read, "Keep our children safe in the sun!"

Alex quickly scanned the crowd, but she wasn't able to determine if there were more signs supporting Resettlement or against it.

"Citizens of *New Haven*," Councilman Stearns began. "Today, we make a historic decision, one that will determine the future of the human race. Before we do, I'd like to present Councilman Fleming to make his case for Resettlement; then I will say a few words about why I, along with the majority of the Council, believe in staying aboard *New Haven*."

Fleming took the podium, and the contrast between him and Stearns couldn't have been more stark. While Stearns looked every inch the statesman, he also looked...well, old. The few strands of hair remaining on his head stood out against his scalp in bright white. His face showed the lines of every one of his nearly seventy years. Fleming, on the other hand, positively radiated youth and energy. His jet-black hair was carefully styled, and his wide smile revealed perfect teeth. Fleming looked calm, confident, and strong, while Stearns's demeanor revealed his displeasure at this morning's vote.

Alex wondered how much that would affect the outcome today. Would people see Resettlement as the future, in part because they saw Fleming that way?

The younger councilman kept his statement brief. "Fellow citizens, one hundred and fifty years ago, our birthright was taken from us. The majority of humanity was destroyed as waves of pure, savage evil poured over the Earth. But the Remnants, our ancestors, escaped through ingenuity and brilliance. Those same qualities flow strongly in our veins. We now have the weapons to take back the Earth. Only one question remains: do we have the courage? Do we have the grit to leave our comfortable prison and claim our birthright? I know the answers to these questions, and I think you do, too. I'm confident you will vote for courage over fear, for the future over the past. We will do what it takes to provide a safe and permanent home for our children. They deserve it."

A wave of cheers and boos echoed through the speakers as he left the podium.

"Damn right," Drew muttered. "Let's do this thing."

Councilman Stearns took the podium, a few beads of sweat standing on his forehead. "Citizens, I ask this morning that you avoid the allure of change for the sake of change. For one and a half centuries, we've been safe aboard this ship. As Councilman Fleming pointed out, we hold the future of humanity in our hands today. Is Resettlement in our future? I believe it is. But not like this. A safe return to Earth will take decades of preparation. I know that's probably not what you want to hear, but it's the truth. Our ancestors handed us a very precious gift, but it's a fragile one. We have to treat it as such.

"Humanity fell to the vampires quickly. Even though humans vastly outnumbered the vampires, the fight did not last long. It's more accurate to call it a slaughter than a war. Today, the vampires may not even know of our city's existence. We have to consider the consequences very carefully before we do anything to change that. Otherwise, we could be risking not only any resettlement of Earth, but also of *New Haven* itself.

"We are safe, we are secure, and as long as we stay aboard *New Haven*, we will remain so. No one here goes hungry. The wars and violence that have plagued humanity throughout our history are a thing of the past. I have grand hopes for future, hopes of what we can become. If we persevere, if we hold the course, we can grow a future even more wonderful than the storied world before the vampires. But if we are rash, we will end up as nothing more than a meal for the creatures that now infest the Earth. I ask that you use caution, use wisdom, and vote to finish what the Remnants started. Vote against immediate Resettlement."

He stepped back from the podium and the crowd once again erupted in a cacophony of support and dissent. Through the small speaker on the screen, it was impossible to tell whether the cheers or boos were louder.

"It's gonna be a close one," Owl said.

The image of the crowd on the screen disappeared and was replaced with a message: *Activate with key card to vote.*

Drew stood up and pushed back his chair. "Hope no one minds if I go first."

He marched to the screen and held his ID card up to the card reader next to it. The image on the screen changed again. Now the text said, *Vote on the matter of the immediate resettlement of Earth.* Two buttons were shown below the text. One said, *For,* the other said *Against.*

Drew dramatically drew back his finger, then pressed it to the *For* button. "One vote for killing vampires. Who's next?"

As the team voted one by one, the tension in the room grew. It was somehow becoming more real by the moment. If the vote passed, the GMT's role would likely change quickly and dramatically. No longer would they serve as a salvage team who ran dangerous but infrequent missions to the surface. They'd be the first line of defense, a group that would need to grow quickly. They would probably be called on to train others, and, once Resettlement took place, combat with vampires would become a much more frequent occurrence. Alex was beginning to feel the responsibility that would fall on their shoulders. Humanity's survival would depend on them in a much more immediate and direct way.

Still, when Alex's turn came, she hesitated for only a moment before selecting *For.*

It only took about thirty minutes before every adult in *New Haven* had cast their vote. The results appeared on the screen and a shocked hush fell over the room.

The screen showed 51 percent For, 49 percent Against.

Resettlement had passed.

———

AN HOUR LATER, Alex was in the gym, lifting weights and trying not to think too hard about what came next. She was happy about the results. This would mean a real future; it would mean the rest of her life wouldn't be spent in the oppressive safety of this flying can.

She imagined what it would be like. There'd have to be a city with high walls and active defense systems. Maybe the walls would be lined with Brian's lights, as he'd suggested during his demonstration. They'd have to stay behind the walls at night.

But what about during the day? Would she be able to roam the countryside? Swim in a real lake? Feel real Earth-grown grass between her toes? She didn't see why not. And that, in and of itself, was pretty amazing to imagine. That was how humans were meant to live.

She focused on that. There would be plenty of time to think about the hard work that lay ahead, the danger, later.

Simmons was spotting her on the bench press. He'd been quiet since the results were announced. To his credit, he hadn't complained. He'd simply accepted it. But there was a troubled look on his face.

A loud, familiar tone filled the room, and the screen on the wall came to life. Once again, it showed Councilman Stearns. This time, he was sitting behind a desk rather than standing behind a podium.

"Sweet," Alex said. "Maybe he's gonna talk about the timeline."

Simmons didn't respond. A dark shadow crossed his face.

Alex toweled off as she waited for the councilman to speak.

"My fellow citizens, a historic vote was cast today. With this vote, you let your voice be heard, loud and clear. The City Council hears and understands that a majority of the people of *New Haven* wish to return to the surface. Your voices have been heard."

Alex got to her feet and stepped closer to the screen.

Something about the careful way Stearns was phrasing things struck her as odd.

"Alex, this is not going to be good," Simmons said.

Stearns continued. "After the vote, the City Council met to discuss the results. As the last of our kind, we have a grave responsibility to the future, and it's one we do not take lightly. As you may know, our city charter grants the Council the ability to override a popular vote if there is a clear and present danger to humanity. We have determined that such a threat exists today."

"Oh shit," Alex whispered.

"While we will continue to explore the possibility of Resettlement in the coming years, returning to the surface is not in the best interests of humanity at this time. As such, we are hereby declaring this proposal an immediate threat to humanity and overruling the results. The proposal for immediate Resettlement has been rejected."

12

ALEX FELT Simmons's hand settle on her shoulder.

"Alex, we have to be smart now. People are going to be upset."

She shrugged off his hand. "You think? Hell, I'm upset." She threw her towel into the laundry basket near the door to the locker room. "The Council is supposed to follow the will of the people, right? How can they do this?"

Simmons answered her softly, his voice even more careful and measured than it had been before. "Fifty-one percent of the people feel just like you do. Actually, more than that. I voted against Resettlement, and this decision makes me nervous."

The thought of swimming in a lake, feeling the cool water on her skin, once again passed through her mind. "Oh, I'm pretty far past nervous."

"That's exactly the problem. No offense, but you're rash enough, even when you're not mad. Remember, we work for the Council, like it or not. Don't do anything you'll regret."

"Funny, I thought we worked for the people." She headed for the locker room. She'd had enough of this.

"Hey, I thought you were going to spot me. Where you going?"

She answered without turning back. "To find people who understand."

———

GENERAL CRAIG STOOD in the City Council meeting chambers at the end of a large, u-shaped table. The Council members were seated before him. All but one.

"Dare I ask why Councilman Fleming isn't present?" he asked.

Stearns exchanged glances with Harriet Yates, the Councilwoman sitting to his left. "After the vote, we had a rather... spirited debate. Fleming wasn't pleased to lose the discussion eleven to one. He left."

"Stormed out, is more like it," Yates said. Like Stearns, she was on the far side of sixty-five.

"In truth, I'm not entirely sure if we'll be seeing him in these chambers again," Stearns said.

The general blinked hard. If Fleming left the Council, would his followers still stand behind him? If so, that could make for a dangerous situation. Fleming didn't seem like the type to go quietly. "Understood. It probably goes without saying, but I'll say it anyway. Whatever happens next, the Council has the full support of the Ground Mission Team and the police force."

Eleven expressions of surprise stared back at him. He had the sudden, sinking feeling that the Council didn't comprehend the severity of what they'd done. They didn't understand the potential repercussions.

Stearns cleared his throat. "Well, yes, thank you, General Craig. As you say, that probably didn't need to be said."

"Understood. In that case, would you be open to suggestions for mitigating the risks of this potentially tumultuous time?"

Eleven blank stares. Jesus, they really had no idea how their decision was going to be perceived.

Stearns leaned forward. "All right, Craig. What would you recommend?"

"Increased badge presence on the streets for at least the next week. You should also double your personal security detail."

Yates drummed her fingers on the desk. "Is that necessary? I assume we'd be paying overtime?"

"Better to have it and not need it."

"Fine," Stearns said. "But if the people are going to be as upset as you seem to think, perhaps what they really need is good news. Engineering tells us the temperature regulation in Sparrow's Ridge is still a little off, even with the motors your team brought back. With the proper parts, we could solve this problem. Jessica has records that indicate a likely location on the surface."

The general nodded sharply. "Understood. I'll prep the Ground Mission Team."

————

ALEX SLIPPED into the meeting just as it was about to start and stood near the back. She was dressed more like a farmer from Sparrow's Ridge then a lieutenant in the GMT. That was by design. She was here because she was frustrated and didn't know what else to do, not because she wanted to make a political statement on behalf of her team.

Sarah was sitting in front of the room near Fleming. She spotted Alex, smiled, and waved. Alex cringed a little, hoping no one would notice her, but she waved back. Fleming didn't seem to see her, which was good.

They were in a small community meeting room in Sparrow's Ridge. This place was used for weddings and parties by the people who didn't have the resources to book one of the fancier locations in the Hub. It was designed to hold maybe two hundred people, but there had to be at least four hundred here. They were jammed in, shoulder to shoulder, most of them standing. Sarah had said this was only for Fleming's most trusted supporters and it wouldn't be open to the public. Alex had expected maybe thirty or forty people. This was a bit overwhelming.

Alex hadn't been sure if she should come, but she was glad she had. It felt good to be with all these people, to see her frustration reflected in so many faces. To feel the anger that she felt amplified hundreds of times in this room.

Fleming stood up and was met with thunderous applause. He held up his hands to quiet the room. "Thanks very much, but this is hardly the time for celebrating. If anything, it's a day for mourning. Since the time of the Remnants, the City Council of *New Haven* has acted as the servant of the people. That changed today."

A rumble ran through the crowd. Somebody near the front yelled, "What are we gonna do about it?"

"Maybe we should remind them who's in charge!" someone else said.

A few scattered voices mumbled their agreement.

Fleming again held up a hand, and the crowd fell silent. "What are we going to do about it? That's a great question, Steven, and it's exactly what we're here to discuss. To start with, I walked out on the Council today. I won't be going back anytime soon."

"You're resigning?" a woman shouted.

"Not at all. As far as I'm concerned, the Council stopped being a legitimate government the moment they refused to follow the will of the people. Since I joined the Council, one thing has become clear to me: the Council is only interested in protecting its power. Today proved that even more. Now we must take the necessary steps to put the power back where it truly belongs."

This time, the room stayed silent when he paused. But it was an electric silence, a silence filled with the potential energy of things unsaid.

"This is no longer just a movement of Sparrow's Ridge. We have in our ranks people in important positions that I hope they will be willing to use for our cause." His eyes rested on Alex for a moment before he continued. "If we all work together, I think you'll all be amazed at what's possible. This is not the end of the Resettlement movement. It's just the beginning."

13

THE NEXT FEW days proved the general's suspicions correct. Even with the increased police presence, protests were turning violent. Three protesters and four badges had to be hospitalized after the third night.

Alex was in bed with Simmons when they heard the news of the protests-turned-riots. He nodded toward the screen showing the report. "This is what you wanted to be part of?"

Her stomach turned. She'd been open with Simmons about her views and her frustration at the Council's decision, but she hadn't told him she'd gone to Fleming's meeting. Or about the conversations she'd had with Sarah since then and what she'd agreed to do for Fleming's cause. "I said I was for Resettlement. I didn't say I was for rioting. Just because someone acts out doesn't mean their opinions are wrong. They're just frustrated."

"Is that what you call attacking cops? Acting out? Come on, Alex, you're smarter than this."

Alex had never seen Simmons this angry. He was always

calm and composed. Even on missions. Especially on missions. She felt her own anger rise to match his.

"What are they supposed to do? They tried following the rules, and you see what that got them. I'm not saying they're right, but they've just found out they don't have a voice in their government."

Simmons shook his head, clearly disgusted. "That would be us out there, if we weren't prepping for the mission tomorrow. They'll probably send us to help control the crowds when we get back. I hope your understanding makes you feel better when they're bashing your head in."

"Jesus, Simmons, relax. Nobody's bashing anybody's head in. Are things out of hand? Of course! They should lock up anybody who attacks a cop. I'm not saying anything different."

"A second ago you were defending them!"

Alex threw back the covers and got up. She didn't need this right now. Not with everything else going on. And Simmons lumping her in with those people rioting? That wasn't fair. What she was doing was far different. It wasn't just acting out without purpose. There was a method to her role, and it could do real good for everyone.

She found her bra and put it on. "I should go."

Simmons sighed. "You don't have to do that. Stay. It's okay for us to disagree."

"Sure it is. We don't even have to get along. It's not like you're my boyfriend."

Simmons lay back down and rolled away from her. "So that's how it is?"

"I guess." She didn't want to hurt his feelings. Okay, maybe she did, a little. But more importantly, she had somewhere she was supposed to be.

"After everything, this is still just a booty call to you?" he asked.

"Can we not, right now? It is what it is. I'm having fun, and I thought you were too. Let's not ruin it by thinking too much. Besides, we have a mission tomorrow. Get some sleep."

She left without waiting for him to say goodbye.

———

SARAH WAS WAITING in the R&D lab when Alex arrived. It was past midnight, and most of the lights were off. A single bulb shone over Sarah's table, and two duffle bags sat in front of her. Alex made her way toward the light.

"Wow, this is the first time I've ever been here that Brian hasn't. Doesn't he usually sleep in his office?"

Sarah nodded. "Sometimes. I really had to put the pressure on him. I told him he was starting to look like crap, and that you'd said something about the dark circles under his eyes."

Alex stifled a laugh. "Seriously?"

"Desperate times." She patted the bags in front of her. "I've done my part. Now it's all you." She pushed the bags toward Alex. "You sure this is the right move? I mean, they'll know it was you. And it won't be hard for them to figure out it was me."

Alex picked up the bags. They were lighter than she'd expected. "That doesn't matter. If this works the way we hope it will, it'll be a big step toward convincing the Council."

"Or starting a civil war."

"Let's hope it doesn't come to that. Stay safe." Alex headed toward the door, then called over her shoulder. "Oh, and have Fleming tell his people to chill. Rioting isn't a good look."

ALEX MOVED through the hangar quietly, but purposefully. Considering the time of night, she felt pretty safe. There was rarely anyone here at this hour. And even if someone did show up, people were so used to seeing her in the hangar that they probably wouldn't question her presence. She had a cover story ready, just in case. She followed Sarah's lead by leaving as many lights off as possible.

Sarah was right. Even if this went perfectly, every person on the GMT would know who had done this the moment the mission started. CB would tell the general, even if every other member of the team would cover for her. It was possible that CB or the general would remove her from the team for this, but she was willing to risk it.

CB had accused her of being rash, of putting her desires ahead of the needs of the team when she'd taken the jet pack outside and when she'd used the rover on the factory door in Buenos Aires, but the truth was she'd been thinking of nothing but the team on both occasions. She was putting the needs of the team far above her own safety. In the case of the jet pack, she'd known the Council was hesitant to approve any new spending, so she'd put her career at risk to give them a thrilling enough demonstration to move the needle. In the case of Buenos Aires, she'd known immediately that they'd need to bust into the factory. Better to get it done quickly before team morale wavered.

Both of those had been risky maneuvers, but both had paid off for the team. She hoped and believed this time would be no different.

She reached the away ship and typed Owl's security code into the control panel next to the door. Alex had watched Owl enter the code last month and filed it away, not intending to use it, but putting it in her mental *just in case* file. She had her own passcode, but Owl was incredibly touchy about her ship. Alex wouldn't have been surprised if she had a safety measure built in that alerted her when anyone else boarded.

The ship door unlocked with a hiss of air, and Alex pulled it open and stepped onto the away ship.

The lights in the interior of the ship were motion activated, and she imagined she could almost hear them click as she entered each new section of the ship. It felt odd to be here alone. Usually, the ship was buzzing with the excitement and tension of the upcoming mission when she boarded. Walking through it now, she felt a bit of that excitement spark inside her, as if the residue of so many missions still hung in the air. But mostly the ship felt like a dead thing, like she was exploring the preserved carcass of some great beast long extinct.

She made her way to the passenger section where she and the rest of the crew sat during flights. She went to the starboard side where she always sat and wedged her fingers under the bench seat. The seat detached with a snap, revealing a large space inside the bench. This area had been designed for storage, Alex knew, but they never used it as such. The GMT was small enough that there was always plenty of room, and it was easier to just stow their gear in the cargo hold and grab it on the way out. To Alex's knowledge, this would be the first time these benches would be used for their intended purpose.

She stared at the storage area for a long moment. Like it or not, she had to admit she was crossing a line here. This wasn't just flying a jet pack outside, instead of in the hangar. This was smuggling. Any way she wanted to defend it to herself, this was putting politics ahead of her team.

But, for the citizens of *New Haven*, it had to be done.

She placed the two black bags into the seat and replaced the bench.

Twenty minutes later, she was back in her quarters, lying in bed and waiting for morning.

14

CB WAS on his morning run when his earpiece chirped. He sighed and touched the radio on his belt. "Brickman."

For CB, morning runs were sacred. As the field commander for the most elite team on *New Haven*, very little of his time was his own. He often felt pulled in a dozen different directions. General Craig needed updated budget projections. R&D wanted his sign-off on new gear. One of his team members had gotten into a fight at Tankards and punched a patron. He had to show up at the gym and lift with the team, so that they didn't think he was slacking off. And that was the average Tuesday before ten a.m.

But this forty-five-minute run was for him. He guarded this time jealously, and he even went for the run on mission days, when things were three times as hectic. Everyone who worked with him, everyone who had access to this radio channel, knew about the holiness of his morning run, and they damn sure wouldn't interrupt it unless there was no choice.

So, he was more than a little surprised when the voice of Brian McElroy came through his radio.

"Sorry to bother you, Captain. You need to come down to R&D right away. We've got a situation."

Ten minutes later, he was changed into his fatigues and on his way to R&D.

Brian met him at the door. "This isn't good, sir."

CB brushed past him and into the lab. He didn't know what he'd find there, but he had his gun on his hip just in case. "Care to elaborate?"

Brian followed close behind. From the quiver in his voice, CB could tell he was about to lose it. The kid was brilliant, but he wasn't exactly calm under pressure. "I've looked everywhere, and I can't find them. Which is insane, because they were here at eleven last night when I locked up. I know because I was trying a new casing for them, one that would make them more useful in the field."

CB stopped and turned toward Brian. "Son, slow down and tell me what you're talking about."

Brian nodded frantically, then took a deep breath before speaking again. "Okay, sorry, I'm a little freaked out."

"Something's missing?"

Brian nodded again, but this time it didn't look as much like his head was out of control on a spring. "It's the Daylights, sir. The ones that replicate sunlight. They're gone."

CB cursed softly. "You're kidding."

"I wish, sir."

If the general found out about this, he'd blow a gasket. The mission would be canceled, and the place would go into lockdown. This was the piece of tech that had caused this whole Resettlement resurgence, after all.

CB pointed up at the cameras mounted all over the room. "You checked the tape?"

Brian shook his head. Clearly, he hadn't even considered

that. "I'll get right on it."

"Good. While you do that, I'm going to see what I can dig up."

CB glanced at his watch. He had three hours until he needed to report to the away ship. He'd tell the general about the Daylights before that if he had to, but he wanted to try recovering the lights on the down low first. He had a pretty good idea where to start looking.

———

CB HAD GROWN up in Sparrow's Ridge. His father had died when CB was four, and his mother had worked a low-level job in the nuclear sector. Like everyone in *New Haven*, their most basic needs were guaranteed, so CB never went hungry or naked, but he spent most of his younger years wearing thin, City-Council-issued handout clothes, which the other kids took every opportunity to taunt him for.

His mother had passed five years ago, and he hadn't spent any real time in the Ridge since, but he still knew his way around. Enough old-timers remembered him that he was able to get someone to point him to Fleming's makeshift headquarters—the Council-in-exile, they were calling it, apparently.

CB barely recognized the place. Back in his day, it had been a general community center, mostly used for poor kids' birthday parties and old people's card clubs. Now, it was transformed. Dozens of desks filled the room, and the walls were lined with even more workers jammed together at tables. There must have been one hundred people crowded into the room. And at the head of it all, sitting at a large desk at the front of the room, was Fleming.

CB marched right up to the desk, ignoring the three

young men who tried to stop him with polite offers of help. He planted both hands on the desk and leaned forward.

Fleming looked up, clearly surprised to see this fireplug of a man in his face, but he quickly recovered and gave CB his signature smile. "Captain. Pleasure seeing you here. Come to join the movement?"

"Cut the shit, Fleming. I want to know what you did with them."

Fleming's gaze darted behind CB, and CB glanced over his shoulder to see a small group of men was gathering behind him. Probably what passed for the tough guys in this pathetic assortment of would-be rebels.

Fleming looked back at CB. "You're going to have to be a little more specific, Captain."

CB grimaced. He didn't have time for this nonsense. If Fleming wanted to play coy, fine, but CB sure wasn't going to. "The Daylights, Councilman. I know you have them."

Fleming's smiled didn't waver, but CB was almost certain he saw a spark of recognition in the councilman's eyes. "We don't have your lights. If you've misplaced them, that's not my concern."

"I didn't misplace them, asshole. You took them."

CB felt a hand on his shoulder. He turned to see the biggest of the men looming over him.

"Okay, time to leave, buddy."

The guy had eight inches on CB, and he held himself like a man used to getting his way. CB was fairly certain he could drop this idiot in one punch, if it came to that.

He shrugged the man's hand off his shoulder and glared at him. "Touch me again, and I'll break your fingers."

"It's okay, Phil," Fleming said. "Captain, I'm sorry your equipment was stolen, but you are seriously misplacing your suspicion. And, frankly, it's a little insulting that you'd leap to this conclusion. These people you see before you are all volunteers, graciously giving their time to help us raise support. We're focused on putting pressure on the City Council to do their duty and listen to the will of the people, and I promise you, that is more than job enough for all of us. We don't have time to break into Ground Mission Team headquarters to steal equipment."

CB smiled. "That so? I guess your people don't have anything to do with the protests that have been going on? With the riots?"

"I'll admit, things have gotten a little out of hand, but these are extraordinary times."

"That they are. I never thought I'd see the day when a member of the City Council would steal equipment from the GMT."

Fleming shook his head as if disappointed. "Look around, Captain. What use would the Daylights be to us? I said it before, and I'm only going to say it one more time. We don't have your lights. Now I think it's time for you to go. Unless you'd like to sign our petition first?"

Others had joined the men behind CB. There must have been twenty of them. And every other eye in the room was watching.

CB knew many of these people were Sparrow's Ridge lifers, hardscrabble folk who were no strangers to a barroom brawl. Still, he was pretty sure he could drop four or five of these guys before they took him down. And he was armed.

But the clock was ticking. He didn't have time to fool around. He turned back to Fleming. "I'm sure you know that, at this point, the Council is just looking for an excuse to officially remove you. If I find out you had anything to do with those lights going missing, they'll have it."

Fleming flashed his most brilliant politician's smile. "If

you're threatening to remove me from power, best of luck, Captain Brickman. You're going to need it."

———

BRIAN SAT in front of the monitor, fast-forwarding through last night's footage. He couldn't believe someone had stolen the Daylights, but there was no other explanation for their disappearance. As upset as he was about the theft, he was even more worried about what he was going to find on the security tape.

The thing he hadn't mentioned to Captain Brickman was that the list of possible suspects was quite small. Only ten people worked in R&D, and only five of them had keys. There were a few others who had access—janitorial staff, a few select Engineering people, the general himself—but the list wasn't long. Whoever had done this, it would be a gut punch.

He slowed the recording as a shape appeared. The figure was familiar, and Brian's heart sank. Sarah. He'd suspected as much. She'd been talking about Resettlement for months, and lately she'd been spending all her free time with Fleming and his supporters. Brian knew she'd been indoctrinated to Fleming's radical views, but he didn't think she'd go this far.

He scrolled further through the tape and watched as she gathered the Daylights and stowed them in black duffle bags.

Brian grabbed his radio off the desk. Time to tell Captain Brickman he'd found the culprit.

Before he could turn on the radio, another figure joined Sarah on the screen, and Brian let out a gasp.

"Oh, Alex, how could you?"

15

Alex was the last one to the locker room that morning. Somehow, in spite of everything that was going on, with the mission, the Daylights, the rising tension between the Council and the Resettlement supporters, she'd fallen asleep almost the moment her head hit the pillow the previous night, and she'd slept hard. She'd woken disoriented and groggy, and now, she was ten minutes late to mission prep.

Grabbing her stuff out of her stocked locker, she threw on her silver mail suit and her fatigues. She gave herself one final check to make sure she had everything—pistols, sword, tactical knives—and then she headed out.

Alex knew something was wrong as soon as she approached the away ship. There were people around the ship, the same way there always were before a mission, but they weren't bustling around. They stood, working slowly, methodically, and every one of them looked at her as she approached.

Brian exited the ship and startled when he saw her.

"Hey, man," she said.

"Hi, Alex." His voice was distant and cold, and his eyes were heavy with heartbreak.

She was caught, and she knew it.

But what were her options? Turn tail and run? How far would she get? No, she had to face the music.

She stepped into the ship, brushed past a tech from R&D, and headed for the passenger section. When she got there, the other GMT members were standing around the area. The bench seats were removed. Every eye turned toward her as she entered.

Silence hung thick in the air.

Emotion played openly on the faces of her teammates. Simmons wore a disappointed look. Drew looked shocked. Firefly looked angry.

Only CB's face was blank, as if it were carved from stone. "You've pulled some shit in your day, Goddard," he said, "but this is one step too far. Come with me. We're going to see the general."

Alex nodded. She tried to keep the emotion out of her voice when she said, "Yes, sir."

As they turned to go, Drew said, "How could you, Alex? You know we need you on this team. We need you down there. Anything happens to us, it's on you."

"What were you trying to accomplish here?" Owl asked.

Alex considered whether to answer that or plead ignorance, but only for a moment. Her team deserved the truth. "I thought if we could demonstrate the Daylights, if we could show how effective they are, it might help change the Council's mind."

"*You* thought?" Simmons said. "We all know this wasn't your idea. You're so far in Fleming's pocket you don't even know what you're doing anymore. You don't even realize you're a traitor."

Alex turned back at that, her eyes suddenly alive with anger. "A traitor? How about the Council? They were elected to serve the will of the people."

Simmons laughed dryly. "See what I mean?"

Firefly glared at Alex. "If they say we can't go on the mission because of you, I'm gonna kick your ass. Girl or not."

"I think we both know what would happen if you tried," Alex answered.

"That's enough!" CB yelled.

The ship fell silent.

He turned back toward the cargo hold. "GMT needs the ship. Everyone else, clear out."

They waited a minute in silence as the R&D techs left. When they were alone, CB said, "The general and the Council will decide how to address what Alex did. It starts and ends with them. This city is tearing itself apart. I won't have this team do the same thing. I already lost one team." He paused, looking around, meeting each of their gazes. "It's time I tell you how it happened."

"IT HAPPENED WHEN I WAS TWENTY-FIVE," CB began. "I was in charge of demolitions for the GMT, at the time. We had a strong group. Lots of years of experience, more than we have now, even. The captain was this grizzled old woman named Murphy." He paused and chuckled. "Well, she seemed old at the time. Come to think of it, she was probably about fifty, same as I am now.

"The thing you young people gotta know is, this isn't the first time the idea of Resettlement has gained popularity. Seems to crop up every generation or so. Back then, our sniper was this dude about a year younger than me named Kravitz. He was a cocky SOB, but damn if he wasn't good enough to back up his confidence. He was also a big proponent of Resettlement, and, even more importantly, he had Murphy's ear. Maybe more than her ear, if you want to believe the rumors that were flying around then.

"I don't know how he did it, but Kravitz somehow convinced Murphy to allow us to give a little demonstration of how effectively we could deal with vampires. Thought was, if we were successful, it would be quite a boon to the Resettlement movement. It'd show people maybe the idea wasn't so farfetched after all.

"So, we headed down to the surface, an old city in the northern hemisphere called Quebec. It was supposed to be a routine mission to gather some parts for Engineering, but we had other ideas.

"Our pilot set us down right in the old center of the city, in the middle of a mess of buildings. We all stayed near the ship, safely in the light. We'd brought a supply of human blood with us, quarts of the stuff. We spread it all around us in a circle. And, sure enough, soon the vampires began to appear.

"They stayed in the doorways of the buildings, in the shadows, but it was like they couldn't resist. They came right up to the edge of the light and stopped, pretty as a picture. I'll tell you what, it was like target practice. We spent hours killing vampire after vampire. Every time we'd blow one's head off, another one would drag the body out of the way and take its place.

"At first it was exciting. We were killing dozens, hundreds of them, and hardly breaking a sweat doing it. But after a while, I started to feel numb. Then, a few hours on, the nervousness started to creep in. See, the whole idea was for us to prove we could clear out this whole city center. Make it a vampire-free-zone, you know? But no matter how many we killed, they just kept coming. I couldn't help but wonder, if there were this many just in the few buildings around our ship, how many were there in the city? In the world? Still, I have to admit, I was enjoying myself.

"We'd started clearing them out around midday, and the work dragged on for hours and hours. Shoot one. Wait for another vampire. Shoot that one. Reload as needed. Repeat. Thankfully, Captain Murphy had thought to bring an ungodly amount of ammo. Even with all the vampires, we weren't in much danger of running out. We'd periodically send one of us back into the ship to restock the team.

"As the day wore on and the sun moved across the sky, the shadows on the west side of the street grew longer, and the vampires were able to move out of the doorways and into the street. Still, we were safely in the sun, and we were happy to be able to kill them in a new location. Since they were in the open, I was able to use some explosives, which everyone enjoyed. It's the only time in my life I remember being on the surface and feeling comfortable. It was so easy. We were just killing dumb animals. I started to consider why I'd been so afraid of vampires all my life. Why anyone was.

"Somehow, in the midst of the mind-numbing repetition and the violence, we lost track of time and didn't realize how quickly dusk was approaching. I can't explain it other than to say we felt invincible. For the first time in my life, night didn't seem the least bit scary.

"Murphy sent me back to the ship to restock everyone's ammo, and as I was walking toward the ship, the sun dipped behind a building, a shadow fell across the ship, and all hell broke loose.

"Vampires poured out of the buildings and attacked the team. Still, the team held their own. They circled up quickly and killed the vampires racing toward them. It felt like no big deal.

I was almost at the ship, and the team seemed to have the vamps in hand, so I ducked inside to grab the ammo. When I stepped back out, that's when everything changed. The sun set.

"It was as if the vampires suddenly woke up. I don't know how else to explain it. In an instant, they were different. They moved with power and speed like I've never seen, before or since. They seemed like a different species than the creatures we'd been facing all day.

"The team kept attacking, but now their shots weren't landing. The creatures moved almost too fast to see, let alone to shoot. In a matter of seconds, two of my team members were down, their throats torn out. The fresh blood brought even more of the creatures from other buildings. They weren't even using doors anymore; they'd just burst through the buildings' concrete walls.

"Murphy shouted for the team to retreat and everyone started running toward the ship. I tried to cover their escape, launching grenades from the door of the ship into the mass of vampires. But Murphy waved me inside, told me to get the ship into the air the moment everyone was aboard.

"I stumbled my way to the cockpit, dazed from the sudden turn the fight had taken. I was trained to operate the away ship, but it had been a while since I'd even sat in the pilot's seat. I somehow managed to activate the exterior cameras, and I watched in horror as my team was overrun and devoured.

"Somehow I managed to keep my wits about me enough to remember to shut the doors to the ship just before the vampires reached it. The creatures jumped onto the exterior of the ship and began clawing at it, trying to tear it apart.

"I shakily managed to get the ship off the ground and raced toward the sun. The vampires on the ship burned in that light, and I'm not ashamed to say that I reveled in their screams. I somehow managed to get the ship back to *New Haven* and into the hangar before I broke down and wept, the last living member of the Ground Mission Team."

———

CB PLACED a hand against the wall to steady himself as he finished his tale.

Alex blinked hard, trying to take in everything she'd just heard. She'd known CB had faced vampires after sundown, and he'd told them time and time again that vampires were different at night, but she had never imagined he'd lost his entire team. That he'd had to watch as they were torn to shreds.

"That's what we're up against," he said. "I understand your overconfidence. You haven't seen what I have. Hell, I felt the same way before I saw it with my own eyes. But I'm the only person alive who witnessed it up close, and I can tell you that it is much worse down there than you've been taught. The vampires are everywhere, and Resettlement is suicide."

16

AFTER THE STORY, tensions seemed to relax a bit. CB announced that the mission would be delayed a day. This was met with a nominal amount of grumbling, but not nearly as much as Alex would have expected. It also gave her reason for hope. If the mission were today, she'd definitely be left behind. Maybe by tomorrow, cooler heads would prevail, and she'd be allowed to keep her place on the team.

CB left her alone for a few minutes while he went to find the general. Alex felt like she was a little girl waiting for her dad to come home from work and hand out her punishment. It didn't take long; CB soon returned and told her the general was with the City Council. He was taking her to see them.

As they rode in CB's cart toward the Hub, Alex thought about the story he'd just told. She couldn't imagine what it must have been like to experience that, to have to leave his teammates behind. It also made her think a little more deeply about the idea of Resettlement. According to what CB had said, vampires were able to bust through concrete walls at night. They moved almost too quickly for the human eye to follow. How could humanity stand up to something like that? Had she been wrong to support Fleming and his ideals?

"Can I ask you something?" she said.

"Sure." He didn't exactly sound excited about the possibility.

"What happened when you got back to *Haven*? After the mission, I mean. Why'd they allow you to stay on the GMT after your team had disobeyed the mission orders and provoked the vampires?"

There was a long silence before he answered. "I lied."

Alex's eyebrows shot up in surprise at that. She felt like she knew the captain pretty well, and she couldn't imagine him lying to leadership.

"I didn't want my team to be remembered like that," he said. "As disobedient fools who brought death on themselves. So, I told the general that the mission took longer than expected and we didn't make it back to the ship before sundown. He treated me like a hero. Promoted me and let me help train the new members of the Ground Mission Team."

They were passing through the Engineering section of the ship by then, and workers in green jumpsuits, the uniform of the Engineering Corp, filed past.

"Look, Alex, I understand you better than you think I do. Hell, I was very much like you once upon a time. But I'm done lying. I can't hide this from the Council."

"I understand." And she did. It wasn't CB's fault she was in trouble. She was a big girl. She'd take her medicine.

"I don't know what the Council's going to decide, but if you remain on the GMT, I'll ask that you learn from my mistakes. Don't underestimate the creatures on the surface.

I lost one team already. I'm not sure I could handle losing another."

Before Alex could reply, a siren started blaring. For a moment, she thought it was the siren that sounded every time the hangar door was opened. But no, this one was different. Higher-pitched, and more frantic.

"That's nearby," CB said. He turned the cart down the next side street and headed toward the siren.

A moment later, a larger vehicle raced past them. Alex recognized it was the Emergency Response Team, the group in charge of providing emergency medical assistance and battling fires.

"This can't be good," Alex said.

"Let's check it out," CB said.

"What about the Council?"

"The Council can wait."

———

CHADWICK STEARNS and the other Council members— minus the still-absent Daniel Fleming—stared up at the Head of Engineering, Jessica Bowen.

"What's the report, Jessica?" Stearns asked.

"It's bad, sir."

Stearns grimaced. At least she was being straightforward. That was one of the things he liked about Jessica: she never sugarcoated anything.

"The fire damaged a pretty large swath of equipment," she said. "Most of it is salvageable, or not vital to the ship's viability. The real concern is the nuclear reactor. The main control panel was damaged beyond repair."

"Holy hell," one of the councilmen muttered.

"The ship can continue to fly. For now. But without the

reactor, our power cells will decrease daily, and that will adversely affect our ability to maintain altitude."

Stearns leaned forward. "Bottom line it for me."

"I've run the numbers. We have thirty days to get the reactor back online. Otherwise, we'll have to land and find a way to survive on the surface."

17

CB ENTERED the room and looked around, not sure where he was supposed to go. Most of the thirty or so seats in the room were filled. Finally, he caught General Craig's eye, and the general nodded him over.

They were in the City Council headquarters building, in the largest conference room in the city. The group sat around a massive square table. A quick scan of the room gave CB an idea of the scope of the dilemma they were facing. Jessica Bowen, Director of Engineering, was present, as was Tom Horace, the ship's chief pilot. Williams, Director of Agriculture, was there, too. On the other side of the general sat Henry Kurtz, the captain of the badges, the *New Haven* police force.

And then there was the Council. Every one of them but Fleming. They wore pale, gaunt expressions, and the dark circles under their eyes indicated they probably hadn't slept since the incident in Engineering the day before.

Councilman Stearns called the meeting to order and asked Jessica to brief the room. She stood up, her face the picture of seriousness. Clearly, she wasn't intimidated by the group seated before her.

The general had already given CB a high-level briefing on the incident, and he'd seen enough first-hand to have a pretty good idea what had happened. But he didn't know everything Jessica told them now.

"As most of you know, the damage caused by the fire is not easily fixable. Given enough time and the right parts, we could make it happen. But we have neither. We only have two options. Fix the nuclear reactor or land the ship."

"Sure, land the ship," Horace muttered loudly enough for everyone to hear. "And give those Resettlement bastards exactly what they want? No way."

Stearns held up a hand. "Horace, please. We don't know who did this. We don't even know that the fire was intentional. Let's not jump to conclusions."

"It doesn't take a genius to narrow down the list of suspects." Horace turned to Kurtz. "How about it? Send some badges to talk to Fleming and his pathetic followers. Maybe don't ask so nice, and I'll bet you'll get answers pretty quickly."

A murmur of agreement rumbled through the group.

"I said, that's enough," Stearns said. "We're here to make plans, not to start a mob. Jessica, please continue. What's the likelihood of finding the parts you need to repair the ship?"

Jessica stared at the ceiling for a long moment before answering; CB could practically see her wheels turning. She was cute when she was thinking. He'd always thought so, though he'd never shared these thoughts with anyone. Certainly not her.

"It wouldn't be easy," she said. "We'd need to get them from a reactor on the surface. Then, if we're lucky, we might be able to retrofit them for our system. That's assuming we find a plant that was properly shut down during the vampires' attacks and didn't go critical. Even then...it's a bit of a crapshoot, but it's the only chance we've got."

"Lovely," Stearns said. "So just find a functional reactor, get the parts, and hope they fit?"

The general nodded to Stearns. "Our GMT is willing to give it a try."

"Damn right, we are," CB said. Of course, they'd do the job, if needed, but despite his bluster, it wasn't a job he'd relish. A nuclear facility had to be huge. Lots of dark places for vampires to hide.

"Good," Stearns said. "But before we decide on going that route, let's discuss the other possibility. Landing the ship."

That was met with a heavy silence.

"I know no one wants to give the Resettlers what they want, but this is the survival of humanity we're talking about, here. The Council overrode the vote because Resettlement was the most dangerous option. Now it seems it may have become the safest one. So, let's at least talk about it. How would we go about it?"

"It would have to be somewhere safe," Williams said. "Remote. Maybe we could land just long enough to fix the reactor, then head back up."

"We'd be lucky to last long enough to fix anything," CB said.

"And getting this beast back up off the ground would be no easy feat," Horace added.

"What about Antarctica?" one of the other Council members said. CB thought her name was Kara, but he could never remember.

"Could work," the general said. "The extremely low

population before the vampire attacks means there would be very few vampires there now. If any."

Williams shook his head at that. "No way we could keep the crops alive in those temperatures. The crops die, so do we."

"Not to mention the ship components," Jessica said. "Some of them won't function in subzero weather without the reactor keeping things warm."

"Other remote locations, then?" Stearns asked.

There was a long pause. CB had been holding back until now, not wanting to overstep, but he decided, what the hell. "That's exactly the problem. We know what areas were sparsely populated one hundred fifty years ago, but not now. I once ran a mission to the Australian outback for some satellite equipment. Supposedly, extremely low populations back in the day, but I saw one of the largest hordes of my life there. Vampires are unpredictable, and they like to roam. Point is, wherever we land, we're taking a risk."

Rising despair filled the faces staring back at CB when he finished.

"Other options?" Stearns said.

Horace leaned forward and stretched his beard. "What about lightening the load up here? Could we extend the thirty days if we dumped all nonessential items?"

All eyes turned to Jessica.

"Possibly. Especially if some departments cut down on energy consumption." She stared pointedly at Williams.

"We can cut back a little, but I'm not putting the crops at risk," Williams said. "We run out of food, we're just as dead as if the vampires get us."

"Fair point," Stearns said. "All the same, do what you can to reduce energy usage. That goes for everyone here. The Council will begin looking into the matter of reducing weight. We'll get rid of as much as we can. Jessica, you and your team start looking for old reactors on the surface that might fit the bill for what we need. Horace, you and your team scout for possible landing locations, just in case."

"Can I ask a question, sir?" It was Kurtz. This was the first time he'd spoken in this meeting, and his rich baritone voice echoed in the room. "How much are you going to tell the people?"

That question clearly caught Stearns off guard. "As little as we can. We don't want to cause a panic."

"The people aren't stupid, Councilman," General Craig said. "They know there was a large fire in Engineering. If we start taking measures to lighten the ship, they're going to know something's up."

"Then we'll deal with it," Stearns said. "We only need thirty days, for better or worse."

There was another long pause, and then Jessica said, "Due respect, but is now the best time to be keeping secrets? Trust for the Council is at an all-time low, and my department was just attacked to force our hand."

"We don't know that!" Stearns snapped. "It may have been a simple accident."

"That's hardly likely," Jessica said.

CB exchanged a glance with the general. Clearly, Stearns didn't want to admit the seriousness of this situation.

The general turned to Stearns. "Councilman, our badges are stretched to the breaking point already. If the tension grows any more, these protests are going to turn into serious riots. If that happens, we may not have to worry about the ship landing in thirty days. The people will take the controls and land the damn thing themselves."

Stearns shook his head. "That's a little dramatic, General. I expected a cooler head from you, of all people." He turned to the other Council members. "Here's what I propose. We put as many resources as we can into helping Jessica find her replacement parts. Overtime, extra people, whatever it takes. Meantime, we'll meet tonight to discuss the weight situation. Let's get *Haven* as light as we can and keep her afloat. All in agreement?"

The other Council members voiced their approval.

"Good. Thank you, everyone. We're adjourned."

As people began to file out, CB leaned in and whispered to General Craig and Kurtz. "Jesus, I knew the Council was clueless, but this situation is going real bad real quick."

"Tell me about it," Kurtz said. "My guys are gonna take a serious beating from the crowds tonight. I'll be lucky if they don't walk out on me. What do we do, General?"

Craig grimaced. "We do what we always do. We follow orders and try our damnedest to get the job done. And CB? If Bowen locates replacement parts, we sure as hell better get them back here."

―――――

GENERAL CRAIG WAS ALMOST to the door when Councilman Stearns called to him. He let the rest of the people move past him to the exit, then made his way to the councilman.

"There's something else I need you to do," Stearns said. "Do you have people you trust in your department?"

"Of course, sir."

Councilman Stearns appeared to think for a long moment before continuing. The general waited him out.

"I need you to find proof that Fleming and his people were behind the fire."

Craig nodded. "Kurtz's pretty short-staffed, but I'm sure he can find someone."

"No," Stearns said. "Don't just farm this out to any old badge. There's a reason I didn't bring this up in front of everyone. I'm not sure who I can trust. Aside from you."

"I appreciate that, sir."

"We go way back. If you were going to betray me, you would have done it by now."

"You think Fleming has ears at this level?"

The councilman sighed. "Honestly? I don't. But he found out about the Daylights, didn't he?"

"He certainly did." The general was loath to admit it, but he didn't want Stearns going on a witch-hunt over the Daylights. CB had told the general an assistant in R&D was involved, but the general hadn't had time to look into it any more deeply yet.

"It's not just that. Fleming has seemed one step ahead of me for months. He's got a lot of supporters, and some of them are smart enough not to wear his colors on their sleeves."

"I understand, sir. We can trust Kurtz and CB. I'll talk to them and see who they recommend."

"Good. And when we do find proof, are you willing to do what's necessary?"

The look in Stearns's eye told Craig there was weight behind this question. "What are you asking me, sir?"

"I think you know. If this cult of personality keeps gaining steam, we'll have to take measures to stop it. I believe that eliminating Fleming and a few of his highest-profile supporters could end this thing."

Craig put a hand on the table to steady himself. During the meeting, he'd thought Stearns clueless to the dangers they were facing. That hadn't been true, he now realized. Stearns was just downplaying it for the room. "Eliminating political rivals? That's like something out of the old stories from the surface days."

"This isn't about politics. This is about the survival of our species. Fleming has no idea what it's really like down there. The vampires are theoretical to him, just a problem to be overcome. I'll ask again. When we have proof, will you do what needs to be done?"

General Craig was surprised at how quickly and easily the words came to his lips. "Yes, sir, I will."

18

TWO DAYS LATER, the Ground Mission Team gathered in their briefing room.

Alex had been out at the library when she'd gotten the radio call letting her know about the meeting, and she'd had to race back to her quarters, rinse off in the shower for two minutes, and quickly throw on some clothes to get there in time. She was still the last to arrive. When she got there, CB, the general, and the entire GMT team were seated around the table. Jessica Bowen from Engineering and Brian McElroy were there, too.

Alex tried to enter as inconspicuously as possible. She slipped through the doorway and crept to her seat, but CB decided to call her out.

"Ah, our little princess has decided to grace us with her presence."

The GMT laughed. Jessica was busy flipping through some papers and didn't seem to catch the joke, but Brian looked wildly uncomfortable. He looked at Alex with wide eyes, as if he was both surprised and disappointed to see her.

He was probably still pissed about her stealing the Daylights, she realized. They hadn't talked since it happened. She silently cursed herself for not apologizing to him at some point over the past two days, but honestly, it hadn't even crossed her mind.

"Sorry, sir," she said as she slid into her seat.

She'd only seen CB once since the fire in Engineering. He'd called the team together the day before to brief them on the status of the reactor. He'd sworn them to secrecy and told them to prepare for the possibility of being asked to help with crowd control at the protests, being sent on another ground mission, or both. The fact that Jessica was here made Alex think it was probably a ground mission, which was way better than crowd control.

CB hadn't mentioned the Daylights incident to Alex since the fire, and she was all too happy to let it be swept under the rug. In revealing the status of the reactor and asking them to keep it secret, he'd shown that he still trusted her. She silently vowed to live up to that trust. She just hoped her teammates would forgive her as quickly.

The general turned to Jessica. "Director Bowen, whenever you're ready."

Jessica nodded, then activated an overhead projector. The image on the screen was an aerial view of a heavily forested area with some large, ugly structures jutting out of the trees.

"This is Bay City, Texas. Or it was, back in the pre-vamp days. Today, it's home to lots of abandoned structures, including a pair of nuclear reactors. Records are pretty shoddy, but we do know this was among the last parts of North America to fall to the vampires. That gives us reason to believe the reactors were likely shut down properly. Which means the parts should still work."

"Should or will?" Simmons asked.

Jessica met his skeptical gaze. "Should. There are no guarantees here, but this is the best shot we have."

"Texas is North America," Brian said. "It's winter in the northern hemisphere, so that means shorter days."

The team grumbled at that.

"How long will we have?" CB asked.

"There's only about ten hours of daylight there. By the time you factor in flying the away ship to the location, it'll be more like nine."

"And I'm guessing the control panel we need isn't sitting next to the front door."

"No, it is not," Jessica said. "I imagine you'll need to make your way deep into the facility."

"Thanks, Director Bowen," CB said. He turned to the team. "Let's talk logistics."

Alex settled in. This was going to be a long meeting.

———

AFTER THE BRIEFING, Brian pulled CB aside. The captain was surprised at the fire in the usually meek man's eyes.

"What's going on?" he asked.

"A lot. You're going to have to narrow that down."

For the briefest of moments, CB thought Brian was going to hit him. It wouldn't have gone well for the young scientist, but CB would have respected the effort.

"I'm talking about Alex. What the hell is she still doing here?"

CB grabbed hold of Brian's arm and pulled him toward the corner where they'd be less likely to be heard. "Listen, I understand why you're upset, but we need her on the team right now."

"Does the Council even know about what she did?"

"No, and I'd appreciate it if we kept it that way."

"I'll bet you would." Brian was three inches taller than CB, and he glared down at him.

"Watch yourself, Mr. McElroy." CB had never seen this side of Brian before, and he kind of liked it. Still, he couldn't have this guy talking back to him.

Brian backed up just a hair, then slouched into his usual stance.

CB hadn't told the general or the Council about Alex's role in the theft of the Daylights. As far as they knew, Sarah had acted alone. Maybe if it hadn't been for the fire, they would have seen through that. After all, why would Sarah hide the Daylights under the seats on the away ship unless someone on the mission knew they were there? As crazy as everything was, no one had thought to look for an accomplice. Not yet, anyway.

Sarah hadn't returned to the R&D lab since the night she and Alex took the Daylights.

"So that's how it is?" Brian asked. "Alex gets to carry on like nothing happened while Sarah is hunted by the police?"

"Don't be so dramatic, kid. I didn't say Alex is going to get away with it. I just said we're not turning her in right now. Let's make sure life can continue on *New Haven* first. Then we'll deal with her."

———

ALEX MARCHED into the hangar and saw the team's gear carefully arranged on six tables for their inspection. The R&D team would later collect this gear, give it a final check, and set it up in their lockers for easy load out in the morning, but CB insisted that each GMT member carefully go over the equipment themselves first.

He'd often told the team, "Don't trust an egghead to check your gear. Hell, don't trust me. In the end, your equipment is your responsibility, and if a vampire gets you because there was a hole in the neck of your silver mail suit, that's on you."

Alex made her way to her table and began looking over her equipment. The silver mail suit was laid out in the middle of the table. The guns were arranged to the left. Alex started on the right side, at her favorite item, the sword.

The last time she'd seen this beauty, it had been covered in black goo and severely nicked. Now, it looked perfect. As she was inspecting the sword, she noticed Owl out of the corner of her eye. The woman stomped up to her table and snatched her silver mail suit.

"You okay?" Alex asked.

Owl gave her a long look, as if trying to decide whether to speak to her. "Far from it, actually."

"You pissed at me, too?"

"Yes." She began inspecting her silver mail suit, looking over it closely, going inch by inch. "But not just you. This whole damn city. Everything going on out there, it's like people have forgotten how to be decent to each other. We're the last of our species, right? Maybe we should treat each other with respect."

"Damn right." Simmons was at the table on the other side of Owl, cleaning his disassembled rifle. "Politics is one thing, but this is survival. We gotta keep *New Haven* afloat. We can all agree on that."

Firefly had been watching the conversation, and apparently decided he'd had enough. "Come down off your moral high ground and take a look at the real world, Simmons.

You call it politics, like it's some game, but this affects people's lives, man. The Council betrayed the will of the people, and there's no getting around that."

"It's not that simple," Simmons said. "I'm talking about the fate of humanity."

"So am I!" Firefly strode toward Simmons. "You want humanity to survive long-term? We ain't gonna be able to hide up here forever. We want to survive, then vampires have to go. All of them."

Simmons stepped right up to Firefly. Their faces were mere inches away from each other now. "You're missing the point. I'm not talking about long-term. You want to take back the Earth? Okay, fine, but we also have to survive now. And that means fixing the ship."

"Sure, let's delay Resettlement until the ship's fixed. After that, they'll come up with another reason it's not the right time. And another after that. And so on, until our grandkids are looking for their own excuses why Resettlement can't happen."

Alex had had enough of this. She swung her sword overhead and brought it down exactly between Simmons and Firefly, stopping it between their noses. "This isn't the men's room; you can have your pissing contest later. For now, we have work to do, yeah?"

Simmons glared at Firefly for another moment, then turned back to his rifle. "She's right. CB will be back soon. We'd better finish up here."

Firefly shook his head at Alex. "I thought you of all people would have my back on Resettlement after what you did."

Alex ignored the comment. As she was turning back to her equipment, she saw Brian marching purposefully across the hangar. She put down her sword and ran to meet him.

"Hey, Brian, hold up."

He stopped and waited but didn't look at her.

"Listen, I just wanted to apologize about the Daylights. That was way—"

Brian held up a hand to stop her. "Honestly, I don't want to hear it."

She blinked hard, taken aback.

"You want to apologize because you feel bad," he said. "I'm not interested in helping you feel better. You betrayed us, Alex. You betrayed the Council." He stopped there, but the sentiment was written all over his face. She'd betrayed *him*.

"I know I did. And I was wrong. That's why I'm apologizing."

He let out a sardonic chuckle. "You just keep getting away with everything, don't you? That won't last forever. It'll catch up with you, Alex. I guarantee it."

"Brian, it was a stupid move, and I should have realized—"

He turned and walked away before she could finish.

19

DANIEL FLEMING and Sarah were in Fleming's new private quarters hidden away in the depths of Sparrow's Ridge. They were hunched over a table, as they were all too often these days. This time, they were working together on a statement that Fleming was planning to give to his supporters the following day.

It had been three days since Sarah helped Alex plant the Daylights on the away ship. Three days since she'd left the life she'd known and gone on the run. She'd loved her job and her coworkers—especially Brian, as goofy as he was—and she'd been proud to be part of the Ground Mission Team's support unit. It was an important job, and she felt like she'd made a real difference there.

Now she was marked a traitor and in hiding from the very government she'd spent her adult life working for. She couldn't reach out to friends or family. If given a list of these circumstances, Sarah would have expected she'd be distraught, but, to her surprise, she couldn't remember a time she'd felt so alive. Every morning, she woke energized and excited about what the day might bring. She'd felt like she was making a difference in her lab job, but now she *knew* she was. She was helping humanity reclaim its rightful place on the surface of the Earth.

But, if she were being honest with herself, she'd have to admit that was only part of the reason she was on a constant high. The other reason was Daniel.

Their relationship wasn't sexual. She wouldn't be opposed to taking things in that direction, and she occasionally fantasized about it, but in all the time they'd spent alone together over the past few weeks, he'd never so much as put a hand on her knee. Sarah sometimes wondered why— she'd never had trouble attracting men—but she honestly didn't mind. The fact that he didn't fall into the lecherous politician stereotype made him even more attractive.

But her sexual attraction to him was only a side effect, not the real reason she was here. Daniel Fleming was the most focused, passionate person she'd ever met. He believed in the cause of Resettlement in a way that was both inspiring and contagious. His dedication was almost scary sometimes, and he worked long hours and seemed to have little interest in anything outside the city's future.

He reminded her a little of Brian McElroy in that way. But where Brian was insular and would prefer to be left alone to complete his work, Fleming drew people in, made them part of his cause. And once he'd drawn them in, he knew how to keep them there.

Take this speech, for example. Fleming knew that his people were fired up. They needed two things from him: fuel for their enthusiasm and direction for their anger. This speech tomorrow would give them both.

There was a knock at the door. Fleming looked up from

his paper and tapped a button on the keyboard next to him. The monitor on his desk flashed to life, showing the person at the door. It was a tall, thin young man in his early twenties. Steven Harper.

Fleming pressed another button and the door let out a soft beep as it unlocked. The door opened, and Steven marched in.

The guy did not look good. Not the most kempt individual at the best of times, today he looked positively disheveled, as if he'd just rolled out of bed after five hours of tossing and turning.

Still, Fleming turned his million-watt smile on the young man. "Steven! Pleased to see you."

Steven blinked hard, as if dazed by Fleming's presence. "Thanks, Councilman. It's good to you see you, too. And you, Sarah."

"Hi Steven," she said. Sarah was annoyed by the interruption, and it was a struggle to inject a bit of friendliness into her tone.

Fleming gestured to the chair across the table from him. "Have a seat."

Steven nodded his thanks and sat down. "Sorry for dropping by so late."

Fleming waved the thought away. "What brings you by this evening?"

"I, uh, wanted to ask you something, sir. About the fire in Engineering. Were you behind it? I mean, were we?" He scratched at the stubble on his chin. "I'm sorry if it's rude to ask, but I need to know. I joined this cause because I want to help people and because I want a better life. If this stuff, hurting people and starting fires, is what we're about, then I don't want to be part of this thing."

"I understand," Fleming said. He set down his pen and pushed the paper on the table to the side, giving Steven his full attention.

Sarah was tempted to speak up in Fleming's defense, but she knew that wasn't wise. Fleming could do a much better job defusing this. Steven was important to the cause, Sarah knew. He was their man in Engineering. He had passed along a few juicy details about how his boss, Jessica Bowen, responded to the Council's vote and the things she had been working on since. So, it was important that they didn't lose this young man.

"It's not a rude question, Steven," Fleming said. "It's an important one, and I'm glad you asked it. I've heard the whispers. I know people are speculating about whether we were involved, but very few have had the courage to come right out and ask. I thank you for that."

Steven sat up a bit straighter in his seat. "You're welcome, sir."

It was an effort for Sarah to keep the smile off her face. Fleming was already rebuilding Steven's confidence.

"The answer to your question is no," Fleming said. "I didn't light that fire, nor did anyone acting on my orders. It might have been an accident. It might have been the act of an insane lone wolf. Or it may have been the Council trying to frame us. I don't know, and in the end, it doesn't matter. Because I'll tell you something else, Steven. I'm glad it happened."

Steven's eyes widened.

"Don't get me wrong. I don't want anyone to get hurt. But this fire is going to force the Council's hand, and it will make people pick a side. The Council showed their true colors when they went against the will of the people, and now they'll continue down the path they started. It doesn't matter if I set the fire. The Council will pin it on me and use it as an excuse to discredit us. Then we'll find out who's really dedicated to this cause."

"You think they'll come after you for this?" Steven asked.

"I know they will. Sometime in the next few days, they'll announce I'm suspected of the crime and then they'll come after me. If they find us, and they will, I need strong leaders like you and Sarah to step up in my place." He paused and regarded Steven as if considering something. "Can I trust you, Steven?"

"Of course, sir."

"Good. What I'm about to tell you doesn't leave this room. We know that the fire damaged our nuclear reactor's control unit."

Steven didn't reply, but from the look on his face, Sarah knew this information wasn't news to him.

Fleming continued. "The reason we're telling you this is because we have to speed up our timeline. Decisions will need to be made quickly now. If they can fix the ship, fine, but I think there's a good chance they will not be able to do so. Having sat on the Council, I firmly believe they will never land *New Haven*, no matter the consequences. That's when we'll have to make some tough decisions."

"What kind of decisions?" Steven asked.

"You said when you came in here that you don't want to take part in violence, and I applaud your sense of morals. But I hope you can see now that things have changed. Protesting may not be enough. We may have to take the Council by force. I know that sounds extreme, but it's for the survival of our species."

Before Steven could reply, there was a knock at the door. Fleming's gaze shot to the monitor, and he visibly relaxed when he saw who it was. He pressed a button and the door beeped. "Don't worry. It's a friend."

The door opened and Firefly walked in.

"Sorry I'm late," he said. "I had a meeting with the team, and I didn't want to make anyone suspicious."

20

ALEX HAD trouble sleeping that night. Every time she drifted off, she had another dream of *New Haven* crashing to the Earth in a fiery blaze, the last of humanity extinguished in a collision of earth and fire. She gave up at oh five hundred and decided to go for a run.

The streets were nearly empty at this hour, and she ran in the center of them, enjoying the luxury of having so much space. The sun shone bright and hot through the glass dome above as it always did regardless of the hour. Sometimes on these runs, Alex would consider what it would be like to run at night. True night, like they had on the surface, with darkness and stars. Part of her thought that it would be frightening to be surrounded by a black void of nothingness above and around her, but another part thought it would be exhilarating. It would feel like she could fall right off the Earth and drift into the darkness at any moment.

This morning, she didn't think about those things. Her thoughts were on vampires.

On her last mission, she'd thought it was possible they might encounter some vampires; on this mission, she *knew* they would. They'd be entering the depths of a nuclear facility with plenty of dark spaces. A haven for vampires. From her experience last time, she knew she could handle it. Still, there were no guarantees. Even with all her training, her top-notch equipment, and her team watching her back, all it would take was a single slip-up, and she'd be a beverage for the undead hordes.

They'd be well protected on this mission. In addition to their usual gear, CB had informed them last night that the Council had approved them to bring the Daylights. Alex had laughed out loud at that. After everything she'd gone through to try to smuggle them aboard, now they were coming along legally. What a difference a few days and the threat of the destruction of humanity could bring. They'd also be wearing the jet packs.

When she got back to her quarters, she found Simmons waiting at the door. He was dressed in sweatpants and a tee shirt, and he nodded at her as she approached. "Hey. Mind if I come in for a minute?"

"Yeah, sure."

Alex reached past him and unlocked her door. Other than a few group conversations with the whole team, she hadn't talked to him since the Daylights incident. She knew he wasn't happy with her, but she hadn't taken the time to gauge his anger. As usual, she'd been wrapped up in her own stuff.

Was he here to break up with her? Could you even break up with someone if you were just occasionally hooking up? And if he was here to break up, why would he do it now, right before the mission? The only explanation she could come up with was that he was so angry he needed to get it off his chest, so that it didn't distract him down on the surface.

He followed her into her room and shut the door. She sat down on the bed, leaving enough room for him next to her, but he chose the chair across the room.

"So, what's up?" she asked.

"I wanted to talk. Before the mission."

Yeah. Just as she'd thought. Better to nip this in the bud. "Listen, I know you're pissed, and I know you don't understand why I did it. If you want me to explain, I'll try, but I'm not sure I have the energy for it now. I've spent the last few days apologizing, and right now I need to stay focused. But if you need to get something off your chest, I understand that, too. Go for it."

Simmons nodded. "Thanks. I do have something to get off my chest. It's about the day you took the Daylights."

Great. She knew it. She took a deep breath and vowed to let him vent. She owed him that. If she could rein her emotions in and avoid an argument, this would be over soon, and they'd both feel better. Well, *he* would.

"When I found out what happened that morning, that you'd smuggled the Daylights aboard the ship, I was pissed."

"I know you were."

"Let me finish. I was pissed at CB for letting the whole team find out like that. He could have taken you aside and talked to you in private."

Well, that wasn't what she'd expected to hear.

"Then I got even angrier when he hauled you off to see the Council. I sat in my quarters, stewing. I came dangerously close to heading to the Hub to see if there was anything I could do. I swear, if they'd thrown you in a cell, I would have grabbed Firefly and headed over to blast you out."

Through sheer force of will, she kept her mouth shut. She'd promised herself she'd let him have his say before responding.

"It wasn't until later, when I heard Drew and Owl talking, that I realized I wasn't angry with you for betraying the team. It never even crossed my mind. I was too worried about you. I guess what I'm saying is, this whole thing made me realize how much I care about you. These late-night booty calls are great, and I don't want that to go away, but I want something meaningful even more. I'm willing to risk it. You're worth it."

Alex had never seen Simmons look so vulnerable. She waited a moment, forming her words carefully in her mind before she spoke. "Thank you. That means a lot, especially right now."

He smiled weakly. "You're welcome. But *thank you* wasn't exactly the response I was hoping for."

"I know. Honestly, I'm so messed up in the head right now that *thank you* is all I can give." She held up a hand before he could respond. "I want to talk about this, I really do, but it has to wait until after the mission. Is that cool?"

He nodded, his smile a little more confident now. "I'm just glad you didn't kick me out for talking about my feelings."

"It was kinda girly. Now, if you don't mind, I need to take a shower before I head down to the hangar."

She stood up and peeled off her tee shirt.

Simmons watched as a bead of sweat dripped down her neck, onto her chest, and disappeared into the depths of her athletic bra. His eyes lingered there for a long moment.

She stepped toward him and took him by the hand. "Care to join me?"

He did not object.

———

AN HOUR AND A HALF LATER, the majority of the team was geared up and gathered in the hangar outside the away ship.

Things felt different this morning to Alex. The familiar excitement and nervousness hung in the air the same way it did before every mission. The political tension was gone now, replaced by the gravity of the job at hand. For the first time in days, they felt like a team again.

Owl shifted her weight nervously from foot to foot. As both the pilot of the away ship and the driver of the rover, a lot of the responsibility for this mission would fall to her. She'd have to navigate the versatile, but still large, rover into the dark depths of the facility. While others would be able to duck around corners and slip into doorways when the fighting came, she'd be stuck behind the wheel.

Alex put a hand on her shoulder. "You ready to do this, girl?"

Owl put on a brave smile. "You know it. Can I count on you to keep the vamps off me while I'm driving?"

Alex smiled. "I won't let them get you. That would look really bad on my record."

"Right, 'cause it's so spotless, now."

"You know me. Always toeing the line."

Firefly came up to the ship and nodded a curt greeting. Unlike the rest of the team, he wore a dour expression, and he moved sluggishly.

"Rough night, Firefly?" Drew said. "What was her name?"

"And can Drew have her apartment number?" Simmons threw in.

"Ugh, no thank you. Firefly and me have different taste in women. I like mine alive."

Firefly ignored the ribbing and brushed past them, setting down his bag of explosives near the door of the ship.

CB soon joined them. His fatigues always looked crisper than the rest of the team's, for some reason, and today was no exception. He always looked like he'd come directly from ironing them. His cap was pulled low over his eyes, and he crossed the hangar at a brisk military clip. A stack of papers was secured snugly under his arm.

He stopped in front of the group and waited for them to come to attention. "All right, I've just received my final orders from the general. We're a go for the mission."

He looked down the line, giving them each a quick visual inspection.

"Before we head out there, I want to let you all know something. I'm proud of you."

That caught Alex by surprise. CB expected his team to perform well, and he wasn't one to throw around praise, earned or not. First Simmons had shared his emotions, and now CB was doing the same? There must have been something in the air.

"I know I don't tell you that much."

"Ever," Drew said, and the team laughed.

"But you deserve to hear it now and again. You're one hell of a team. You proved that in Buenos Aires, and you proved it again by hanging together the last few days."

Alex suddenly realized what he meant by that. None of them had ratted her out to the general. God, she hadn't even realized or thought to thank them.

"You all know that this mission is going to be different.

We'll be in a vast facility filled with dark, tight places. There *will* be vampires, and we *will* have to kill them. There's no doubt about that. Even once we locate the reactor control panel we're looking for, there are no guarantees what condition it will be in and how long it will take to remove it.

"I need everyone to keep a close eye on the time. Get paranoid. There's no such thing as checking it too much. We'll be working on a shortened day to begin with, and the facility won't have a lot of windows. It would be easy to lose track of time. That ain't happening to this team.

"I also need you to be disciplined. No one goes rogue this time." He glanced at Alex, but, thankfully, only for a moment. "You don't hear the order come from my lips, you don't do it. Got it?"

A chorus of, "Yes, sir!" rang out.

"Good. I don't need to tell you any more about the challenge we'll face. No doubt it's been running through your minds all night. But I will tell you one more thing. This mission is the reason this team exists. I've been running to the surface for going on twenty-seven years now, and nothing I've done comes close to the importance of what we're doing here."

He cocked his thumb over his shoulder, toward the city behind him. "Not to put too fine a point on it, but if we don't succeed, they die. We resettle, we die, Daylights or no. And we can't stay up here without the parts. We talk a lot about the Remnants up here. About how brave and brilliant they were, and how they saved humanity. We have the same chance; *you* have the same chance, today. I'm not saying they'll be learning your names in history class, 'cause that's not how we do it in the GMT. That's not *why* we do it. But you damn well better believe that if we succeed, they'll be talking about the events of today."

He paused and turned his gaze to the sky. "And if we fail? There won't be any more history classes. There won't be any more history."

CB let the weight of his statement hang over the team for a moment. Then he said, "All right, time to board. We're going to Texas."

21

FLEMING WAS ALREADY THERE by the time Sarah arrived in the Resettlement headquarters that morning. Try as she might, she was never able to beat him to work. It was as if the man didn't sleep. No one else had arrived yet, which was a good thing. She might not be as dedicated as the councilman, but she was his most dedicated supporter.

She approached his desk at the front of his room, where he was once again poring over the speech that they'd written together the previous night.

He looked up at her, his eyes alive with excitement. "Whenever I write something I'm happy with, I always go to bed afraid that it won't seem as good in the morning."

Well, at least that confirmed that he actually slept.

He slammed his hand down on the papers in front of him. "These are even better than I thought! We did well, Sarah. Very well. This is going to move the needle. It will help them understand that something big has to be done, and we can't wait much longer to do it."

Sarah leaned over and scanned the paper. "I'm still not sure about that opening. You don't think it's too bold?"

"If now's not the time to be bold, when is?"

She couldn't disagree.

The first ten supporters arrived not long after Sarah. Most were the faithful from Sparrow's Ridge, which made Sarah a little anxious. Not that she didn't appreciate every one of them, but she hoped some of Fleming's supporters in more powerful positions would show up, too. People like Steven. Firefly was on a mission today, so of course, he wouldn't be in attendance. And Alex. If she was still staying strong. Sarah hadn't seen her in days, so she wasn't sure if she was still supporting Resettlement or if getting caught had scared her back to the straight and narrow. Firefly said she hadn't spoken a word against Resettlement to him, which was a good sign.

Sarah glanced up from the speech text and saw Fleming staring at the door with wide eyes. She followed his gaze and what she saw made her gasp.

General Isaiah Craig stood in the middle of the hall, two dozen police officers at his back.

"You're a difficult man to find, Fleming," the general said.

———

GENERAL CRAIG HAD DISCOVERED Fleming's location in the usual way—someone had talked.

A badge named Franklin had hauled in a young man for smuggling government supplies in one of the less savory sections of Sparrow's Ridge. Thinking he might be part of a larger operation, Franklin had sat him down in an interrogation room to find out what he knew. The interrogation had turned up some unexpected information. Franklin had passed the info up the chain until it got to Captain Kurtz, who had immediately called General Craig.

Craig could have let Kurtz and his men handle this bust, but something about it, about the way Fleming and his followers had most likely put the entire ship at risk by starting the fire in Engineering, felt personal. The general would have wanted to be there, even if Councilman Stearns hadn't asked him to take care of it personally.

When they'd arrived, they'd been surprised to find no guard outside the door. Quite the contrary—the doors had been propped open. Apparently, there was a meeting starting soon.

Then they'd stepped inside and found only a dozen people. He'd exchanged glances with Kurtz. Maybe this movement wasn't as big as Stearns had made it sound.

On the plus side, the way Fleming went pale when he spotted them was entirely satisfying.

"You're a hard man to find, Fleming," the general said.

Fleming quickly regained his composure. He stood up and clapped his hands together. "General Craig! Welcome. Have you come to join the Resettlement movement?"

"I'm afraid not. We need to ask you some questions about a fire."

Fleming nodded sagely, as if he'd expected nothing less. "Of course. In that case, I'm afraid you're going to be disappointed. I don't have any information on the matter. Still, if you have questions, ask away."

General Craig felt himself bristle at this man's hubris. To Craig, Fleming had the smug air of a guilty man who believed he would not be caught. "Not here. I need you to accompany us back the Hub. We'll talk at badge headquarters."

Some of the others in the room started to stand, but

Fleming waved them back into their seats. Craig was suddenly glad he'd brought so many badges.

"I'm afraid I'll have to decline."

The general took a step forward. "That wasn't a request."

Fleming shook his head sadly. "So that's how it is?" He looked behind the general, and his eyes lit up. "Ah, friends, come in! The more the merrier."

The general glanced over his shoulder, then cursed at what he saw: another dozen Resettlement supports arriving.

Kurtz leaned close. "General, let's get this over with. They're still coming."

Craig nodded his agreement. "Fleming, let's go."

Fleming chuckled—actually chuckled! Craig couldn't believe this man. He could feel the fury building inside, and he knew it would be a struggle to keep it contained.

"You'll forgive me if I'm a little skeptical of the Council's intentions," Fleming said. "I'm not going to sit in one of their jails. There's too great a chance I'll never get out."

Kurtz leaned in again. "Maybe this isn't the time."

General Craig ignored him. "Badges, place this man under arrest."

The woman next to Fleming stood up. "You heard Councilman Fleming, General. Get the hell out of here!"

The Resettlement supporters around the room vocally let their agreement be known.

It took Craig a moment to recognize the woman in this setting, but her voice made the connection for him. "And arrest her for theft of government equipment. Lovely to see you, Sarah."

"General," Kurtz said, "are you sure—"

The general brushed the man's hand off his shoulder. "Badges, let's go."

The police moved forward. As they did, one of the

supporters on their left threw something. The general couldn't see what it was from his angle—a piece of metal or concrete maybe. Whatever it was, it connected with Kurtz's head and sent the police captain reeling. He managed to keep his feet, but when he rose back up, there was a nasty two-inch gash above his left eye.

"You son of a bitch!" The words came from a short, stocky badge—Craig didn't know his name. The badge charged at the man who'd thrown the object, pulled back his fist, and punched him in the jaw.

Then all hell broke loose.

The supporters leaped from their seats and came at the police. The badges turned and met their attackers with equal fury.

The general observed the scene with mounting panic. This was turning into a street fight. He glanced toward the exit and saw it was clogged with Resettlement supporters who were surging forward.

Craig cursed. They wouldn't be able to retreat even if they wanted to.

Many of the supporters were pushing their way toward Fleming, forming a human shield between him and the police. One of them reached out and shoved General Craig. Before he even realized what he was doing, he threw a punch in return, sending the man staggering backward before he fell on his ass.

Craig stepped back and took a deep breath. As much as he wanted to knock out more of these idiots, he had a job to do. His priority was to protect his badges. Badges didn't carry guns, but the general did. He looked around and saw that, while they all carried batons, only two were using them. Whether that was because they hadn't thought to use them or because they didn't want to seriously hurt these people, he didn't know, and it didn't matter. They were outnumbered and the exit was blocked; they were in serious trouble—there was no time for caution.

"Badges!" he yelled. "Batons!"

The police officers heard him, but so did the Resettlement supporters; they attacked with renewed fury.

Franklin, the officer who'd found out about this place, was standing on General Craig's right, and he drew his baton at the general's command. He raised the weapon and moved to his left, going to help an officer who was trying to fight off two men. The general saw the man coming from Franklin's right, knife in hand, but he was too slow to stop it.

The man lunged forward and sank the blade into Franklin's back.

Franklin shouted in pain and reached a hand toward the wound.

Enough. It was time to end this.

General Craig drew his gun, aimed at the man with the knife, and fired.

The contents of the man's head exited the back of his skull and splattered onto the people behind him, badge and supporter alike. He fell backward, his body suddenly limp.

Craig saw movement out of the corner of his eye. He spun and saw a man rushing toward him.

The general fired again, hitting the charging man in the chest. He fell to the ground with a gasp.

Craig suddenly realized everyone else had stopped fighting. They were all watching him. It was silent but for the ringing the gunfire had left in his ears.

After a moment, Fleming's voice cut through the silence. "General, how dare you come into my—"

That was as far as he got before General Craig spun toward him and trained his gun on his chest. It wasn't

Craig's fault this had happened. It was Fleming's. All of it was Fleming's fault. If only he'd come quietly, as the general had ordered. If only he'd worked with the Council, instead of against them.

Councilman Stearn's words echoed in Craig's mind. *"For the survival of our species..."*

Craig fired.

But the woman next to Fleming was already moving. Sarah. She was stepping in front of Fleming.

The bullet struck her in the chest.

"No!" Fleming yelled. He dropped to his knees next to the fallen woman.

Nobody moved. Again, the hall was silent.

Sarah was alive. She stared up at the ceiling, wide-eyed, but the sucking sound coming from her chest meant the bullet had hit her lung.

Fleming clutched Sarah in his arms while she wheezed and struggled for air.

General Craig looked at the damage around him, knowing everything in *New Haven* had just changed.

22

IT TOOK the team two hours to reach their landing point. To get there, they had to not only head north across the equator, but also race west, chasing the edge of the morning. The days were short in North America at this time of year, and they needed every moment of sunlight they could get.

Alex stared out the window as they approached, and Owl gave her traditional rundown in their headsets.

"The South Texas Nuclear Project Electric Generating Station. The station went live in 1989 and provided energy to the Houston and San Antonio areas from then until the fall of humanity. The station is located on the Colorado River in Bay City, Texas. Based on my research, there was a popular musical act in the late twentieth century called the Bay City Rollers. This appears to be unrelated to Bay City, Texas, and the South Texas Nuclear Project. Just thought it was interesting."

"Truly fascinating stuff," Drew said, his voice thick with sarcasm.

Owl continued. "As we approach, you'll notice there are two reactors; these were known as South Texas 1 and South

Texas 2. You'll also notice the seven-thousand-acre reservoir next to the reactor. In the early days of nuclear power, when Pressurized Water Reactors were in use, this reservoir was used to cool the reactors."

Alex glanced around at her teammates. Owl's informational speech aside, there was less joking in this flight than was usual before a mission. The faces of her teammates were serious. Whether this was because of the importance of their mission or the danger they were about to face, she did not know.

"We're now approaching the facility, lady and gentlemen. Please stay buckled in until we have finished landing. And remember the words of our beloved captain: ours is not to question why..."

"Just to be prepared to die," the team said in unison.

"That's the spirit. See you on the surface."

They dropped down from the clouds, and Alex got her first look at the facility. It was massive. Two monstrous domed buildings dominated the landscape. These were the reactors, Alex knew. They looked like two enormous bullets sitting on end, their tips jutting into the sky. The reactors were each surrounded by a collection of smaller square buildings. The reservoir Owl had mentioned sat behind the reactors, a still lake surrounded by dense forest on one side and a nuclear power station on the other.

The reservoir reminded Alex of her Resettlement fantasy of a few days earlier. Walking on the surface, carefree, feeling the sun on her skin and grass on her bare feet. Swimming in a lake, though preferably, not one next to a nuclear station. Even though it had only been a few days ago she'd dreamed of all that, it seemed naive to her now. If Resettlement did somehow happen, whether because of the will of the people or because the ship was forced to land, life on the surface would be a constant battle for survival.

The ship landed, and the crew gathered outside. It was a chilly morning, and the wind bit Alex's face. Another mark in favor of life aboard *New Haven*, where the temperature was always pleasant.

CB huddled them together and gave them the rundown. "Two reactors here. That means two control panels. We don't know if either is still in working condition, so we need them both. First order of business is to find them. The good news is the reactors should both be set up the same way. That means we find one, we'll know where to look in the other building.

"As I said topside, days are short, and time is against us. As much as I hate to do it, we're gonna need to split up to search most effectively. Firefly and I will take reactor 1. Drew and Alex, you're on reactor 2."

Drew smiled at Alex. "You and me, girl."

"Yeah," Alex said," because that went so well last time."

"You start at the east end of your building and work your way west," CB said. "We'll start west and work east. We'll stay in constant radio contact."

He glanced toward Owl and Simmons. "You two are on rover duty. Get the vehicle out here and be ready to bring it inside the moment either team finds their reactor's control panel." He turned back to Drew and Alex. "We have to work fast, but we also have to work smart. No doubt there are vampires living in here, but they should be sleeping. Don't do anything to wake them." He looked pointedly at Drew. "And, for the love of Christ, if you cut yourself, sprint toward the exit. Got it?"

"Yes, sir," Drew said.

"Always be aware of your closest exits in case you get

into trouble. I want lots of radio chatter. Check in every five minutes tops. Questions?"

There were none.

"Good. Let's save humanity."

————

ALEX AND DREW found the entrance on the east side of reactor two. They quickly exchanged a glance as they stood in the entryway. Alex touched her radio and spoke into her whisper mic.

"CB, remember how we were discussing whether we'd have to blow the doors open to get inside? That's not going to be a problem."

The doors to the reactor were gone. One metal door lay fifteen feet from the entrance. It was battered with huge dents as if someone with incredible strength had punched it repeatedly. She thought about CB's story and how the vampires had been able to break through concrete after sundown.

Her earpiece squeaked CB's response. "Same at reactor one. Vamps ripped the doors right off."

"Okay, Captain. We're going in." She looked at Drew. "Whatever happens, let's make sure they don't catch us off guard, okay?"

Drew was already reaching for his shotgun. "No argument there."

They entered the station, Alex with her pistol drawn and Drew holding his shotgun at the ready.

They walked past what must have once been a security checkpoint. Alex wondered what it would have been like to work here back in the good old pre-vamp days. She was sure those people had plenty of fears. Maybe they'd laid awake at night worrying what would happen if they lost their jobs and weren't able to feed their families. Maybe they worried about an accident at one of the reactors.

Whatever it was that they worried about, Alex was willing to bet it wasn't vampires. It was a lesson she often tried to remember: it's no use worrying because you're not going to see the thing that gets you. It's always a blindside.

Drew elbowed her and pointed to his left with the shotgun. "Check out this shit."

Alex paused at what she saw. "Lovely. I guess we found their cafeteria."

It was a pile of animal bones, six feet wide and three feet high. Alex was no expert on animals. There were none aboard *New Haven*, and what little knowledge she had came from picture books she'd read as a kid and a couple of Earth nature documentaries she'd seen years ago. She had no idea what types of animals these bones had belonged to, but it appeared to be a pretty wide assortment. She spotted tiny skulls the size of her thumb and large skulls adorned with huge racks of pointed antlers.

Looking at the pile, Alex took comfort in the fact that the bones looked old. There weren't any fresh carcasses among them. Maybe the vampires had moved on from this particular spot. CB said the hordes roved from location to location in an unpredictable manner, after all.

On the other hand, she knew almost nothing about how vampires fed. She knew they drank the blood, but what happened after that? Did they eat the flesh, too? Suck the marrow from the bones? She had no idea. For all she knew, these animals could have been killed yesterday.

"Well," she said to Drew, "at least there aren't dirt piles everywhere, like in Buenos Aires. Wherever they're sleeping, it's not in this room."

"Somehow, that doesn't make me feel entirely better."

As they moved deeper into the lobby, they saw bullet holes scattered along the walls. Some walls had holes torn in them. Others were marred by long claw marks.

Alex remembered what CB had said. Constant radio contact. She was done going rogue; today she was going to play it straight. She grabbed the radio off her shoulder.

"Hey CB, we've got signs of a battle here. Lots of bullet holes and vampire damage to the walls."

"Yeah, us too. I'm hoping that'll make our job easier. Maybe the vampires ripped off all the locked doors."

"We've got lots of animal bones in here, too," Alex said. "All piled up, like this is some kind of feeding area."

"We haven't seen anything like that yet," CB said. "We didn't go in the main entrance, though, so maybe we'll come across something similar. Thanks for the report. Stay in touch. Out."

As they progressed, the placement of the bullet holes in the wall told the story of what had happened here. People had been inside, and the vampires had invaded. The humans had tried to fight them off.

"Can you imagine what it must have been like?" Alex asked. "Holed up in here, trying to fight off the vampires as they poured in?"

"Honestly?" Drew said. "I'd rather be trying to fight them off than to be in our shoes. At least they knew where the vamps were coming in. We're headed into a dark facility, with no real clue where we're going and no idea where the vampires might be hiding."

"Way to bolster my confidence, buddy," Alex said.

They reached the end of the lobby, turned on their headlamps, and headed west into the reactor.

CB AND FIREFLY walked through a long hallway, pitch-black but for the pale beams of their headlamps. There were signs of battle everywhere. Massive holes ripped straight through the walls, destruction that must have come from high-caliber assault weapons.

Firefly hadn't talked much since they entered the reactor. He was clearly disappointed that the exterior doors had already been removed and he hadn't had the chance to blow them off the hinges himself. CB was grateful for the silence. He needed to remain completely aware, not only for his own sake, but he also had to keep his ears open for communications from his team.

Up ahead, something caught his eye, and he raised his head so that his lamp illuminated it. The light revealed three sets of elevators at the end of the hall. Without electricity, they wouldn't be functional, but they were still worth checking out. He motioned Firefly forward.

Something was jammed between the twin doors of the elevator on the left, propping them open. CB crouched down and took a closer look at the object. It was a dark green, military-style helmet. That fit with the bullet holes. This place had been heavily defended. The bodies would have been devoured by the vampires long ago, but it was nice to see there was still some sign of the battle where so many men and women died.

The elevator car was on this floor. CB turned to Firefly. "Hang tight for a minute. I'm going to peek inside."

He twisted his way through the door, carefully stepping over the helmet. He didn't think the doors would slam shut and cut him in half if the helmet was moved, but he wasn't taking any chances. Who knew, with this ancient technology?

The elevator was empty save for a smattering of bullet holes. He pointed his headlamp at the elevator control panel. The buttons showed three floors, but what was really interesting was that below that. The numbers continued below 1 in reverse order, each with a G in front of them. G1, G2, and so on. All the way to G10.

CB grabbed his radio and spoke into it. "Folks, we found an elevator. It seems the facility has ten underground levels. This place is much bigger than we thought."

He heard both Alex and Simmons curse into their radios.

"It's gonna be one hell of a task to get a control panel from ten stories underground, Captain," Owl said.

"That's why we brought the rover. Besides, we don't know it's that far down." He thought for a moment. "Here's what we'll do. Firefly and I will start working our way down. Alex and Drew, you check out the upper levels, then report back."

"Roger that, Captain," Alex said.

CB wormed his way out of the elevator and found Firefly standing next to a red door. He gestured toward the sign next to it. "Check it out."

The sign said, *Stairs*.

"Excellent. Let's head down."

Firefly turned the knob and pushed on the door, then frowned. It didn't budge. He pushed again and got the same result.

"It's not locked," Firefly said, "but it's not moving either."

"Could be jammed. A lot of these doors warp over time. Might have to force it open."

Firefly nodded. "That I can do." He took a big step back and drew a deep breath, then kicked the door hard.

The door flew open and slammed against the wall. It sounded like a gunshot. The crash echoed down the stairway.

CB and Firefly froze, listening.

A hideous, unnatural roar came from somewhere far down the staircase.

"Shit," Firefly said.

CB grabbed his radio. "Folks, change of plans. We have confirmation of an active vampire in Reactor 1."

23

At CB's command, Simmons and Owl joined him and Firefly in Reactor 1. He told Drew and Alex to continue their above-ground search in Reactor 2. After they'd checked to ensure the control panel wasn't above ground, the team would reconvene. In the meantime, the crew in Reactor 1 would carefully begin working their way downward.

"Owl, my gut tells me we're going to find the control panel underground," CB said.

"Same," Simmons echoed. "Why build ten stories underground if you're not going to put the most vital equipment down there?"

"Lovely," Owl said. "So, I'm gonna be driving the rover down this dark staircase where we know there are vampires awake? Sounds safe."

"That's why I called you in here," CB said. "We're going to do something about that. We've got six Daylights, right?"

"Yes, sir."

"We need you to set up five of them, one on each landing down to the fifth floor. Cover as much of the darkness as you can. If we get down to five and still haven't found the control panel, we'll start spacing them out, one every other floor."

"What about the sixth light?" Owl asked.

"That we'll mount on the rover itself. It won't be perfect, but it'll give us some coverage. If shit goes south, we'll have some light to cover us on our retreat."

"I like that idea," Owl said. "The rover will make it upstairs, but it ain't exactly speedy."

"Simmons, you stay with Owl. Cover her while she's working, just in case something happens. I agree with your sentiment that it's more likely on one of the lowest levels, but so was that vampire we heard. In the interest of safety, we're going to start at G1 and work our way down rather than starting at the bottom. I'm not sending the team down to risk their lives on G10 only to find out the control panel was on G2. Firefly and I are going to search those floors as quickly and quietly as possible. *Quiet* is the operative word, hear me, Firefly?"

Firefly nodded.

"Good. Let's make it happen."

Owl got to work. No one mentioned that the Daylights hadn't been field-tested. They were counting on the hypothesis that real living vampires reacted the same way to the lights as the samples had in Brian's lab.

Once Owl had the Daylight set up on the first underground floor, CB decided it was time for him and Firefly to head into G1 and search for the control panel. They made their way past the Daylight Owl had set up. This door was jammed too, and since it swung inward, they didn't have the luxury of kicking it in. After futilely tugging on it a few times, they took the door off its hinges.

As soon as they pulled down the door, the powerful odor of death and decay wafted out.

CB took one last breath of the relatively fresh air in the stairwell and stepped through the doorway.

———

ALEX AND DREW'S search of the first floor of Reactor 2 was uneventful, but more time-consuming than they would have liked. The place was a labyrinthine collection of corridors. Each was marked with a different color, apparently a system to make it easier to navigate the facility. But it wasn't entirely helpful, since Alex and Drew had no idea what the colors meant, and they had to double back a few times to make sure they hadn't missed any areas of the floor.

It took them nearly thirty minutes to check the first level. As they covered more and more ground without incident, they had to resist the natural inclination to relax, to drop their guard. There could be a vampire around any corner, and it wouldn't stop and give Alex and Drew time to collect themselves before attacking.

If Alex were being honest, she'd have to admit that she was a little jealous of the crew in the other reactor. While Alex and Drew searched empty offices, they were plunging down into the unknown depths of the facility. They would likely find both vampires and the control panel, while she and Drew would find nothing at all.

Still, she fought the urge to rush through these floors. Not only would that open up the possibility of being attacked, but it would also increase the chances of their missing the very piece of equipment they were here to find.

Alex finally figured out the color-coding system just as they finished their search of the first level. There was a central hub in the middle of the building that contained what seemed to be the most important offices, and each wing off the hub was marked with a different color.

As they made their way back to the staircase, Alex spoke into her microphone. "First floor's clear, Captain. Moving on to the second floor."

"Roger that." The response was given in a whisper. He and Firefly must have begun their search of G1.

Alex deactivated her microphone and said, "Oh, sure, we have to tell him when we're progressing to a new area, but he doesn't tell us?"

Drew sighed. "Don't start. The last thing we need today is you going off on one of your—"

"Relax, big guy. I'm kidding."

"Oh. Sorry."

"No need to apologize. I get it. Things have been a little weird lately. But I just want to put it behind me and get back to good old-fashioned ass kicking. Cool with you?"

He chuckled. "Very."

They went up the stairs to level two, moving carefully, sweeping the light from their headlamps across each area and making sure it was clear before progressing.

The second floor was laid out exactly like the first. Since they now had a grasp on the color-coding system and the layout, they were able to move much more quickly. After ten minutes, they'd covered nearly half the floor.

They were sweeping through a cluster of offices in the blue section when Drew suddenly froze. "Alex, check this out."

He was looking through an open door into an interior office that seemed indistinguishable from any of the others. She leaned in for a closer look and quickly saw what he'd been referring to.

A body was slumped in the corner of the room. For a

moment, Alex considered that it might be a human, one of the people who'd worked and died here. Maybe his body hadn't been found, or he'd been one of the last to die. But she quickly realized that didn't make any sense. If it were human, the vampires would have devoured it years ago along with all the other casualties here.

"You think it's sleeping?" Drew whispered.

She considered that. It wasn't attacking them, so that was a mark in the *sleeping* column. On the other hand, who ever heard of a vampire sleeping exposed like this? They were supposed to sleep covered in dirt, like the vamps they'd found in Buenos Aires.

"Not sleeping," Alex said.

Drew gripped his shotgun tightly. "Maybe we should—"

The vampire sprang up and lunged at them, letting out an ear-splitting hiss as it came.

This time, Drew was ready. He brought up his shotgun and fired. The vampire fell backward as if hit by a truck. It landed on its back and didn't get up again. The gaping hole in its chest told the tale; Drew had hit it in the heart with one of his silver slugs.

Alex blinked hard, momentarily stunned by the shotgun firing in such close quarters. She drew her sword and pressed her back to Drew's. He was probably as stunned as she was, and she wanted to make sure they could at least see, in case something came at them from either direction.

After a moment, the roar in her ears turned into an annoying ringing.

She stood perfectly still, listening. Then she drew a sharp breath at what she heard.

There was movement in the halls. In both directions. She also heard a distant, angry grunt. Apparently, they weren't the only ones who'd been affected by the sound of the shotgun blast. Something else—multiple something elses—had been made aware of their presence.

Just then, CB's voice came through her earpiece. "Team, I've found something. Let's reconvene at the ship."

"Thank God," Drew whispered.

They made their way quickly to the nearest staircase and headed down.

24

Fifteen minutes later, the team gathered outside the ship. Alex and Drew told the others about their vampire encounter.

"Maybe that'll be our excitement for the day," Drew said.

CB frowned. "Somehow, I doubt it."

"How'd it go for you?" Alex asked.

"We made it all the way down to the fifth underground level. We didn't encounter any vampires, other than the one we heard when we banged the door open. They'd definitely been there recently, though. We could smell them."

"That's a good thing, right?" Alex said. "They gotta be sleeping."

"Perhaps," CB said. "But we didn't find any sleeping, either."

Alex had to admit that this was a bit troubling.

"These are dumb animals we're dealing with," Firefly said. "They operate on instinct. Maybe they burrow as far below the Earth as they can. Maybe they're all sleeping on Gio."

"Could be," CB allowed. "If so, we're going to be

bumping right up against them."

He then showed the team what he and Firefly had found. It was a blueprint of the facility that showed the layout of each floor, as well as what was on each of them. It showed the reactor control room was in the center of G9.

"Guess we're going almost all the way down," Alex said.

"Yes," CB said. "I'd like us to concentrate our efforts. Everyone together in Reactor 1, now. Once we get the control panel out, we'll head back to Reactor 2, if there's time." He glanced at his watch. "We have five and a half hours before sunset. Should be plenty of time to get them out, but if worse comes to worst, we can always make a return trip for the second control panel, if Director Bowen thinks she needs it."

The team studied the blueprint in silence for a moment. Then Owl said, "The doors are gonna be a problem. The rover is six feet wide. It'll fit through the double doors on the ground floor, but the doors to each underground level are much smaller. No way it's squeezing through those."

"I can widen those doors for you," Firefly said.

"Those walls are solid concrete," Simmons said, "and the frames are steel."

Firefly grinned. "Not a problem. I can blow a hole in the wall wide enough for two rovers to pass side by side."

"Maybe so, but it would make one hell of a racket," CB said. "Besides, an explosion that big could compromise the stairs. We can't risk it. We'll have to dismantle the control panel and bring it out to the rover piece by piece."

Firefly didn't look happy, but he didn't voice a complaint, either.

"We're going to do this safely," CB said. "Firefly and I have already swept floors G1 through G5. We're going to sweep G6, 7, and 8 before we get to work on 9."

"You sure we have time for that, Captain?" Drew asked.

"We're making time for it. The last thing we want is to find out we have vampires between us and our exit."

"We've got the Daylights covering our escape path, too," Alex said.

"Yes," CB said. "But, remember, they only have a twenty-minute battery life. We have to leave them turned off until we need them. That's Owl's job."

Owl nodded. "I've got them all rigged up on a remote. I can click them all on at once from the rover if shit goes sideways."

CB folded up the blueprint and stuck it in his vest. "Drew, Firefly, Alex, and I will go on ahead to sweep floors G6 through G8. Simmons, you stay with Owl and watch her back. The two of you work on getting the rover down the stairs. You got any questions, now's the time, because once we're in there, we'll need to be as quiet as possible."

He waited a moment and heard no questions.

"Good. Let's move out."

―――――

BEFORE HEADING BACK DOWN, the team checked the three above-ground levels. Unlike in Reactor 2, no vampires were lurking up there. They did, however, find a massive hole in the ceiling of level 3. It looked like a cannon had shot through the domed roof. The gap had to be fifteen feet wide.

"Okay," CB said. "Looks like we're clear up here. Let's head down where the darkness lives."

Levels G6, G7, and G8 were much like the other levels CB and Firefly had described: empty and smelling of death. Since there were four of them working together now, they were able to search all three floors thoroughly in less than an hour. Owl drove the eight-wheeled rover down the stairs, waiting one landing behind the team until CB had declared the next level safe and given her the all-clear to proceed. Simmons waited with her, his rifle at the ready in case trouble came from below.

They reached level G9 and headed in. With the blueprint, they knew the exact location of the control room, but once again, CB wanted to err on the side of caution and swept the rest of the floor before proceeding to their destination. Alex kept her sword in hand; if they did encounter a stray vampire, as they had in Reactor 2, she'd try to take it out quietly.

Alex was starting to think perhaps they were being overly cautious. Maybe there weren't that many vampires in this facility to begin with, and any that were here were sleeping. But she forced herself to be like CB, to put caution ahead of all else. Besides, CB and Firefly had heard a vampire roar, so there was at least one awake and unaccounted for in this reactor.

After clearing the rest of the level, CB, Alex, Drew, and Firefly prepared to enter the control room. Alex stood in front of the double doors, sword in hand. CB hunched next to her, pistols at the ready. He counted them down with his fingers, and on three Firefly and Drew threw the doors wide.

Two vampires crouched on the floor near the massive control panel ten feet from the door. They whipped their heads in the direction of the door and trained their inhuman eyes on the team.

Alex leaped forward, sword raised. She heard three gunshots ring out as she reached the vampire. She swung her sword hard, and it hit the target, slicing into the vampire's neck and cleanly removing its head.

She spun toward the other vampire, but it was already

prone, a trio of closely grouped bullet holes in the center of its chest.

CB stood at the door, his pistol still trained on the downed creature.

Firefly and Drew dashed inside, one going left and the other going right, and cleared the room. There were no other vampires.

"Nice work, Alex," CB said.

"You too, Captain."

"Let's just hope the gunfire didn't wake up any of their friends."

"Holy hell," Drew said.

Alex turned and saw that he was looking at the control panel. She whistled, echoing Drew's sentiment.

The control panel ran all the way to the ceiling, along the entire back wall of the room. Alex guessed it was twelve feet high and fifteen feet wide. Three feet above the floor, the panel angled out at forty-five degrees, presumably so the operator could sit in a chair while monitoring it. The entire surface was covered in tightly grouped rows of knobs and dials, with the occasional monitor mounted in seemingly random spots across the panel.

"You sure this is all Director Bowen needs, Captain?" Drew asked. "She doesn't want us to bring back anything else? Like maybe the Statue of Liberty?"

CB didn't reply, but it was clear from the look on his face he was as overwhelmed as the rest of them. The control panel on *New Haven* was one third the size of this beast.

"Okay," CB said. "Same rules apply here. Caution above all else. We dismantle this thing methodically. I'd rather have to come back for another day down here than do it wrong. Last thing we want is to get back to the ship and find out we broke this damn thing. First thing—"

A flash of movement in the doorway caught everyone's eyes. Alex spun toward the door. A vampire was sprinting toward them, its fangs bared. Alex raised her sword, ready to meet the creature, but Firefly was already on it. He shot the vampire five times in the chest before it reached the door.

"Nice shooting," Alex said.

Firefly holstered his weapon. "And you guys thought I could only blow things up."

"Damn," Drew said. "Where'd he come from? We swept the floor."

"Must have come from G10," CB said. "Looks like Firefly's theory of them wanting to be as far beneath the Earth as possible is proving correct."

Alex took a deep breath to calm her jangled nerves. Owl and Simmons were holding fast in the main stairwell, and she hadn't heard any gunfire from their direction. The vampire must have come through one of the other three stairwells they'd seen.

"We'll keep one person at the door at all times," CB said. "The rest of us will work on dismantling this thing. We'll rotate who's on guard duty every thirty minutes. Let's get to work."

————

THE NEXT THREE hours were filled with the difficult and mentally grueling task of dismantling the control panel while watching their backs for vampires.

Director Bowen had given them detailed, written instructions, but translating her notes to this much larger unit was an arduous process. They'd check the instructions, begin to remove a component, encounter something unexpected, and then have to check the instructions again.

At one point, Drew grumbled, "If we have to come back down here tomorrow, we're bringing Bowen with us. She can dismantle the thing her own damn self."

It was mentally exhausting work. Combine that with carrying the components out to the rover, and they were all starting to get tired.

They'd set up work lights of the standard, non-Daylight variety. CB didn't like putting a spotlight on them for any vampires that might be watching, but it was necessary for the delicate work at hand. They also set up work lights along the path between the control room and the stairwell, and in the stairwell itself, so floors G1 through G10 were all aglow in regular light. The Daylights were set up on every other floor, but were left off, only to be used in an emergency.

Solo vampires attacked three more times while they were working. Twice, in the control room. Alex dispatched one of these attackers with three bullets to the chest. Upon inspection, she was disappointed to see her shots weren't as closely grouped at CB's had been. Drew took care of the second attacker, once again inflicting auditory damage on his teammates by using his shotgun in close quarters. CB told him that next time, he had to bring a pistol, no matter how much he loved that damn shotgun.

The third attack had come in the stairwell. Alex had been in the control room, so she'd missed the excitement that time. The vampire had come up from below, adding more credence to Firefly's theory that the vampires were holed up on G10. Simmons and Owl had heard the door open as soon as the vampire entered the stairwell and Simmons readied his rifle. He'd waited until the creature rounded the stairs and was only ten feet away before taking the thing's head clean off with an explosive round.

As they worked, Alex noticed CB was unusually quiet. He was always serious when they were on the surface, but he was usually quick to bark orders and freely handed out reprimands to those who deserved it. This time, he only spoke when absolutely necessary. It could have been just the nature of the task at hand, but Alex didn't think so.

"You okay, Captain?" she asked him as they were preparing to carry another load of components to the rover. "You've been awfully quiet."

CB grimaced. "Maybe I'm just paranoid, but there's something off about the vampires in this place."

"Nothing seems strange to me, sir," Drew said, his voice strained under that weight of the panel he was carrying. "They keep attacking us like idiots, and we keep putting them down. Business as usual."

"Yeah, but this place is huge." CB's brow creased, as it always did when he was deep in thought. "We've put down, what, six of them? Remember how many were in the little factory in Buenos Aires? There should be hundreds here."

Firefly came back in the control room, having returned from carrying a piece to the rover. "You really complaining about the lack of vampires, sir?"

"Not complaining. Speculating."

"Maybe there just aren't that many here. You said yourself the hordes move unpredictably, right? Maybe most of them have moved on."

"Perhaps." CB turned toward the remaining parts. There were two large components, plus a whole bunch of smaller parts. "We'll be able to get these loaded in plenty of time, but we'll have to come back for Reactor 2 if Jessica says she needs it. Let's load out these bigger pieces and get them out of the way."

It took two of them to haul each of the two large pieces.

Alex and CB went first, carrying one, and Firefly and Drew followed with the second.

Owl groaned when she saw the first big piece come through the door. She and Simmons had just returned from taking a load back to the ship.

They loaded the two large pieces onto the rover. They just barely fit.

"How much more is there?" Owl said.

"Not a lot," CB said. "A handful of smaller components. Altogether maybe half the size of one of these."

"Still won't fit in this load," Simmons said.

Owl nodded her agreement. "We'll take these topside while you gather up the rest."

"Roger that," CB said.

Firefly and Drew headed back to the control room. Alex and CB walked back up with the rover to make sure it made it back to the ground floor, providing cover, since it would be difficult for them to fight while so loaded down.

When the rover was safely at ground level, CB and Alex headed back to G9.

"Can you imagine working down here?" CB asked as they reached the door to G9. "Spending your days surrounded by dirt and concrete?"

"No, sir," Alex admitted. "I gotta wonder if they—"

A series of loud crashes came from both above and below them, cutting off her words.

"The hell is that?" Alex asked. "We cleared those..."

CB's eyes widened. "The control room! Go!"

Alex darted through the door and sprinted toward the control room, CB close behind.

A cacophony of scurrying footsteps, grunting, hissing, and roars filled the air as a horde of vampires poured onto the stairwell and raced toward G9.

25

GENERAL CRAIG and Councilman Stearns stood outside the interrogation room where Daniel Fleming was being held.

Craig was tired, and he felt numb from the morning's events. He'd shot three people, which was three more than he'd shot in a *very* long time.

Stearns didn't look much better than Craig felt.

"This is very bad, Isaiah," Stearns said. "I thought I made myself clear. I wanted proof."

"We don't have it. Not yet." He nodded toward the interrogation room. "But I expect he'll talk if we put a little pressure on him. He's a politician, after all, not a hardened criminal."

"You assume there's a difference."

Craig chuckled. "Glad to see you still have your sense of humor, Councilman."

"Just barely." Stearns shook his head. "I wish he would have come quietly. This whole mess could have been avoided. Honestly, Isaiah, once the fighting started, you should have shot him. At least that would have ended it."

"You really think so? You want to turn him into a martyr for his cause?"

"Cause? Please. They're a bunch of malcontents looking to start trouble. Without a charismatic leader to follow, they'll be back to making moonshine in their bathtubs and gambling away their paychecks by this weekend."

General Craig wasn't sure how to respond to that. It once again struck him that the councilman might not fully understand the gravity of the situation. "Kurtz tells me crowds are already gathering in Sparrow's Ridge. They'll be protesting here within a couple of hours."

"They just need some good news. Let's hope your Ground Mission Team comes back with some." Stearns looked past Craig and smiled. "Ah, speak of the devil! How is it out there, Captain?"

Captain Kurtz approached and greeted them both with a nod. "Not great, sir. The crowds are growing rapidly, as are the rumors. My badges are hearing people say the police busted into Fleming's meeting and started executing people. They're saying the general shot a dozen people himself."

General Craig cursed softly.

"That's not all," Kurtz said. "People have noticed the Council's inspectors weighing things in Engineering and Agriculture. Taking away some of the heavier items. They're putting two and two together, and rumors are circulating that there's something wrong with the ship."

"We can't catch a break," Councilman Stearns said. "Enough of this doom and gloom talk," Stearns said. "Get in there and see what you can get out of him. Meanwhile, I need to make an announcement. It's time to tell the people the truth about the reactor."

———

CRAIG AND KURTZ sat down at the metal table across from Fleming. It was ten degrees warmer in here than in the rest of the ship, and beads of sweat stood out on Fleming's forehead. He wasn't restrained, but he did look smaller sitting in this room than he had when holding court in front of a roomful of supporters. He still had the familiar spark of intelligent defiance in his eye.

He looked long and hard at General Craig, so much so that the general began to wonder if the councilman was going to attack him. That would be an incredibly stupid move. Though the general was thirty years Fleming's senior, he still worked out every day, and he'd spent his life training to be a killer. He had no doubt that he could make short work of the scrawny councilman.

"Are you comfortable, Councilman Fleming?" Kurtz began.

Fleming answered without taking his eyes off the general. "No, not at all. Thank you for asking."

"I was just checking," Kurtz said. "This is our nicest room by quite a long shot. Depending on how this discussion progresses, things can become a bit more comfortable —we can ask that the climate be set to your requested temperature, for example—or they can get a whole lot worse. Again, it all hinges on this discussion. Something for you to keep in mind."

"What exactly are you threatening, Captain Kurtz?"

Kurtz gave his sweetest, most innocent smile. "I'm not threatening anything, Councilman Fleming. I'm merely apprising you of your situation." He set a file folder on the table and flipped it open. "I'd like to discuss the night of the fire in Engineering. I have quite a few questions for you, so please get comfortable."

Fleming shook his head. "Before I answer anything, I want the general to tell me how Sarah's doing. Is she alive?"

"In fairness, I was aiming for you." The general's low voice rumbled in the small room. "She was just dumb enough to think you were worth saving. In answer to your question, she's alive. The doctors give her a fifty-fifty shot of pulling through."

Fleming squeezed his eyes shut. "Damn it. She's a good woman. She doesn't deserve this. Neither did the other people you shot."

"They attacked officers of the law. That has consequences."

Fleming opened his eyes and glared at Craig, his lips curled into a snarl. "You're a murderer, Craig. A stone-cold killer who gunned down people just for trying to make the world a better place. Every fear I had, every nagging suspicion about the underlying corruption of this government, you confirmed it all when you pulled that trigger. This government would rather silence the voices of the people than listen to them."

"Let's get back to the topic at hand," Kurtz said. "Where were you the night of the fire?"

"I was with Sarah and a few others. You can ask her about it when she wakes up."

Kurtz sighed. "Okay, I'm just going ask you straight out, and we'll go from there. Did you start the fire in Engineering?"

"No, I did not. Nor did I order anyone to do so. Nor did I even know about the fire until I heard the emergency broadcast about it." He crossed his arms and leaned back in his chair. "That's all I have to say on the matter. I won't say another word to you gentlemen except that, as a publicly elected official and a citizen of *New Haven*, I ask that you take me before a judge to publicly accuse me of a crime or let me go."

The general shook his head. "I understand, Fleming. Captain Kurtz and I are perfectly happy if you'd like to wait to make your statement. I think you'll find we're incredibly patient. We'll go about our lives, do our jobs, spend time with our families. Meanwhile, you can wait in a cell. We'll check back with you in a couple days to see if you've changed your mind."

The general pushed back his chair, stood up, and left.

26

ALEX AND CB raced through the hallways toward the control room. The floor shook with the movement of the horde of vampires.

Drew stuck his head out of the control room door as they got close. "Why the hell are—"

"Get inside!" CB screamed.

Drew did as he was told, and Alex and CB dashed into the control room. As soon as they were inside, CB slammed the door shut and locked it. Five seconds after it was closed, the first vampire slammed into it. Then a second. And a third.

The bangs continued as more and more vampires began pounding on the door. Soon creatures were banging on the walls, too.

"What the hell happened out there?" Drew said, shouting to be heard over the pounding.

"The vampires rushed us all at once," CB said. "Dozens of them. Maybe a hundred. Hard to tell from just the sounds of them."

Firefly looked stunned.

Drew gave CB and Alex a quick look up and down. "You guys okay?"

Alex understood what he was really asking. "No one's bleeding. It wasn't blood that drew them."

"Then what did?" Drew asked.

"Nothing," CB said. He spoke into his microphone. "Owl, Simmons, you read me?"

Simmons's voice sounded in their ears. "We read you, Captain, but just barely over the background noise. What the hell's going on down there?"

"A shit ton of vampires decided it was feeding time. We're barricaded in the control room, and we should be safe for now. The exits are decidedly inaccessible at the moment, though. You two stay put. Get the equipment loaded on the ship and get it prepared for takeoff while we figure a way out of here."

A long pause, then Simmons said, "Roger that, Captain. Let us know if we can do anything to help."

After Simmons had signed off, Alex tried to gather her thoughts, but it was hard to think with all that pounding on the doors and the walls. She thought of Frank, the vampire on *New Haven*. She wondered if this was how he felt, locked in that steel box with his enemies just outside, just beyond his reach. If he felt at all. After over one hundred and fifty years of fighting them, there was still so little that humanity knew about vampires. And the events of today were calling even what they thought they knew into question.

As if echoing her thoughts, Drew spoke up. "I don't understand. The vampires somehow, what, decided to all hold off until the time was right and attack at the same moment?"

"Seems that way," CB said. "It was a coordinated attack."

"That's impossible," Firefly said. "Vampires are stupid animals. They can't strategize. Right?"

"It would appear they can," CB said.

"Hold on," Drew said. "You guys are saying the vampires purposely cut us off from the rest of our team? That they all waited on G10 for the perfect moment?"

Alex thought about that, then shook her head. "They weren't all on G10. They came from below *and* above."

"They were on the above-ground levels?" Firefly asked.

CB ran a hand over the stubbly hair on his head. "Could be. But I'm thinking they were down here the whole time. I think they moved floor to floor, staying away from us until they were ready."

"That's impossible," Firefly repeated.

The pounding on the door paused for a moment, then continued again in earnest.

"Is that door going to hold?" Alex asked.

"It's steel," CB said. "I think it'll hold for now."

Alex watched the way the door shook with each blow the vampires hit it with. She hoped the captain was right.

"So, what's the plan?" Drew said. "Do we wait them out? Hope they lose interest?"

"We're going to be more proactive than that," CB said. "Sundown is in two hours. When that happens, they'll be able to tear through this door. You saw the holes in the walls upstairs. Those weren't all caused by man-made weapons."

A chill ran through Alex. She hadn't considered that they were on such a tight clock here. She once again thought of Frank, suffering endlessly inside his steel box, while generations of humans waited patiently for him to die. "CB's right. Besides, I doubt immortal creatures are going to lose interest in their first shot at a human meal in a century and a half."

"So, what do we do?" Firefly asked. Of all of them, he seemed the most stunned by this turn of events.

"We come up with a plan," CB said. "I don't know about you, but I'm not waiting for sundown. If I'm going down, I'll go down fighting."

———

SIMMONS AND OWL stood in the cargo hold of the ship. They'd followed CB's instructions and secured the equipment. Owl had prepared the ship for takeoff. They'd gone about their work methodically, professionals unshaken by their teammates' situation. Now that there was no more work to do, they were altogether less calm.

Simmons's stomach clenched as he thought about his teammates trapped down there. Of *Alex* trapped down there.

They waited in silence for a long time, both feeling helpless and neither knowing what to say.

Finally, Owl said what Simmons had been thinking the whole time. "I think in this particular instance, we might need to disobey CB's orders."

Simmons tried to keep his voice calm as he answered. "I think you may be correct, Owl."

"The Daylights are set up in the stairwells. We can turn them on with the remote in the rover. That'll clear the stairs enough for us to get down there. Then it'll just be a matter of fighting our way from the stairwell to the control room."

Simmons didn't answer. There were a thousand objections to her plan. First, they had no idea how many vampires were down there. CB had used the word *horde*. He hadn't described the dozen or so vampires they'd faced in Buenos Aires using that word. And the team wouldn't have turned tail and hidden in the control room if they were just talking about a dozen vampires. *Horde* implied a not-easily countable number of vampires. CB had a far better handle on the situation down there than they did here, and he'd told them to stay put.

And then there was the matter of the Daylights. Yes, they could turn them on with the remote, but their light didn't cover the entire stairwell. There would still be plenty of dark spots for the vampires to cower in. That also assumed the theory that the lights actually killed vampires and that the vampires hadn't destroyed the lights. Owl had mounted them high in the corners, but Simmons had seen vampires jump much higher than ten feet during his tenure on the GMT.

He couldn't imagine vampires taking any interest in darkened lights mounted in stairwell corners, but, before today, he hadn't imagined vampires carrying out a coordinated attack, either.

"You know CB wouldn't leave us down there," Owl said.

She was right, but there was another concern, one Simmons had no choice but to bring up. "Owl, if we go after them and die, this control panel equipment will sit here and rot while *Haven* loses power. They'll be forced to land, and humanity will die."

Owl looked shocked at the suggestion. "You're saying we just leave them down there?"

"Of course not. I'm just saying we have to look at all possibilities. One of which is that we take this equipment back to *Haven* and return with reinforcements in the morning. CB said they're safe for now."

"Did you not hear CB's story about his first team? They may be safe now, but come nightfall, it's going to be a different situation."

"I heard the story, but we're talking about steel doors

and concrete walls. This is a nuclear facility. It was built to withstand disaster."

Owl stepped forward and jabbed a finger into his chest. "First of all, we don't even have all the parts. For all we know, the most important components are still down there. Secondly, if you think I'm going to abandon my friends to die down there, you don't know me very well. I don't care what you do, but I'm going to fight like hell to save them."

Simmons smiled. He was done playing devil's advocate. "I was hoping you'd say that. As soon as our moment comes, we're going in."

———

ALEX, CB, Firefly, and Drew pored over Jessica's instructions one last time, trying to identify the remaining parts to determine what was essential to bring with them. They sifted out what they could fit into their packs. It would mean leaving some of their mission equipment behind, but one way or another, they wouldn't need it. An hour from now, they'd either be dead or safely aboard the ship and headed back toward *New Haven*. Either way, they probably wouldn't need a hand shovel or a multitool.

The group had unanimously agreed they weren't going to wait in here until nightfall. They had no idea how many vampires were out there. Their odds of fighting their way out of the tight spot they were in were incredibly slim indeed, but what choice did they have but to try?

Each moment that they worked through the remaining equipment, the pressure of their quickly diminishing time became heavier. Sundown was in less than an hour. If they were going to act, it needed to be soon.

They'd been so cocky. Splitting up, clearing floors, and

assuming the animals were too dumb to stand a chance against their strategic maneuvers. Over the hours of dismantling the control panel, they'd grown even more comfortable. Firefly's insistence that the vampires were all sleeping on G10 seemed foolish now.

Alex promised herself that if she somehow managed to get out of this mess, she'd never be complacent on the surface again. Next time she came down here, she'd be a holy terror, a vampire hunter without mercy or hesitation.

Her eyes settled on the blueprint of the reactor CB had found. He'd set it on the ground next to Jessica's instructions. She thought about what Simmons had said earlier... that they'd likely put the control room on the lowest floor possible.

She looked up suddenly. "Guys? Why'd they put the control room on G9 instead of G10?"

CB looked at her blankly for a moment. Then he got it. He grabbed the blueprint off the floor, looked at it for a moment, then smiled.

27

THE TEAM HUDDLED CLOSE TOGETHER SO they could hear each other over the clamoring of the vampires.

Alex held up the diagram. "G10 is the utility level. It should be mostly clear. That means if we can get down there, we'll have a straight shot to the stairwell. The vampires are piled up around the door, right?"

Firefly smiled. "I like where you're headed with this."

"What if there are still vampires in the stairwell?" Drew asked. "If we have to stop and fight them, the others will figure out what's up and join the party."

"That's where Simmons and Owl come in," CB said. "They have the rover back in the away ship. Once we give them the signal, they'll activate the Daylights, which should fry the majority of vampires in the stairwell. Then we haul ass topside and get the hell out of here."

Alex looked at the blueprint again. This was their best shot at getting out alive. More importantly, it was their only shot at getting the equipment in their packs back to the ship. She turned to Firefly. "What do you say? Can you put a hole in this floor and get us down to G10?"

"Oh, hell yes." Firefly dove into his demolitions bag and began pulling out equipment.

After a little thought, Firefly decided they would need to drill into the floor, then he'd drop a charge that'd make a hole big enough for them to climb through. The drilling turned out to be no small task; the floor was two feet of solid concrete.

At times, while Firefly worked, Alex worried that maybe the vampires would hear the noise and go down to Gio to check if anything was happening down there. She shouldn't have worried. They kept attacking the door and roaring with impressive vigor and consistency. It was becoming increasingly clear that Drew's idea that they would eventually lose interest and wander off was nothing more than wishful thinking.

There wasn't much for CB, Drew, and Alex to do except wait and watch. The temperature in the small room seemed to be rising by the moment, and the constant noise level of the drill combined with the frenzied vampires began to wear on Alex.

CB filled Simmons and Owl in on the plan over the radio, and he reminded them to stay on the ship and have it ready for takeoff. If things went badly down here, they were to take the parts to *New Haven* and return the following day to see if they could retrieve the remaining components. Owl said she was ready to activate the Daylights when CB gave the signal.

Drew and Alex went over the remaining components again, comparing them to Jessica's instructions to make sure they were bringing the most vital ones that could fit in their packs.

It took Firefly nearly forty minutes of drilling before he was satisfied. His face was slick with sweat, but Alex thought she'd never seen him so happy. He was practically giggling as he set the charge in the floor.

"Sometimes I think he likes his job a little too much," Drew said.

Firefly sauntered back to where CB, Alex, and Drew were huddled behind a piece of sheet metal from the control panel. "We're all set, Captain."

"Good. After the charge goes off, we have to move quickly. No telling how smart these bastards are, and we're not taking anything for granted. Speed and surprise are our only advantages here. Move quickly, kill anything that isn't wearing a black vest, and stay together. Questions?"

"Just one," Alex said. "Why are all our missions so uneventful?"

Drew guffawed, but CB ignored the comment.

"On my mark, Firefly," CB said.

They all crouched low, bracing themselves against the blast.

"Now!" CB yelled.

Firefly detonated the charge.

ALEX ROCKED BACK on her heels, pushed by the force of the concrete debris slamming into the piece of sheet metal. The sound of the blast dwarfed the ongoing clamor from the vampires and even the earlier sound of Drew's shotgun blast. She fleetingly wondered if her eardrums would ever be the same after today.

As the sound of the charge faded, she realized the vampires were in an absolute frenzy now. Bodies slammed against the control room door so quickly that it sounded like fire from an automatic weapon. She hoped that meant that the vampires hadn't understood what they'd done. Even considering that they might understand what the sound of the explosion meant would have been ridiculous twenty-four hours ago; now, she wasn't so sure.

Firefly somersaulted out from behind the sheet metal and scurried toward the hole. He pointed his headlamp down the hole for a moment, then turned back to where his teammates were huddled. "We're good, sir!" He shouted the words, but still Alex could barely discern them over the sound of the vampires.

CB tapped Drew and Alex on the shoulders. "Go, go, go!"

Alex switched her headlamp on and dashed toward the hole. She leaped down without even looking.

She landed with a thud ten feet below and quickly rolled out of the way. She was glad she had a moment later, when Drew slammed down next her. CB and Firefly quickly followed. They both landed gracefully compared to Alex and Drew.

Alex spun around and saw she'd been right about this place. It was wide open with only the occasional tray of electrical and telecommunications wiring between her and the walls in the distance.

The floor was dirt here, and it seemed to be spotted with what must have been one hundred tiny hills. No, she realized a moment later, not hills. Graves. Firefly had been right about one thing—the vampires slept down here.

It took her a moment to get her bearings. She had to look up through the hole to G9 to orient herself. The sound of the vampires abusing the door of the control room up there was muffled here, and she relished the comparative quiet as she figured out which way it was to the main stairwell.

She found it and pointed at it. "There."

"Let's go!" CB shouted.

The team took off, running close together, dodging spools of wiring and hopping over piles of dirt and empty graves. In a few moments, they were at the door to the stairwell.

Alex was the first to reach it. She grabbed the doorknob and turned to Drew, who'd been the next to arrive. "Cover me."

"Roger that." He leveled his shotgun at the door.

Alex stepped out of the way and pulled the door open.

As soon as the door was open, a tall, gangly vampire leaped through, its fangs bared and its claws outstretched, hissing as it came. Drew fired, dropping it before it even passed the threshold.

Another immediately took its place. This time, Alex dropped it with a flurry of shots to the chest. As it fell, she caught a glimpse behind it. The vampires were jammed tight all the way back to the wall with even more on steps.

"Holy shit," she muttered as she shot the next one in line.

"Owl, lights!" CB yelled into his mic.

The Daylights came on with an electric *thum*, and the vampires began to scream. They caught fire as quickly as old parchment under a lit match. They wriggled and staggered as they burned. One stumbled through the door toward the team, and CB put it out of its misery.

The burning only lasted a few moments, then the vampires seemed to dissolve from the outside in. They crumbled, turned to ash, and fell to the ground. A moment later, the stairwell was empty.

"Well, I guess those work," Alex said.

Simmons's voice came from somewhere high up the stairwell. "Guys, you need to hurry!"

"What the hell is he doing?" CB said.

Alex agreed with the sentiment. Simmons and Owl were supposed to wait on the ship and be ready to take off.

"You heard the man," CB said. "Let's go!"

This time, CB led the charge himself. Drew and Firefly stormed after him with Alex pulling up the rear.

The air in the stairwell was thick with dust.

"You guys know we're breathing vampires, right?" Firefly shouted as they dashed up the stairs.

"Dude, shut up!" Drew said.

Alex put the thought out of her mind. She didn't have time to think about the possible implications of breathing well-done vampires into her lungs.

As they passed the open door to G9, Alex looked inside and saw vampires lined at the edge of the Daylight's beam. Some nipped at the air as she passed, clearly furious at their inability to pursue their prey.

When she was almost past the door, something whizzed by her head and hit the wall near her. As it clanked to the ground, she saw it was a piece of wood the size of her head, maybe ripped from one of the old desks. Part of her wanted to shoot the vampires in the doorway just for throwing stuff at her, but her survival instinct won out. She kept running. She was so close to Firefly she was almost stepping on his heels.

As she rounded the steps to the next level, something on G9 caught her eye. She spun just in time to see an old file cabinet soar through the air and smash into the Daylight. The landing went dark.

Through the dim illumination of her headlamp, she saw vampires cascading through the door, crawling over each other to get to the stairs. Many of them were holding objects, old office equipment they must have scavenged from G9.

A vampire carrying an office chair climbed past the others and stopped at the edge of the illumination from the next Daylight. He squinted up at the light, raised the chair, and took aim.

28

SIMMONS STOOD at the landing on G2, his rifle aimed down the stairs. Vampires pushed through the open door to the level, jostling one another to get as close to the light, and the human standing in it, as possible. Simmons trained his rifle on the gap in the center of the stairwell. His team was on G6 now, but the vampires were getting closer. Apparently, they'd figured out to smash the Daylights.

The gap in the center of the stairs wasn't large, but he caught a vampire in his sites and dropped it as it ran past far below. He considered racing down to try to take out more of them, but he'd likely get in the way of the team's retreat and do more harm than good.

It had taken a Herculean effort to convince Owl to stay back in the ship while he came to help. After CB had told them the plan, they'd spent a frustrating few hours aboard the ship, unable to do much more than twiddle their thumbs and hope for the best. When CB had said they were ready to retreat, there was no way Simmons was waiting on the ship. Yet, they'd had to think practically, too. The sunlight was fading fast, and it was likely they'd have to cut a fast retreat. Owl needed to stay behind and be ready to get the ship off the ground the moment the last member of the team stepped aboard.

Now Simmons was wondering about the wisdom of his plan. He wasn't doing much good here. The quarters were just too tight for his rifle to be useful. The last thing he wanted to do was get in his teammates' way. He had to admit his best bet would be to head back to ground level and wait in the lobby. That way he'd be able to cover his teammates where there was a little more space, if the vampires did manage to smash the remaining Daylights.

He ran back up to ground level, looked out of the door, and froze. More vampires were in the lobby than he'd seen in any of the other floors he'd passed. They crowded in the doorway, pushing one another into the light in an effort to get closer to Simmons. He had to dodge out of the way as one caught fire and nearly stumbled into him.

He turned just in time to see a vampire barreling down the stairs from level 2. Cursing, he slung his rifle over his back and grabbed his pistol. He wasn't as accurate with the smaller weapon, but it was much more manageable in this tight space. He dropped the vampire and gazed up the stairs into the darkness.

What the hell were they going to do? The team could probably clear the lobby, given enough time, but time wasn't on their side. Besides, if the vampires below smashed the rest of the Daylights while they were fighting the vampires in the lobby, they'd be trapped between two hordes. But what other choice did they have? He gazed up into the dark stairwell. Then he remembered something.

He spoke into his microphone. "Captain, the lobby's a no-go. The vampires somehow beat us to it. There's a shit ton of them in there."

An impressive string of curse words was the only response.

"Sir, you remember the hole in the ceiling on level 3?" Simmons said.

There was a pause, then CB said, "Owl, get the ship in the air. Hover it above the building and open the cargo door."

"Roger that, sir," Owl replied.

Simmons took one last look through the door to the lobby. Far past the vampires, he could see the exit, and it sent a chill through him. The light looked far dimmer than it had only ten minutes ago. He heard a crash from below that he knew was another one of the Daylights breaking. No time to waste. He switched on his headlamp and ran up the stairs.

After what he'd seen today, Simmons was hesitant to even begin to guess how the vampires' minds worked. He had no idea how much they were able to reason and how much they operated by pure instinct. However they'd come to their conclusion, they appeared to be focusing on blocking the team's retreat through the lobby. Even if they were smart enough to think through other possible escape routes, they didn't know about the team's secret weapon.

All told, Simmons encountered five vampires on his way up to level 3. He'd only ever killed four of the creatures before this mission, but somehow, five didn't seem like a terribly difficult task after considering the horde he'd just seen in the lobby.

When he finally got to level 3, he dashed through the door, then quickly skidded to a stop.

Apparently, he'd sold the vampires short yet again. They had considered alternative exits. At least, some of them had.

A dozen vampires stood fifty yards down the hallway between him and the hub.

Simmons hesitated for only a moment before moving into action. He had no choice. This was their only feasible way out.

He put away his pistol and grabbed his rifle just as the first vampire spotted him and began to charge.

————

ALEX DASHED UP THE STAIRS, rounding the corner up to G7 just as the office chair smashed into the Daylight on G8, knocking it out. There were vampires crowded in the doorway to G7, and they, too, were throwing objects. How the hell had they gotten up here so quickly? They must have been using one of the stairwells on the other end of the building.

She was close at Firefly's heels, racing upward as fast as she could. As long as she stayed in the light, she'd be fine. Well, as long as she didn't get hit by the office equipment that was now flying through the air. Thankfully, the vampires seemed to be focusing their efforts on taking out the Daylights. They were doing a far better job of it than Alex would have thought possible, but the lights were still slowing them down enough that the team would be able to reach the lobby safely.

Simmons's voice spoke in her ear. "Captain, the lobby's a no-go. The vampires somehow beat us to it. There's a shit ton of them in there."

No. That was impossible.

She pushed the panic away.

The captain cursed in her ear, apparently having the same reaction to the news as she was.

There had to be another way. Her mind was churning through the possibilities, but Simmons got to the only other feasible one first.

"Sir, you remember the hole in the ceiling on level 3?" Simmons said.

Yes! Alex thought.

There was a pause, then CB said, "Owl, get the ship in the air. Hover it above the building and open the cargo door."

"Roger that, sir," Owl replied.

Alex pressed onward, her panic giving way to newfound hope. There was a crash as another Daylight smashed two floors below.

The vampires crowded in the doorway of G5 were throwing things too now. Thankfully, they were still hurling small objects and had yet to move on to file cabinets and office chairs. Alex dodged the projectiles and kept going, trying not to think about what would happen if the vampires on one of the levels above them managed to smash the Daylight before they got there.

They kept pressing upward, reaching the ground floor. The sounds of Daylights smashing below grew more frequent as the vampires refined their techniques. How many had Alex heard them smash? Five? Six? She'd lost track, but however many it was, it was too many for comfort.

"Simmons wasn't kidding," Drew said as he passed the lobby.

A moment later, Alex passed the door as well. The largest horde she'd ever seen was gathered there. One of them was holding a large part of a desk, hoisting it above its head, and preparing to throw.

"Shit!" Alex quickly ran out of the way and up to level one. She tripped over a downed vampire, but quickly regained her footing. She'd fallen back from the group a few precious steps, though.

Simmons spoke into her ear again. "Level 3 is clear. Hurry up. I'll cover you."

"That's what I like to hear," CB said.

As they reached level 3, Alex heard a loud crash from only a couple of levels below. The Daylight on level one.

"Go!" she yelled. "They're coming!"

CB, Drew, and Firefly all passed through the door to level 3 and ran down the hallway toward the hub and its promised escape. Alex was only a few steps back, but the vampires were thundering up the steps behind her, moving more quickly than she ever could.

She reached the door and sprinted through. Far down the hallway, Simmons stood, his rifle raised and ready.

He fired, and she heard a whine close behind her as a vampire fell.

Shit! She'd had no idea they were that close.

Simmons fired again, and another vampire behind her fell. She didn't dare look back, but this one seemed closer still.

As she ran, she noticed the hallway was littered with what had to be fifteen vampire corpses. Had Simmons taken out all these himself?

CB reached the hub and looked back at her. What he saw behind her caused his eyes to widen.

"Don't wait for me!" she shouted. "Go!"

He nodded briskly and pressed his thumb against a button in his glove. His jet pack fired to life and he shot upward, disappearing through the hole in the ceiling. Firefly quickly followed.

Drew stared back at Alex. He raised his shotgun, but

even he had to know it would be ineffective at this range. No way he could hit a vampire without also hitting Alex.

"Go!" Alex yelled again.

He hesitated only a moment before firing up his jet pack and shooting into the sky.

Simmons fired again and again, not even pausing between shots. Alex felt one of the vampires brush against the back of her legs as it fell victim to his rifle. She wanted to tell him to go, too, but she knew she'd have no chance of escape without him picking off the vampires at her back.

"Let's go, you two!" CB yelled in their ears.

Alex wanted to thank him for his sage advice and say she hadn't thought of leaving until he'd suggested it, but she didn't have the breath.

She reached Simmons's side just as he fired again, and she looked up through the hole. The sky was dimmer than she'd ever seen it. The sun was almost set. She turned to Simmons. "Come on."

He fired again, and a vampire's head exploded in a mist of brain matter and bone. "Right behind you."

They wouldn't be able to hold off the vampires long; there was no time to argue.

She pressed the button in her glove, and her jet pack roared to life. She rocketed upward. The away ship hovered a few hundred feet above the reactor's domed roof. Its cargo door was open, and CB, Drew, and Firefly stood in the open maw of the ship, beckoning her onward. She used her hands to make a minor adjustment to the jet pack's trajectory, like Brian had taught her.

Just before she reached the ship, she glanced at the western horizon. The sun dipped below it. Night had fallen.

She reached the open cargo door and flew inside. She deactivated the jet pack as she entered the ship, fell to the floor, and quickly spun to look back. She was relieved to see Simmons shooting up toward the ship.

She fell to her knees and let out a huge breath. Thank God. She would have killed him if he'd died providing her cover.

Simmons was about one hundred yards away and closing fast. The team was safe.

Suddenly two vampires leaped through the hole in the reactor's dome and shot two hundred feet into the air.

One of the vampires grabbed Simmons's leg. It scurried up his back, climbing him like a ladder. It bared its fangs and bit down on his neck. Its head erupted in flames as its teeth sank into the silver mail. It quickly fell away.

But the other vampire was already on his leg, and, a moment later, his back.

Simmons's jet pack sputtered under the added weight.

Three more vampires leaped through the dome. These easily reached Simmons, piling on. The jet pack couldn't handle the weight, and Simmons sank like a stone, falling back inside the dome even as more vampires leaped on him and dragged him down.

A vampire scurried up his chest and bit the underside of his chin, above where the silver mail stopped. It looked up and howled at the sky, its face wet with blood. As Alex watched, its face began to transform.

Then Simmons and the vampires disappeared into the darkness of the dome.

"No!" Alex screamed.

"Owl, go," CB yelled.

Owl's voice came through her earpiece. "We're not leaving without Simmons."

CB turned and sprinted into the depths of the ship.

Alex stared down into the black emptiness.

Another vampire leaped upward, clutching at the air in an attempt to reach the ship. It only fell short by twenty yards.

The cargo door began to close.

"No!" Alex yelled again. She moved to the window in the cargo door, her gaze fixed on the hole in the dome, hoping against hope that Simmons would appear.

A moment later, the ship shot upward and the dome disappeared below the clouds.

29

ALEX RACED INTO THE SHIP. In the passenger area, the team was silently sinking into their seats and strapping themselves in. Their faces looked hollow, as if some vital piece of them had been left below on the surface. Why weren't they screaming? Why weren't they shouting that they had to go back and get him? She wanted to grab every one of them and shake them. Simmons was part of the team. He was family.

CB shuffled in, looking old and tired, and went to his seat.

"We have to go back," Alex said.

"I'm sorry, Alex, but he's gone." CB reached for the safety belt and pulled it over his shoulder.

"Screw that. We're not leaving him." Alex stormed toward the cockpit. Maybe no one else on this ship cared about their friend, but she did.

CB threw off the safety belt and jumped to his feet. He grabbed her around the shoulders. "Alex, you have to listen to me. He's gone."

She shook her head violently, not willing to believe it.

"He fought off a dozen vampires by himself on level three before we got there. He could be fighting for his life right now. He needs our help."

CB spun her around and held her by the shoulders, his face close to hers. "There were a hundred vampires. The sun is down, and they're at their strongest. There's no way anyone could last two minutes against that horde. Not even Simmons."

She stared into CB's face and knew he was right. Going back was suicide. Simmons was dead.

She stumbled to her seat, her eyes filling with tears. "How did they do that? It was like they were flying." She'd seen vampires jump in Buenos Aires and here today. It had been impressive, but it had been nothing like she'd witnessed when those vampires leaped out of the dome.

"It's like CB's been telling us," Drew said, his voice hollow. "They're different at night."

A heavy silence fell over the ship.

They passed through a cloud and broke out into a sunlit sky. They had caught up with the daylight.

"I was an idiot," Firefly said. "I thought they were just dumb animals. But we just got outsmarted by vampires."

"They surprised all of us," CB said. "Of all people, I should have seen it coming."

Firefly shook his head. "You don't understand. I believed in Resettlement. Like, really believed in it, even after your story. I thought we could wipe them off the face of the Earth."

"Some things you have to see for yourself," CB said.

Alex stared out the window at the clouds far below. Every moment took her farther from Simmons. Or whatever was left of him. He'd saved her life, and she'd failed to save his.

They flew the rest of the way to *New Haven* in silence.

———

THE TEAM WENT through the quarantine and decontamination process in shocked silence. No one said anything to the medical team, but the doctors could count. To their credit, they didn't ask any questions or press the team for information. They just went about their work in silence.

There was a flurry of activity when Drew told them the whole team, barring Owl, had breathed in the dust from dead vampires. The medics talked it over and decided to put the team on a round of strong antibiotics, which Alex took to mean that they had no idea if the dust would do anything to them.

Jessica Bowen was waiting impatiently outside the quarantine area, anxious to take a look at what they'd managed to retrieve. As soon as she was cleared, she ran into the hangar and started digging through the control panel components, which had been unloaded and were now waiting in the hangar.

After decontamination, the team went to the briefing room, where the general was waiting for them. CB recapped the events of the day tersely but thoroughly, his voice devoid of any emotion. Alex respected that. If she'd been called on to speak, she probably would have broken down in a puddle of tears on the briefing room floor.

When CB finished, the general regarded the team. "I want to commend you all for your work today. You are a credit to the GMT and its rich history. I'd also like to say I'm sorry for your loss. Simmons was part of our family, and I promise you, I'll make sure the Council understands his sacrifice and they give him the hero's memorial he deserves.

His name will be on the lips of every man, woman, and child on *Haven*, and they'll damn sure understand he saved every one of their lives."

"He saved mine." Alex's voice came out as a whisper.

The general looked at her quizzically. "I'm sorry, Lieutenant?"

She cleared her throat and tried again. "I said, he saved mine. He died protecting me. If not for him, I wouldn't have made it out."

"None of us would have," CB said.

Alex didn't reply. It was different for her. If it hadn't been for their relationship, maybe Simmons wouldn't have been so careless with his life.

————

ALEX LEFT the debrief and walked toward the gym. She wasn't sure where she was heading, exactly; she certainly didn't feel like working out, after everything her body had been through that day. Her feet kept moving, and she followed where they led, too tired to give it a conscious thought.

"Alex, wait up." It was CB.

She stopped and turned toward him. He looked as tired as she felt.

"I just wanted to let you know I'm proud of how you handled yourself today."

"Thank you, sir," she said automatically.

"I mean it. You were brilliant. We might still be stuck in that control room, if not for you."

And Simmons might still be alive, she wanted to add. But she didn't.

"Losing a teammate...there's nothing like it," CB said.

"And no one who hasn't been through it can understand. Not really. All you can do is give yourself time and allow yourself to grieve. Get some rest, Alex. Take tomorrow morning off. We'll check in after lunch."

"Thanks, Captain." She turned and walked away with no particular destination in mind and absolutely no idea what she was supposed to do next.

30

When Alex woke the following morning, she lay in her bed for a full five minutes, trying to summon the will to get up. For the first time in she didn't remember how long, there was nowhere she needed to be. More disconcertingly, there was nowhere she *wanted* to be.

What she wanted was to curl up into a ball and stay in bed, preferably for a month or two. In here, it was nice and warm, if miserable. Out there, Simmons was still dead, and nothing made sense.

Finally, it was the power of her grief that convinced her to get up. If she stayed in bed now, she might never leave.

She threw on her workout clothes and headed out for a run. She figured that if she were going to be numb anyway, she might as well be numb while doing something productive.

At the first opportunity, she exited the GMT-dominated residential area and headed into Sparrow's Ridge. As soon as she did, she was smacked in the face with the fact that reality had continued here aboard the ship while she and her team had been fighting for their lives in Texas. Even in

Sparrow's Ridge, the streets were normally clean. It was just a part of life on *New Haven*. Due to the limited space, everything had to be kept pretty tidy, out of necessity. But today she was shocked at the condition in which she found the neighborhood.

Homemade signs demanding immediate Resettlement were stuck to buildings all along the street. Graffiti was almost everywhere, most of it reading *Free Fleming*. Garbage littered the streets. Had there been more protests the previous night? And what did *Free Fleming* mean? She had to assume he'd been arrested.

The streets were nearly empty this morning. Apparently, everyone was sleeping off the previous night's drama.

Alex found the Hub was in no better condition. Seeing graffiti in Sparrow's Ridge was surprising, but seeing it on the high-end buildings in the Hub was downright shocking.

She saw a badge walking briskly down the road ahead and vaguely recognized him from her days in law enforcement. What was his name? Matthews? Maddock?

"Murphy," she said, and he looked up and nodded to her.

"Morning, Alex." The man looked bone tired, and dark circles ringed his eyes.

"You working a double?"

"Me and everyone else on the force. Between Stearns's announcement yesterday about the reactor being damaged and Fleming being arrested, we're barely keeping things together."

Damn. So, Fleming had been arrested. She had to give the Council respect for coming clean with the people about the reactor, though.

"Too bad you left the force for a life of thrill-seeking

down on the surface," Murphy said. "We could use you up here."

She let that one go. "Good luck, Murphy. Keep up the good work."

She'd only run another few blocks before an announcement came over the city's communication system.

"Attention citizens. Councilman Stearns will be giving an important address in thirty minutes. Please make every attempt to be near a video monitor. Again, Councilman Stearns will be giving an address in thirty minutes."

Great. What fresh hell would this announcement bring?

She circled her way around the Council Building and briefly considered remaining here. There were monitors set up on the front of the building, and a few people were already gathering, claiming the best spots for viewing Stearns's address. She decided she didn't want to be around people right now. Whatever Stearns was going to say, she didn't think she could handle listening to people complaining about it right now. She picked up her pace and ran back toward her quarters.

She made it back in fifteen minutes, which gave her time for a quick shower before the address. In the shower, she scrubbed herself hard, as if she could wash away the events of the previous day.

By the time the video monitor flipped on and showed Councilman Stearns's face, she was sitting on her bed, dressed, her hair still wet.

Councilman Stearns wore a dour expression, as if he were a man who was being forced to deliver bad news. "Good morning citizens, I know this is a bit early, and I appreciate your flexibility. I have some things to share with you, and I didn't want to wait until evening for you to hear them.

"First, as many of you may have already heard through the rumor mill, Councilman Daniel Fleming has been arrested in connection with the fire in Engineering three days ago. We have evidence the fire was arson, and that Councilman Fleming was involved in ordering this vile act in an attempt to force the Council toward Resettlement.

"Innocent until proven guilty is an important core belief of humans going back hundreds of years, and this will be no exception. I can assure you that Councilman Fleming is being treated with respect and dignity, and he will receive a fair trial. However, we also cannot let someone suspected of these acts run free. If he is indeed behind this crime, we owe it to the people to keep him safely in custody. I ask that you respect the rule of law and allow the process to run its course. Fleming will be proven innocent or guilty in court, and I hope we can all reserve judgment either way, until that happens.

"Secondly, I want to tell you about a mission that took place yesterday. The Ground Mission Team traveled to the surface in an attempt to acquire the parts we need to repair our nuclear reactor. They were successful in their goal. Director Bowen in Engineering has confirmed we now have the parts we need to make the repair and keep this city in the air."

Relief flooded through Alex. Everything they'd done had been worth it. The city was safe.

"The mission was not without cost, however. The GMT sniper, Lincoln Simmons, died in the line of duty during the mission. I'm told he fell while ensuring his teammates made it back to their away ship safely before sundown. He not only saved his team, he saved us all. We owe him the highest debt of gratitude."

Alex's eyes filled with tears. Hearing Simmons's death

announced by Councilman Stearns on the video monitor made it more real, somehow.

"We've been a city divided over the issue of Resettlement in recent weeks. I hope now that the ship is safely repaired, we can reunite and work together. Whatever your stance on Resettlement, we all want the same thing: a better future for humanity. The only thing we disagree on is how to make that happen. I believe we can use our differences of opinions as a strength rather than a weakness, coming together to build the future. I want to take this moment to commend everyone who cares enough to make their voice heard, whether that's through peaceful protest or the voting ballot. We are safe. Now let's build the future."

———

BRIAN WAS the only one in the R&D lab when Alex arrived. He was crouched over a jet pack, working on it with a tiny screwdriver. He did a double take when he saw her.

"A-Alex," he stammered. "Hi. Welcome back. I'm so sorry for your loss." The words tumbled from his lips as if they were half-formed thoughts that he didn't have time to process properly before speaking them.

"Thanks, Brian."

He looked up at her, the pain clear on his face. "Look, about the way we left things—"

She waved off the rest of his comment. "Don't even worry about it. You were right to be pissed. Listen, what happened while I was gone? Fleming's been arrested."

A shadow passed across his face. "It's bad, Alex. The general and Captain Kurtz took a bunch of badges to Fleming's headquarters. Things got out of hand. Fleming's supporters and the badges started fighting and, well, Sarah got shot."

The blood drained from Alex's face. "Is she all right?"

He shook his head. "The bullet got her in the lung. Last I heard, they still weren't sure whether she was going to make it."

Sarah had been perhaps a little too blind in her dedication to Fleming, but she didn't deserve this. Not even close.

"Stearns came clean about the damage to the ship last night," Brian said. "He told the people that the ship can only remain in the air for twenty-eight more days unless we are able to repair it. Between that and Fleming's arrest, it was chaos in the streets last night. Protests everywhere, some of them violent."

"Damn."

Neither of them spoke for a long moment.

Finally, Brian asked the question Alex knew he'd been dying to ask since she'd walked in. "How'd the Daylights work?"

She put a hand on his shoulder. "No joke, man, they saved our lives. None of us would have made it back, if not for them."

Brian smiled widely and he practically glowed with pride. "They burned the vampires?"

"Like noontime sun. But listen, they need more battery power and longer range."

He nodded briskly. "Of course. I'll get to work on that right away. I already have ideas." He pushed the jet pack to the other side of the table and pulled out a pad of paper.

Alex tapped the jet pack. "These saved our lives, too. We wouldn't have gotten out if we weren't wearing them. You might not go on missions, Brian, but as far as I'm concerned, you're as much a part of the team as I am."

His eyes widened in surprise. "I...I don't know what to say. Thank you."

She clapped him on the shoulder. "Say you'll give me a Daylight I can use for more than twenty minutes."

"Of course! I'm on it."

"Something happened down there, Brian. When the vampire bit Simmons, it...changed. Started to, anyway."

"Changed how?"

Alex's radio buzzed.

"You there, Alex?"

She lifted the radio and replied. "I'm here, Captain."

"I know I said I wouldn't bother you this morning, but something's come up. Can you meet me in my office?"

She exchanged a quizzical look with Brian. "Sure thing, sir. I'll be there in five minutes."

———

CB ROSE as Alex entered and gestured to the chair across the desk from him. She sat, looking around hesitantly.

Though she'd been on the team for more than a year, she'd only ever been in CB's office one other time, and that had been her first day, when he'd laid out the ground rules for the team.

In truth, she didn't think CB spent much more time in this place than she did. It was sparsely appointed, with only a monitor, a keyboard, and a picture of a woman Alex had never seen before. CB wasn't married—maybe it was his mother? In short, it had the antiseptic feel of an unused space. The captain spent his time in the gym, the briefing room, and the hangar—the places where his team spent their time. She'd never really appreciated it before, but CB went to a lot of effort to lead the team from among them.

"I won't ask how you're doing," he said. "About as crappy as I am, I'll bet."

"Yes, sir. I'd imagine so."

He gestured toward the dark monitor. "You saw Stearns's speech earlier?"

"Yes, sir. It was a lovely tribute."

"Simmons deserves more. But I'm impressed Stearns is playing it straight with the people. This city's tearing itself in half, and it won't heal if the government keeps hiding things." He waved the thought away. "Enough politics. I have a favor to ask you."

She hadn't been expecting that. She'd thought this would be a mental-health check-in, that CB was probably doing it with the entire team. "Of course, sir. What do you need?"

"I know I promised you a little time off, and you're going to get it. But there's something I need you to do first."

She waited. The way he was beating around the bush, this wasn't going to be pleasant.

"I need you to talk to Councilman Fleming."

Her eyes widened in surprise. She'd thought maybe he was going to ask her to help the badges with crowd control or give a written account of what happened yesterday. But she hadn't expected this. "Pardon me, sir, but I thought Fleming was in jail."

"He is. That's where you need to talk to him."

"I'm confused. If he's already caught, why do you need me to talk to him?"

"Because he likes you." He leaned forward and rested his elbows on the desk. "The general's visited Fleming, as have Captain Kurtz and some of the best interrogators on the force. Fleming's unwilling to cooperate in any way. He still thinks he's in the right."

"How can I change that?"

"You stole the Daylights because he asked you to, right? He respects your integrity. We're hoping if he hears the story of what happened yesterday from you, it might make him reconsider his convictions about Resettlement."

There were probably a few things Alex was less interested in doing this afternoon than visiting Fleming in prison and attempting to talk him into cooperating, but she couldn't think of any. She highly doubted this plan would work, but she understood the reasoning. And this was CB asking.

"Sure thing, Captain. Set it up and I'll be there."

"Thank you. It means a lot that you're willing to try. To me and the general both. And after this? I promise you'll get that time off."

31

THEY HAD FLEMING WAITING in an interrogation room when she arrived. The lieutenant on duty asked if she needed someone to accompany her. Prisoners could be pretty unpredictable, he reminded her. She thought about knocking the lieutenant on his ass, but decided it probably wasn't the smartest move. Instead, she politely declined and asked to be let into the room.

"Okay, but we'll be watching and listening," he said as he unlocked the door. "If you need anything, just start shouting, and we'll be in there in ten seconds flat."

Alex wasn't sure if this was a veiled threat or a statement of support, so she didn't respond.

Fleming's eyebrows shot up in surprise when she sauntered in. He was dressed in a bright blue prison uniform, and he looked thinner than Alex remembered. That couldn't be accurate, because he'd only been in here a day. Must have been one of those men-in-power-seem-bigger things. His hands were cuffed to a d-clip built into the table, which seemed a little unnecessary to Alex, but she wasn't about to ask for him to be released. Let the badges do their thing.

Fleming stared at her with concern. "What are you doing here, Alex?"

Jesus, did he think she was in trouble? Like they'd let a suspect come talk to another suspect in an interrogation room unsupervised.

"I'm here to see you."

"Ah." He looked away, and though he didn't say anything, Alex was certain he was considering whether she'd been sent to pump him for information. "You have to tell me what's going on out there. Can you believe what they've done to me? They'll do anything to try to stamp out the cause of Resettlement."

"That's kinda what I came here to discuss. Listen, Councilman, I went on a mission to the surface yesterday, and I saw some things that made me question whether Resettlement might be a good idea."

His eyes narrowed, and he drew back in his seat. "What things?"

"The vampires yesterday were working together. They hid from us, moving from floor to floor so we wouldn't find them. They waited until we were all exactly where they wanted us, and then they attacked all at once."

Fleming sighed. "Alex, I don't think you're lying. But I do think, sometimes, in the heat of battle, the enemy can seem more intelligent than they are."

"Don't patronize me, asshole. One of my teammates died down there. I know what I saw."

"Fine. But even so, you survived. You proved once again that a properly trained and prepared human force can take out a much larger number of vampires."

Alex wondered how she could have ever believed this

man's rhetoric. Naiveté radiated from him like light. "During the day, sure. But I saw vampires leap two hundred feet in the air moments after sundown."

A brief smile played on his face, and for a moment she glimpsed the cocky Councilman she'd visited that night the week before. "Two hundred feet? I'm guessing you didn't have a measuring tape out at the time."

Alex gritted her teeth, using all her restraint not to attack this man. "I did not. What I did have was a clear view of them leaping through a hole in a roof and piling on top of my friend, who was flying through the air on a jet pack. So, yeah, my estimation might have been ten feet off either way."

The smile disappeared from his face. "I'm sorry about Simmons."

She didn't respond.

"Look, if what you're saying is true, it's all the more reason at least a partial Resettlement is essential. If something happens to the ship and we have to land, those creatures you describe would tear us apart. But if we start work on setting up a colony now and build protective walls and figure out how to defend them, we might stand a chance."

"And what happens when the vampires rip through that colony, Councilman?"

"We learn from our mistakes and build another."

"And when they tear through that? How many people are you willing to sacrifice to trial and error?"

"As many as it takes to ensure the long-term survival of humanity," Fleming said. His lips were curled back in a snarl now. "Yours is an old way of thinking, and we have to move on from it."

"You haven't seen what I have. It'll be a long time before human cities can survive on Earth again." She suddenly realized how much she sounded like CB. She hadn't believed what he'd tried to tell her, so why should she expect that Fleming would believe her?

Fleming let out a little laugh. "This is good. Reasoned debate is important. It's what makes our government run, wouldn't you agree?"

"Sure."

"You'd be surprised how few on the City Council do." He sighed, and suddenly all the weariness came back into his face. He was once again a prisoner, scared and alone. "Whether or not you're right about Resettlement is beside the point. They refused to follow the will of the people, and they attempted to kill me to silence the Resettlement supporters. They have to go."

She screwed up her face in disbelief. Tried to kill him? *Now* who was being dramatic?

"It's true. General Craig took a shot at me. Unfortunately, Sarah stepped in front of the bullet. That brave, stupid woman is barely clinging to life because of your boss."

"No way," Alex said. "I heard what happened. People were attacking the badges, and things got crazy. I'm sure the general wasn't trying to shoot you."

"You heard wrong. The fighting had stopped by then. Your general had already shot two of my friends. Only then, after everything had calmed down, did he point his gun at me."

Alex wasn't sure what to believe. Fleming might be naive, but he wasn't a liar. At least not the kind who'd spout off an easily disprovable fact like this. But she also didn't believe General Craig would shoot a man in cold blood.

She'd had enough of this. Time to wrap it up. "Look, Councilman, I think you need to consider what's actually in the best interests of the people. Maybe the Council acted wrongly, but they did it because they are fighting tooth and nail for humanity's survival. They know Resettlement means death. If you want progress, you have to be smart enough to realize it's not going to happen if the city's tearing itself apart. And you can't be the leader the people need while you're sitting behind bars." She stood up and rapped on the door. "Just something to think about."

"Thank you, Alex. Feel free to stop by anytime. My door's always open to you. So to speak."

The door opened, and Alex marched out. A moment later, she heard the metal door of the interrogation room clang shut, once again trapping Councilman Fleming inside.

———

CB WAS WAITING for her in the lobby of the building, a pillar of stillness in the sea of movement around him. His arms were crossed, and he looked pale. For the first time, Alex considered how losing Simmons must be affecting him. He was the leader of the team, and he'd come back without one of his people. Did he feel responsible? Did he lie awake last night wondering what he could have done differently?

She nodded in greeting as she approached. "That didn't go as well as I'd hoped. I told him what happened in Texas, but I'm not sure he even—"

"We gotta go." There was a shake in his voice as he spoke.

"What's going on?"

"General Craig needs to meet with us. Emergency briefing." He turned and headed for the door.

Alex hustled to catch up with him. "About that time off you promised me—"

"It'll have to wait."

———————

JESSICA BOWEN STOOD before the team. As usual, she cut to the chase. After a day spent listening to politicians—first Stearns's address over the monitor and then Fleming in the interrogation room—Alex appreciated this woman's candor.

"There was a problem with the parts you brought back. I knew the facility in Texas was a water-displacement reactor, which of course is significantly different from our modern-era reactor, but I thought the control panel would be similar enough to make it work. Turns out, I was wrong."

The words were like a punch in the gut to Alex. Simmons had died bringing back those parts, and they were worthless?

"I still believe I can retrofit them to our system," she continued, "but it would take time. More time than we have. At least a month."

A groan went through the room. Alex exchanged a worried glance with Drew.

"What about Stearns's address this morning?" Owl asked.

"It was a bit hasty," Jessica said. "I urged him not to give it until we were sure, but..."

"Yeah," CB said. "He wanted to calm people down."

"What's the Council say about all this?" Firefly asked.

"They're currently discussing the matter," General Craig said. "I need to head over there as soon as we're done."

Jessica spoke up again. "My team is poring over records, looking for another facility that might have what we need. Trouble is, our records are pretty shoddy. We don't have time for another dangerous mission, just to gather the wrong equipment."

The general stood and addressed the team. "I need you

ready to go at a moment's notice. As soon as Jessica gives the word, we want to be ready to move. That means, stay close to your quarters and keep your radios on you at all times." He looked the team over, meeting each person's eyes. "This team's been through a lot, and I'd like nothing more than to give you a break right now, but it'll have to wait a little longer. *New Haven* needs saving, and you're the only ones who can do it."

"Sir," CB said, "we wouldn't have it any other way."

32

THE CITY COUNCIL, the directors, and their department heads were once again gathered in the Council building. Stearns stood at the head of the table, trying to restore order. Things were not going well.

"What in the hell were you thinking, telling the people we had the problem fixed?" Councilwoman Yates asked. "There isn't enough doubt in the trustworthiness of the Council?"

"I was working the best I could with the information I had," Stearns said.

Jessica Bowen leaped from her seat. "Hang on, Stearns. If you're trying to pass this off on me—"

"I'm not!" Stearns threw his hands in the air. "Please, everyone, if we could have some semblance of an orderly discussion. Time is too short to waste it bickering."

CB took a deep breath and fought to maintain his composure. There was too much going on for him to waste his time here. But the general said he was needed, so here he sat.

"What I'd like to know," the general said, "is how

Director Bowen managed to be so wrong about the parts. I lost a good man down there."

"I'm well aware, and I'm very sorry," Jessica said. "Believe me when I tell you that no one feels the weight of my mistake more than I do. We just don't have enough information about the nuclear facilities on the surface to understand whether or not the parts will work."

The mood in the room was tense. Everyone was angry and looking for someone to blame, and there was plenty of blame to go around. First, everyone had blamed Jessica for sending the GMT for the wrong parts, then they'd blamed the GMT for leaving some parts on the surface—CB hadn't even bothered to dignify that with a response—then they'd blamed the Council for voting against the will of the people. They'd also touched on Fleming, his supporters, and Captain Kurtz's badges before circling around to Jessica again.

"As I've said time and time again, there's no use debating the merits of our past actions," Councilman Stearns said.

"Mighty convenient," Horace muttered.

"What matters is the future. What do we do next, Director Bowen?"

The room fell silent. Every eye was on Jessica. CB admired the way she stood before them, unwavering, her jaw set. "My team is working around the clock to find the next most likely location for the parts. Once we do, we'll send the GMT down to bring back the parts to see if they'll work."

"And my people risk their lives for nothing again?" the general said.

"Or to save humanity," she said coolly. "If those parts don't work, we try the next facility on the list." She paused, reading the anger in the room. "I'm sorry, but it's the best plan we have."

"Come up with a better one," Stearns said, "and do it quickly."

———

AFTER THE MEETING, CB approached Jessica. While her face was the picture of calmness, CB had spent his life in the GMT around hard cases who would rather go up against a horde of vampires than betray the slightest hint of their real emotions. He'd long ago learned to look past expressions and tones of voice and toward the smaller, unconscious things that might betray a person's inner life. From the way she was gathering the paper in front of her and the way she was carefully not looking at anyone, he could tell she was furious.

"Hey, Director Bowen."

She looked up sharply, defensively. Another dead giveaway.

"Listen," he said, "I just want you to know that regardless of what these fools in here think, getting the wrong parts wasn't your fault."

She looked back down at her papers and resumed gathering them. "I'm well aware of that, Captain. But thank you."

"The team doesn't harbor you any ill will. They respect the hell out of you, every one of them. So do I."

She paused for a moment when he said that. "Thank you, Captain. I admire your work as well."

He put his hands on the table and leaned down, getting close enough that he was able to lower his voice a little. "You and I both know it's not politicians that'll save this city. It's the boots on the ground. It's us. So, you figure out the most likely location for the parts you need, and my team will fight like hell to get them for you."

"I will. Though there are no guarantees. The only alternative is to stop fighting, and we're certainly not going to do that."

"Yeah." CB wished she'd look up at him again. There was something about her eyes, the way they seemed to dance with curious intensity. It made him ache in a way he hadn't in a long time. "It's a shame there's not a way to get more information about the facilities on the surface. If we had that, we'd know exactly where to get parts, now and in the future."

She paused, then stood up. "Thank you again for the kind words, Captain Brickman. I'll be in touch as soon as we have a mission location."

He caught just a glimpse of those eyes before she turned and headed for the door.

"CB," the general said from behind him. "Let's go."

As they walked toward the exit, the general said, "That was a real shit show in there. Scary to think those people are in charge of the fate of humanity."

"I couldn't agree more, sir."

"Listen, I know the team needs a break after everything they've been through, but we can't afford to give it to them. Not right now. They have to be ready to go at a moment's notice."

CB agreed, but they'd already discussed this. "They're ready, sir."

"No, they're not. You're down a man. We need a full crew for the next mission."

It took CB a moment to realize what General Craig was saying. "Forgive my bluntness, sir, but this is hardly the time to bring on a fresh recruit."

"No one said fresh. You've got five qualified candidates. Pick one and get him working with the team. Today."

CB clenched his jaw to keep from saying something he'd regret. Yes, five badges in Kurtz's department had gone through initial GMT training and been identified as candidates for the next open position. They even ran training exercises with the team every couple of months to stay ready. But there was a damn big difference between passing initial training and being ready to descend into the depths of a nuclear facility, where they might once again be ambushed by a surprisingly strategic horde of vampires. Bringing an unqualified person on a mission like that could cost lives. It wasn't just putting the recruit at risk; it was putting the whole team at risk.

"What's the problem, CB?" the general asked.

"Sir, I'm of the opinion that the team is working together very well right now. I'm hesitant to take someone with no experience on a dangerous mission."

"The missions are how they get experience." The general took a deep breath, and his voice was softer when he spoke again. "Look, this is why we have the training program. So, we're ready when there's a need. What happens if you lose someone else, or two someone elses, on the next mission? Then you have multiple positions to fill with inexperienced people. Fill Simmons's spot, and let the new guy or girl get some reps in on this next mission."

CB didn't like it, but he had to admit the general was right. "Yes, sir. I'll have the spot filled by the end of the day."

———

FIREFLY WAITED in the shadows at the bottom of the stairs outside Engineering. He'd pulled a few strings and called in a few favors to see the schedule, and he'd learned that the person he was hoping to meet was supposed to be off work soon.

The first person who descended the stairs was a woman Firefly had never seen before. He busied himself with a garbage can lid, hoping she'd think he was a janitor. She walked by without comment.

Five minutes later, the man Firefly was looking for came down the steps. He paused at the sight of Firefly, his face suddenly pale. Firefly waited without acknowledging the man. When he reached the bottom, Firefly grabbed him by the arm and pulled him into the shadows.

"What are you doing?" Steven hissed in a whisper. "You know we're not supposed to be seen together."

"I didn't know who else to go to." Sarah had been Firefly's primary contact inside the Resettlement movement, and she was currently hanging on to life in a hospital bed. He would have gone straight to Fleming, but the politician was in no position to hold a discussion either. "Look, you know more people in the opposition than I do. You have to get a message to them."

Steven shook his head. "You're wrong. I'm just a concerned citizen like you. I don't even know who's leading the opposition, with Fleming and Sarah gone."

Firefly tightened his grip on Steven's arm. "Quit playing coy. I'm not trying to set you up, here. I know you've been going to the meetings every night."

Steven's lips tightened in a frown. "Fine. What's the message?"

"Tell them they have to call off the plan. The vampires are stronger than we thought. We have to wait."

Steven shook his head in disbelief. "Are you kidding? After everything we went through to plan this?"

"We don't have a choice, man. You have to tell them."

Steven looked at Firefly for a long moment before replying. "I'll tell them, but that's all I can guarantee. It may be too late to stop it." He shrugged off Firefly's hand. "Don't come here again."

Firefly watched as he walked away, hoping it wasn't too late.

33

ALEX AND DREW were in the gym taking turns spotting one another for their afternoon workout when CB entered. A tall, gangly man in his early twenties followed close behind, running a hand through his unruly shock of blond hair.

Alex immediately knew what was happening. Apparently, Drew did too. He sat up and muttered, "You gotta be kidding me."

CB nodded in greeting. "You two know Wesley Aaron. We're calling him up to the big show."

"Hey Wesley," Alex said.

"Welcome," Drew said.

To Wesley's credit, he looked a little sheepish about the whole situation. Alex understood. After she'd passed initial training, she'd waited nearly a year for a slot to open on the Ground Mission Team. During that time, she would have given just about anything for her shot, but she's never wanted a spot to open up because someone had died. Thankfully, her predecessor had retired peacefully, so she'd joined the team under better circumstances. Even still, she'd endured months of her teammates comparing her to the beloved teammates who'd come before. It would be much worse for Wesley, she knew. Until he put his life on the line to save their asses in the field, he wouldn't hold a candle to Simmons, in the team's estimation.

Still, Alex had to admit he was the correct choice. Out of all five candidates, Wesley had struck the right balance in the training exercises between keeping his mouth shut and following orders and taking initiative. Plus, he showed aptitude as a sniper, so he could fill Simmons's role on the team. As difficult as it was going to be, she promised herself she'd do her best to make him feel welcome.

"Thanks, guys," Wesley said. "Working with you is a dream come true. I can't wait to kill some vampires with you."

Alex wasn't sure how to respond to that. The gap between someone who'd never faced vampires and someone who'd been through what they had only one day prior was too wide.

"Well, you won't have to wait long," CB said. "We're expecting orders any time. Alex, I want you to spend the afternoon with Wesley. Walk him through the mission prep procedures. Take him to R&D and have them gear him out."

"Yes, sir," she said. "Give me five minutes, Wes. I'll hit the shower, and then we'll get to work."

"Thanks. And it's Wesley. No big deal, I just, you know, prefer Wesley."

She sighed and shook her head. GMT 101: Never let your teammates know you hate something. Drew would probably call him Wes for the next twenty years. "Okay, Wesley. I'll be back in five."

They spent the next hour on an in-depth tour of the facilities. He'd been here before and received the trainee's tour, but this was different. She showed him the shortcuts between the briefing rooms, helped him pick out his locker, and showed him where to file reports. She also introduced him to the people he'd now be working with on a daily basis. The support staff, the medical team, and of course the other members of the GMT. He'd met most of them as a trainee, but, again, they acted differently toward him now. He was a teammate who might be assigned to watch their backs in the very near future. For the most part, they treated him professionally, if a bit coolly.

Out of everyone, the only person who came off downright hostile was Firefly. "They couldn't let us grieve for forty-eight hours before they replaced Simmons?"

"Don't be an asshole," Alex said. "We've got a mission coming up any time, and we need a full crew."

"All the more reason I don't want some badge who was writing tickets for littering yesterday watching my back."

Wesley stepped up, a wide but cold smile on his face. "Actually, I was putting down a riot yesterday."

The tough-guy act didn't last long—he was still too intimidated by the GMT members—but both Alex and Firefly appreciated the guts it took for him to make the effort.

Alex took him to R&D last because she knew it would take most of the afternoon. Brian was the opposite of Firefly, immediately giving Wesley a warm welcome and asking him lots of questions about himself. He personally walked Wesley through the weapons-selection process, letting him try out a few models of rifles on the shooting range, and then tweaking his favorite to his exact preferences. He also selected his pistol, knife, and sword.

While Wesley was trying on his silver mail suit, Alex nudged Brian. "Where we at with those replacement Daylights?"

Brian shook his head. "It's going to be at least a few more days before they're ready."

Alex sighed. She didn't know where they'd be sent next, but she was pretty sure it would be less than a few days from now. Looked like they were back to the bad old days of fighting vampires the old-fashioned way.

When they finished in R&D, Alex clapped Wesley on the back. "How you doing?"

He looked at her wide-eyed. "Fine. I mean, it's a lot to take in, but in a good way."

"All right, we're done picking out toys. Let's call it a day. Meet me in the gym at oh six hundred for some sparring."

He raised a skeptical eyebrow as he looked down at her. "Against you?"

"Nah, we'll start you out easy. You can spar against Drew and work your way up to me. In the meantime, I recommend you get some sleep. You'll be glad you did."

She was proven correct when the call came at five the next morning telling them all to head to the briefing room immediately.

———

THE GENERAL, CB, and Director Bowen were standing in front of the room when Alex and Owl arrived. Drew and Firefly showed up together a few minutes later. Wesley was last. He walked in blurry-eyed, his hair still freshly mussed from a night of sleep. Clearly, he hadn't expected to be called in at five in the morning on his first full day on the job.

He looked around the room for a few seconds, apparently trying to detect whether seating was arranged by some sort of pecking order, before Alex took pity on him and waved him over to the empty seat next to her.

For Alex's part, she was glad the waiting was over and it was time to get back to action. She wasn't always the best at working through her emotions in a healthy way, and she felt like facing another swarm of undead monsters in some underground nuclear facility might do her mental health a lot of good.

Alex nodded to Director Bowen. "Director, I take it you've found another likely spot for the parts we need?"

"Actually, no."

That made them all sit up a bit straighter. The room was silent now, all eyes on Bowen.

"Captain Brickman gave me an idea yesterday," she said. "He said he wished there was a way we could get more information on the nuclear facilities on the surface. I believe I've found such a way." She clicked on the overhead projector, and an image of a city appeared, shot from above. "This is Fort Meade, Maryland. Those giant glass buildings are the former headquarters of the National Security Agency, NSA for short. The NSA was an intelligence agency charged with gathering information about threats to the United States. We believe the most thorough information about the nuclear facilities in the United States is housed in this location."

The general tapped the building on the screen. "Your mission is to infiltrate that building, power up their computers, and download all information regarding nuclear facilities."

"Wait," Drew said, "we're not going after the parts to fix the ship?"

"Not on this trip, no." Director Bowen held up a stack of paper. "This is a list of the four hundred and fifty nuclear reactors in the world and the incredibly limited information we have on each of them. We can confidently rule out about forty-seven, but the other four hundred and ten are all potential candidates."

"Rather than having you risk your lives at random reactors until we stumble across the right parts," General Craig said, "we're going to gather the information we need to know exactly where to go next."

"This information will be valuable long after our current crisis," Bowen said. "In all honesty, we should have done this years ago. We'll be reaping the benefits of this mission for years to come."

Owl raised her hand. "Um, maybe I'm missing something. I assume the NSA computers are fairly secure. I'm a pretty big nerd, but I'm not sure I'm up to squaring off against the guys who were literally in charge of computer security for the most powerful nation of the pre-vampire era."

"He is," CB said, pointing at Brian. "Tell them, Mr. McElroy."

Brian stood up. "Thanks, Captain, but it didn't take much effort. Many of the Remnants were former US government. Some of those original nerds you're referring to were aboard this ship, Owl. So, using their records, I was able to put this together." He held up a tablet computer. "Power up the computers in the data center, connect the tablet, and the rest is automatic. No nerding required."

"That's what I like to hear," Drew said.

General Craig stepped in front of the projector. The faint image of Fort Meade, Maryland, was visible on his dress shirt. "I don't have to tell you what's at stake here. You're the best we have. That's why we're sending you. Do your jobs, come home safe, and bring us back the info. We roll out immediately."

Alex glanced over at Wesley. The poor kid looked a little shell-shocked. She patted him on the shoulder. "Chin up, man. Your dreams are about to come true. We're about to go fight a bunch of vampires."

A slow smile grew on his face. "Yeah. This is gonna be awesome."

Alex wasn't sure if that's how she'd describe it, but she had to admire his enthusiasm. "Come on. Let's gear up."

34

As the away ship descended through the dense cloud cover, Owl began her usual routine.

"We're now approaching the city of Fort Meade, Maryland, a place that at its peak held a population of around ten thousand people, but also housed many important military facilities, including the NSA headquarters we will be visiting today. Notable former residents include twentieth-century science fiction and comic book writer Peter David."

The crew waited for more, but none came.

"Hang on, Owl," Drew said. "That's it? That's all you've got for us? A comic book writer and the population?"

"Cut me some slack. I just found out about this mission ninety minutes ago. I only had time to glance at one almanac."

"Captain," Alex said, "I'd like to officially make a complaint about Owl's lack of preparedness for this mission."

"Duly noted," CB said.

Alex glanced across the aisle toward Wesley. Now that they were only moments away from the real thing, his bravado was gone. His face was pale, and he gazed off into space with a thousand-yard stare. She wondered if she'd looked that way on her first mission. She kinda doubted it. Her nervousness manifested itself in other ways. She'd probably driven everyone crazy with bad jokes.

They broke through the clouds, and Alex saw their destination below: two massive buildings, one taller and boxier, the other a shorter but far longer structure. Both sported glass walls.

"At least there will be plenty of sunlight," Drew said.

Owl set them down gently next to the buildings. As soon as they touched down, everyone leaped to their feet and started gathering gear. Alex noticed Wesley fumbling with his equipment with shaky hands.

"Hey," she said. "You're gonna be great. Just watch your buddy's back, and he'll do the same."

"Thanks," he said, but his eyes were distant.

She slapped him on the arm. "Look at me." He did, and she saw fear in his eyes plain as day. "If you could handle those idiots rioting in Sparrow's Ridge, you can handle this. Unlike the rioters, you're allowed to shoot the vampires."

He smiled and gave a weak chuckle. "I guess you're right. They probably won't be chanting any dumb political slogans, either."

"Let's hope not," Alex said. "I can forgive a creature who tries to drink my blood, but I'll never forgive a bad rhyme."

She glanced over and saw CB watching her, a poorly concealed smile on his face.

The team convened outside the ship, and CB pulled them together. "It's nine a.m., and this place is goddamn massive. That means we don't have a lot of time for sightseeing. Director Bowen believes the data center is more likely to be in the taller building. I wish we had more to go on, but that's what we've got. We'll start at the bottom and work our way up."

Wesley raised his hand.

"It's not grade school," CB said. "Speak your mind, son."

"Ah, yes, sir. Sorry. I was just thinking maybe we could get more information in there." He pointed at a building off to his right. The sign said *Visitor Center*. "Just a thought."

CB shook his head and chuckled. "You're pulling your weight already."

The door to the Visitor Center was locked, so CB told Firefly to blow it off for him. Firefly was thrilled at this chance to ply his trade so early in the mission, and probably used a little more explosive than was strictly necessary for the job. Still, they were far enough from the two main buildings that Alex doubted the explosion woke any sleeping vampires.

The team moved through the small, two-story structure, quickly ascertaining that there were no vampires here.

Owl stopped in front of a large informational plaque near the front door. "Holy hell. Check this out, you guys."

Alex skimmed the first few paragraphs. The buildings were dedicated in 1986 by President Ronald Reagan. Housed over ten thousand employees. Blah blah blah. "That's great, Owl. Those facts will come in handy in the unlikely event we ever need to return here."

"It's the last sentence that's capturing my attention."

Alex saw what her friend was talking about. "Holy hell, indeed. CB?"

The captain wandered over, and they pointed at the last sentence on the plaque. In addition to the two structures, the Nation Security Headquarters also boasts an estimated 10 acres of underground facilities.

"Well," CB said, "I guess we'd better get started."

Alex gripped her pistol as they entered the stairwell and headed down to the first underground level. They were in the taller of the two large buildings, which was called OPS2A according to the information they'd found in the Visitor Center. Unlike in Texas, the team stayed together. They didn't sweep the upper floors before heading down, either. For one, they'd learned in Texas that the vampires were smart enough to move from floor to floor to avoid detection. Secondly, and more importantly, there simply wasn't time. Another nugget of information gleaned in the Visitor Center: the complex boasted over sixty-eight acres of floor space, four times as much as the U.S. Capitol building. They couldn't possibly hope to search all of it and get back to the ship in the next seven hours.

So they stayed together and headed downstairs.

The place looked less like a war zone than the reactor in Texas had, but just barely. Once, Alex had to imagine this had been one of the most secure buildings in the United States. Now, the doors at the dozens of security checkpoints they passed were ripped right off their hinges. The key card readers were still mounted on the walls next to gaping holes where the doors had once been.

Even though the building was enormous, they were able to narrow their search relatively quickly. So-called *red corridors*, areas open to visitors who had worn distinctive red badges, were clearly marked, so they knew they could skip those. They also had a pretty good idea that the data center would be on one of the lowest floors. They decided to head straight to the bottom level and work their way up from there.

The first vampire attacked them five levels down. It

leaped out of a doorway just after they'd passed, cutting off their retreat up the stairs. Drew was at the rear of the pack, carrying a small generator on his back for powering up the computers, and there was no way he was going to be caught off guard.

Alex kept her eyes on Wesley, wanting to see how he'd react. He brought up his assault rifle, aiming it in the general direction of Drew and the creature, but Drew already had his shotgun pointed at the vampire's head. He pulled the trigger and the contents of the creature's head splattered on the wall behind it.

Wesley was breathing heavily after the encounter, but at least he hadn't wet himself. She walked next to him as the group continued on and spoke softly so the others wouldn't hear. "Hey, nice job having Drew's back. Remember, though, you gotta trust your teammates. Tight quarters like this, you gotta let the closest guy take the shot, unless he's in serious trouble. Last thing we need is one of us getting taken out by friendly fire."

Wesley's eyes widened. "I would never—"

"Relax. You're doing fine. Watch where you point that thing, is all I'm saying."

As they descended the stairs, Firefly set small charges along the ground. They didn't have the Daylights this time, and they'd need a way to clear the path if this went sideways again.

Twelve floors down, they reached the bottom. The doorway was open, and an eighteen-inch-thick steel door lay on the floor a few feet away.

"Let's hope whoever did that is napping," CB said.

As they swept through the level looking for the data center, there were clear signs of vampire activity. The damaged walls, doors ripped off their hinges, and the lingering smell of death all told the tale that this place was occupied by residents that were perhaps being a bit shy, but were definitely home. They found proof of the theory near the center of the floor. Dozens and dozens of graves—all of them empty.

Drew whispered into his microphone from up ahead. "Over here."

The others trotted over to him and saw a door marked *Data Center*.

"This is going a little too well," Alex said.

"It won't last," CB said. "Looks like these vampires are attempting the same strategy their cousins down south pulled on us. Difference is, this time we'll be ready."

35

THE DATA CENTER WAS A LARGE, mostly open room filled with servers. There were two entrances, one on each end of the room. As Owl started setting up to do her work, Alex investigated both of them. For the most part, she liked what she saw. While the doors had long ago been removed, both exits led to long, narrow hallways. It was a highly defensible position for a small group facing a larger attacking force. Hopefully, it wouldn't come to that, but she was glad to know they'd have a chance if it did.

Drew hauled the generator to the room's power supply, and he and Owl hooked it up. A few moments later, the servers blinked to life.

"You sure you can do this, Owl?" CB asked. "I thought you said you weren't that big of a computer nerd."

"I'm not," she said, "but Brian is. Besides, this is ancient technology. A modern toaster could probably hack it." She pulled out her tablet and connected it to the nearest server.

Alex sauntered over to Wesley, who stood rigidly, holding his assault rifle at the ready. "How you doing?"

"Excellent," he said. He glanced toward CB, who was

busy staring over Owl's shoulder. "It's not what I expected, seeing one up close. The smell...I can still taste it in the air, you know?"

"I know," she said.

"And its face? It's different than in the pictures." He was talking faster now, getting excited. "It's pure animal, but there was some humanity in its eyes, too. Like I could almost see the person it used to be."

Alex had never noticed that. To her, it was difficult to imagine they'd ever been human. "Well, you're doing great. Just stay ready. We'll face more of them before this is over."

"How's it going, Owl?" CB asked.

Owl sounded distracted when she answered. "Well, I take back what I said about the toaster. The security on this thing is no joke."

"Are you telling me you can't get the info?" CB asked, rising alarm in his voice.

"No. I'll get it. I could probably hijack *New Haven* and crash it into the ocean with all the programs Brian loaded on this tablet."

"I vote we don't do that," Drew said.

"It's just going to take a little longer than I'd hoped."

CB sighed. "Okay, keep at it. In the meantime, the rest of you stay frosty. Alex, Drew, you keep an eye out in the north corridor. Wesley, you come with me in the south hallway. Firefly, you stay with Owl and watch her back so she can keep her head down.

The first pair of vampires attacked ten minutes later. They came down the north hallway, howling in rage as they ran.

Alex saw them when they were still thirty feet away, and she took her time aiming. She dropped the first one with an explosive round to the head at twenty feet, and the other with three shots to the heart at ten feet.

"Nice shooting," Drew said.

"Thanks." Even though she'd easily fought off the attack, she found it disquieting. It was too much like the control room in Texas. A few vampires had attacked in singles and pairs, testing their defenses before the main assault.

From inside the Data Center, Owl let out a triumphant laugh. "Ha! I'm in. Now I just need to download the information."

"How long?" CB asked.

"Looks like about twenty minutes."

"We'll be home in time for dinner," Firefly said.

The others didn't respond to that. They didn't want to jinx it.

Two vampires attacked the south entrance five minutes later. Alex heard the howl of their approach, a cluster of automatic gunfire, a pistol, and then Wesley's voice.

"I got one!"

"That you did," CB said. "Took his damn head off, too. Nice shooting, kid."

"Well, it took me twenty rounds. You took yours down with three."

"Practice makes perfect."

Alex touched the radio on her chest. "CB, you see how they're attacking? A couple scouts testing each approach?"

"I sure do. It's just like last time. How much longer, Owl?"

"Ten minutes," she answered. "Fifteen if we want to take this generator back with us."

"Good," CB said. "Maybe they won't launch their big attack until we're already out the door."

A moment later, the rumble of dozens of approaching

feet, seemingly from every corner of the building, put that idea to rest.

"Okay," CB said. "Guess it's time to earn our pay. Let's kill some vampires."

———

ALEX AND DREW stood back to back in the middle of the north hallway. They had no way to tell which direction the vampires would be coming from, but, based on experience, Alex expected they'd come from both directions at once.

Fighting back to back, relying on your teammate to handle his side of the hallway while you handled yours, required great faith. Alex would have her hands full taking care of her side, and she wouldn't have time to look over her shoulder and make sure Drew was taking care of business. She'd just have to trust that he was. The same would be true for him. It was a level of trust she wouldn't have had in anyone a few years ago.

She gave a fleeting thought to CB on the other side of the hallway, back to back with Wesley, who'd been a member of the team for about twenty minutes. The thought made her shudder, and she momentarily wished she'd switched places with CB when she had the chance. Not that he would have let her. He'd promoted Wesley to the team, so he'd insist on paying the consequences if the guy couldn't handle it.

She pushed the thought away. It was time to focus.

"Drew, my good man, how do you intend to deal with the approaching horde of undead monsters?"

The ground was shaking now. The vampires were almost upon them.

"Ah, I'm glad you asked, dear lady." He spoke in the

mock-careful cadence of the Hub elite. "I thought I'd begin the evening's festivities with a silver shrapnel grenade tossed into their midst as they approach. Then I'll move on to a generous portion of robust shotgun shells. Should our guests still have an appetite after that, I shall finish with my pistol. Yourself?"

She started to answer that she too would begin with some light grenade work, but before she could, the vampires rounded the corner thirty feet ahead.

"Here we go!" Drew yelled.

Alex pulled the pin on her grenade and hurled it as far as she could down the corridor. As it reached the vampires, a hand shot up and snatched it from the air.

For a terrible moment, Alex thought it might throw the grenade back at her. Instead, the creature studied the strange object in its hand. It exploded, and the three closest vampires fell to the ground. Five others moaned in pain as silver shrapnel dug into their leathery hides. It didn't stop them from continuing to charge.

By then, Alex had her pistol ready. Most of them were running on all fours, their hearts blocked from her view, so she was forced to go for head shots. It was a lower-percentage target, and she missed twice as many as she hit. Still, she dropped a good number of them, and their companions were forced to slow down and scurry over the fallen bodies, which gave her a bit more time to aim at her next attacker.

Drew's shotgun fired blast after blast behind her. Neither of them spoke. They were professionals doing their job. The time for wisecracks had ended the moment the first vampire rounded the corner.

She tried to count how many were left in the hallway. She'd taken out eight, so far. She thought there were ten more, but the way they moved and wriggled over each other made it difficult to keep an accurate count.

She took down two more, but they were almost to her now. She grimaced, shifted the gun to her left hand, and used the right one to draw her sword.

There were, what, eight left rushing toward her? This was a narrow hallway; those things operated best in open spaces, where their wild, frantic movements were an asset rather than a liability. In this hallway, the way they leaped around, they could only fit two at a time.

Alex liked her odds.

She raised her sword and went to work.

———

CB WAS STANDING in the south hallway, his back nearly touching Wesley's when he heard a grenade go off, quickly followed by another. The vampires on the other side were a bit quicker, apparently. Or was this strategy? An attempt to drive the humans toward this hallway, where an even larger horde would be waiting, maybe?

He turned his head and spoke over his shoulder. "Lob your grenade at them when they round the corner, then start firing. You've got an automatic weapon there, and enough ammo to kill every vampire between here and Washington D.C. Don't be stingy with it."

"Yes, sir." There was a shake in the kid's voice. Not that CB blamed him. This was one hell of a first mission. Still, if either of them was going to survive this, Wesley needed to get past the nerves. No way to tell if that was going to happen until the shooting started.

"Hey, Wesley, you were born to do this. I knew it the

moment I saw you work out with the team for the first time. Do what you were brought here to do."

"Yes, sir." His voice was more confident this time.

CB wasn't normally one to blow smoke, but he wasn't above it, from time to time. Especially when his life was on the line. The roar of the approaching vampires was almost upon them now. It was startling how quickly it had gone from a distant sound to right around the corner. "Here we go, Wesley."

CB threw his grenade as soon as he saw the first vampire. It was coming too fast to stop even if it had the smarts to realize what had just been thrown at it. Ten other vampires followed close on the first one's heels, and the grenade exploded at the perfect moment, right in the middle of all of them. Four of them were killed on impact, but the other six kept coming, pushed by the others following close behind.

A quick count told him sixteen vampires remained upright at his end of the hallway. This was more than he'd expected. He raised his pistols and shot the closest vampire, then started working his way back.

He knew from the sound of Wesley's gun he was in trouble. He was shooting in short controlled bursts, which was fine for the firing range, but he had a horde of vampires charging him. He should have been laying on the trigger, sweeping the weapon back and forth for maximum damage to every creature in that hallway.

CB silently cursed himself. He never should have put the kid in this position the first time out. As he fired with his right hand, he touched the radio on his chest with his left. "Firefly, get out here. We need help."

The respond was an immediate, "Yes, sir!"

CB had his vampires momentarily under control, their

way blocked by the bodies of their fallen brethren. It would only slow them for a moment, but CB risked a look over his shoulder.

Shit.

It was worse than he'd imagined. Twenty vampires filled the hallway, and the first two were less than ten feet away. Many of them had ugly wounds in their legs, arms, and stomachs, but none of the injuries appeared to be fatal to the vampire biology. How had the kid failed to take out a single vampire?

CB pulled another grenade off his vest and tossed it down his side of the hallway—hopefully, that would take out another one or two—and then turned to help Wesley. He dropped the closest two in five seconds.

Firefly jumped through the doorway and paused a fraction of a second—clearly shocked at the situation—then began firing on the vampires in front of Wesley.

It wasn't going to be enough. There were too many vampires, and they were too close. CB, Wesley, and Firefly were going to have to fall back.

CB opened his mouth to give the order, but something grabbed him from behind and slammed him against the wall. His right arm was pinned awkwardly behind him, and he felt it snap as he hit the wall. He let out a soft groan but rolled quickly, raising the pistol in his left hand and pointing it at the vampire who'd somehow caught him off guard.

The vampire's hand snaked out almost too quickly for CB's eyes to follow and smacked the gun out of his hand. The creature lunged at him, leading with his teeth. CB went for his knife, but he knew there was no way he'd get to it in time. The vampire had him.

Suddenly, a flash of light seemed to slice through the

creature's neck. Its head fell from its shoulders and landed on the floor with a wet *thud*.

Alex stared down at him, her sword still held high. Drew was close behind her. He ran into the hallway and went to work with his shotgun.

Alex spun, turning her back to CB, protecting him with her body. She moved like a dervish, slicing through any vampire that foolishly wandered within six feet of her. They had claws and teeth, but her blade was sharper.

Drew focused on the vampires just outside of Alex's range, while Firefly turned his attention to the creatures a bit further down the hall. Firefly barked orders at Wesley, telling him which vampires to shoot.

In another two minutes, it was over. The team stood panting in the hallway, checking themselves and each other for injury.

Alex turned toward CB. "You okay, Captain?"

He struggled to his feet. "It's just my arm. You didn't have to coddle me."

Alex grinned at him. "You're welcome."

"Didn't you two have enough vampires on your side?"

"We had a fair number," Drew said. "I guess we killed them too quickly."

"Thank God for that," Wesley muttered.

Drew clapped him on the shoulder. "I consider saving your ass to be a duty and an honor, Wes. One I presume I'll have the pleasure of repeating many times in the coming months."

Owl appeared in the doorway. She raised an eyebrow as she gazed at the team, covered in sweat and black, inky blood, vampire corpses strewn across the floor around them. "Huh." She shrugged and held up the tablet. "I got the information. Who wants to go home?"

36

As soon as the team landed in the hangar, Alex stormed up to the cockpit. Owl's eyes widened at the intrusion. Alex had only been in the cockpit once before, on her initial tour of the ship two years ago, and she'd never been in it on a mission.

"What's up?" Owl asked.

Alex nodded toward Owl's pack on the floor next to her, which she knew held the tablet with the information they'd just mined from NSA headquarters. "We can't be waiting for fifteen minutes like we usually do while medical takes their sweet time getting around to checking us. Bowen needs that tablet, and every moment counts. Not only that, we got CB in the back, his arm as crooked as a dirty politician. The thing's broken in at least two places."

"Yeah, I radioed ahead that we had an injury. Look, I'm sure they're getting things set up as fast as they can."

Alex glared at her.

"What?" Owl said. "You want me to yell at them? I have to work with these people every day."

"I don't." Alex reached across Owl before the pilot could

object and grabbed the radio off the control panel. She held it up to her mouth. "Hello, this is Lieutenant Alexandria Goddard. Who am I speaking with, please?"

"This is Sergeant Russell, ma'am. Hang tight. We're getting to you as fast as we can."

"Is that so? Who's in charge there, Sergeant?"

"I am, ma'am. We've met like five times. I've given briefings to your—"

"Excellent. I just wanted to make sure I knew where the buck stopped. For when I give my report to the Council. We have information vital to the safety of *New Haven* aboard, and every moment is crucial."

"I understand, ma'am. That's why we're—"

"Not only that, but we've got a hero aboard, gritting his teeth while he clutches his broken arm. I don't know about you, Sergeant, but when I stand before the statue of this man that they will inevitably erect outside the hangar one day, I don't want to be thinking about how I made him wait fifteen minutes longer than was necessary in his hour of goddamn need."

"Ma'am, if you'd just—"

"And I'll tell you something, Sergeant Russell. If you keep us waiting for another five minutes while you twiddle your thumbs and tell dick jokes, the Council will be the least of your problems. I'll knock you on your ass so hard, you'll sink right on down to the surface. Do I make myself clear, Sergeant Russell?"

There was the briefest of pauses. "Yes, ma'am. Sending the medical team to retrieve the information and the injured soldier immediately, ma'am."

"I'm counting the seconds." She put the radio down and winked at Owl.

Owl laughed at shook her head. "You're going to make a hellacious commanding officer someday."

By the time they got back to the passenger hold, the cargo door was opening, and medical techs in hazmat suits were climbing aboard.

"Whoa, record time!" Drew said.

Alex nodded to CB. "You hanging in there, sir?"

"I told you, it's just my arm," he snarled. "Don't be such a mother hen."

The first medical tech reached him and asked to see the arm.

CB brushed him off. "Maybe we can do this inside?" He stood up and marched off the ship, and the confused tech followed after him.

Shirley came and got Alex a few minutes later.

Alex went through the decontamination process in near silence.

When they were nearly finished, Shirley said, "You don't have any jokes today. You feeling all right?"

"Wow, Shirley," she said with a smile, "I think that's the first time you've ever asked me a question that wasn't strictly mission-related."

"It's the first time I've had to. Normally, you won't shut up."

Shirley had a point. For some reason, Alex didn't feel all that much like talking. How many vampires had she killed in those hallways? She should know the answer to that question. CB would. But they'd all been people once, many of them probably government servants like her. Maybe they'd been infected at work and never left, or maybe they'd gotten bit elsewhere and returned to take out vengeance on their coworkers. Either way, they didn't deserve to go out like that, chopped down by some soldier after one hundred and fifty years of darkness and hunger. Now their black blood was being sprayed off Alex's skin and dripping thickly down the drain.

Part of her melancholy was the knowledge that if they'd gotten the information Jessica Bowen needed, it would just mean the GMT would be going out again very soon. They'd once again be fighting for their lives in some dark hole in the ground, scavenging ancient equipment from a dead civilization.

After she'd been cleaned and cleared, she went back to the hangar. The medical crew was still decontaminating the ship.

A tall, thick man with close-cropped red hair was marking items off on a clipboard. He glanced up at her warily, and it took her a moment to place him. Sergeant Russell.

She almost apologized for yelling at him, but the fear and respect she saw in his eyes made her reconsider. Maybe it wasn't such a bad thing to have some people think you were an asshole.

He dropped his clipboard to his side and fired off a crisp salute as she approached.

"Where's Captain Brickman?" she asked.

"He was taken to the hospital in the Hub, ma'am. They needed to reset his fractured arm. He'll be out in a few hours."

"Thanks, Sergeant." She turned and walked away without waiting for him to say more.

Firefly and Drew were waiting for her outside the hangar.

"Hey," Firefly said. "We're thinking about heading out for a drink and bite to eat. Wanna come?"

Of course, she did. Before they'd asked, she would have

said she didn't want to talk to anyone for at least forty-eight hours. But these guys had been through it with her. *Them,* she could talk to. "Should we invite Owl?"

"Nah," Drew said. "She went off with Brian and Director Bowen to look at the data she mined. She's in nerd heaven."

Alex glanced over and saw Wesley standing near the door, just within earshot. "How about you? Up for a drink with the team?"

His puppy-like look of gratitude almost made her sorry she'd asked.

————

THEY WENT to their respective quarters to change into something other than gym shorts and tee shirts, then reconvened at Tankards. Drew and Firefly were already waiting at their usual table when Alex arrived. She joined them and found a drink waiting for her. There was one set up for Wesley, as well.

It was clear from the way he stepped through the door that Wesley had been in this bar before. He walked with a confidence he hadn't displayed in the hangar or down on the surface. Alex waved him over.

They clinked glasses and toasted to their safe return and CB's quick recovery.

Drew slammed his mug on the table and dragged the back of his arm across his face. His shirt sleeve soaked up the beer on his stubbly face. "So, Wes, what did you think of your first mission?"

Wesley shook his head and whistled. "Man, I don't know where to start."

"Better question," Alex said. "What'd you learn?"

When he hesitated, Firefly jumped in.

"I'll tell you what you *need* to learn. You were way too precious with your ammo in that hallway. You get in that situation again, aim for the legs and let her rip. Don't let up on the trigger 'til all them bastards are on the floor. It won't kill them, but it'll slow them down long enough for you to get a handle on your situation. Then you can lob a grenade at them, take your time shooting them in the head, whatever."

Wesley leaned forward, listening intently and nodding along with every word. He might as well have been taking notes.

"Better lesson," Alex said. "You get in trouble like that again, say something. We're a team. That means we have to talk constantly. It's tough to ask for help, but it's necessary if you're gonna last."

Firefly shook his head and laughed. "Man, CB's really got you brainwashed. I think he gave me that same speech once or twice."

"You're not the only one," Alex said. "And he's right. Teamwork keeps us alive."

Drew nudged Wesley. "She was on the team ten months before she even saw her first vampire. That was one hell of a job for your first mission."

"Hear, hear," Alex said, raising her glass.

They toasted again, this time in Wesley's honor.

After they'd set their glasses down, Wesley said, "You guys see all the protestors on the way in here?"

"It was hard to miss them," Drew said.

Alex nodded her agreement. It seemed like the whole situation had spun even further out of control during the few hours they'd been away. A couple of days ago, it had just been the Resettlers who'd been protesting, but now there were just as many people holding signs speaking out against Fleming and his followers.

"Coming back from that mission today and seeing the crap going on up here?" Alex said. "I gotta admit, it's a little disheartening. This ship is weeks away from breaking down, and they're fighting about the politics of it all? Simmons gave his life to protect this place, but I didn't see a single sign thanking him."

"That's the way of it," Drew said. "That'd rather hold signs about what they hate than what they love."

"It's not just the protestors, though. It's the politicians, too. Fleming, Stearns, all of them. Trying to prove how smart they are and how wrong their opponents are, instead of solving problems."

Wesley shook his head sadly. "I know, right? The medics told me Fleming's trial is scheduled for tomorrow."

Alex slapped a hand on the table. "That's exactly what I'm saying! The ship is going down! Is this really the priority right now? How about we save the ship, *then* figure out who's guilty and who's innocent?"

Firefly stared at her blankly as he drained his mug.

"What, you disagree?" she asked.

He shrugged. "Of course, saving the ship is the most important thing. But the Council betrayed the people's will, and they shot up a meeting of Fleming's followers. They threw the man behind bars, just for disagreeing with them."

"That's just politics, man," Drew said. "It's always been that way and always will."

"No, that's way beyond petty politics." Firefly's voice was getting louder now, filling with passion. "Yeah, we gotta fix the ship, but we can't let them sweep this betrayal under the rug, either. And, I'll tell you, there are plenty of people in this city that'll make sure what they've done isn't forgotten."

Wesley looked a little uncomfortable at the political discussion. Alex laughed. "Relax, Wesley, if you can't fight about religion and politics with your friends, who can you fight about them with?"

"Fight vampires by days, philosophize by night," Drew said. "It's the GMT way."

Wesley leaned forward and looked at Firefly, a thin smile on his face. "Well, in that case, I hope Fleming and all his whiny followers take a walk off the west end of the cornfield and don't stop until they hit the surface."

Drew, Firefly, and Alex stared at each other in shocked silence for a long moment. Then all three burst out in a wild fit of laughter.

"Where did that come from?" Alex wheezed between laughs.

Drew clapped Wesley on the back. "You're all right, kid. Welcome to the team."

37

THE NEXT MORNING, Alex stopped by CB's quarters to see how he was doing. His arm was encased in a cast that started at the shoulder and went all the way down to the wrist. He looked decidedly less pale than the last time Alex had seen him, but he was no less feisty.

"My arm was broken in two places, and they wanted to do surgery. I told them to set it and put me in something mobile, so I'd still be able to lead my team in the field. They insisted on putting me in this monstrosity."

"Well, I'm glad you're all right."

"Thanks." He gestured toward a chair next to him. "You want to stay and watch the trial?"

She'd been planning on heading over to Drew's and watching it with the team, but CB looked like he could use the company. "Sure thing, Captain."

She sat down and looked at the monitor, which was currently displaying a shot of the courtroom. The City Council was filing in, one seat on their bench conspicuously empty. "The Council appointed this judge, right?"

"Yes," CB said. "If they find him guilty, his supporters will certainly take issue with the question of impartiality."

They watched in silence for a moment, then CB said, "Listen, Alex, Director Bowen is poring through the information you brought back right now. We'll have our target for the next mission within the next couple days. With this cast, I'd be a liability down there. I'll be staying behind."

"I think that's the right move, sir. No offense."

He nodded, but the pain of missing their most crucial mission was clear on his face. "I want you to lead the team."

It was so surprising, so outside of the realm of what she'd expected him to say, that she simply had no response.

"I saw the way you were with Wesley yesterday. And the way you took charge when I got hurt. It has to be you, Alex."

She thought about that for a moment. Other than Wesley, she was the most junior member of the team. On the other hand, who else would it be? Drew wouldn't want the leadership role even if it were offered. Firefly? No way, he'd tell the team to wait in the ship while he blew up whatever building they were supposed to be infiltrating. Owl? She was a great pilot and had a level head, but she was more interested in interacting with machines than people.

As much as Alex hated to admit it, CB was right. It had to be her. And she was surprised to find that she wanted it this way, too.

"Thank you, Captain. I won't let you down."

"You'd better not." He gestured toward the TV. "It's starting."

The trial lasted less than an hour. Councilman Stearns opened the proceedings by reading the charge against Fleming. He was accused of treason against *New Haven*. He'd have a chance to defend himself, and witnesses would be called both for and against him. Then the judge would make his decision.

Director Bowen was the first witness. She told the story of the fire in Engineering and how, in her opinion, it had been arson. She also relayed the damage done to the reactor and how all of *New Haven* was put in imminent danger because of the fire.

Captain Kurtz was the next witness. He detailed the investigation of the fire and how the badges had determined that it was, indeed, arson. He then told the story of Fleming's arrest and said the man had incited violence among his followers rather than coming along quietly.

At Fleming's request, two of his followers also took the stand. They both recounted the story of Fleming's arrest and told how General Craig had started shooting. They made a special point to detail how the general had attempted to shoot Fleming after the fight had calmed down.

Fleming also called Sarah's doctor to the stand. He testified about the extent of her injuries and told the court she was still clinging to life. It looked like she would survive, but her path to recovery would be neither easy, nor assured.

When all the witnesses had been called, Councilman Stearns spoke.

"Daniel Fleming has only been on the Council six months, but in that time, we've seen him quickly become radicalized on the issue of Resettlement. He made a point of arguing for it in every meeting, and he wouldn't be swayed by logic, tradition, or the very real threat of vampires. It became clear he was willing to push for Resettlement by any means necessary.

"When the Council decided to deny the people's request for Resettlement, Councilman Fleming absolutely lost his mind. Rather than stay and fight for his beliefs, he stormed out of the Council chambers, and he never returned. Days later, the fire happened, giving Councilman Fleming exactly what he wanted. It was nothing more and nothing less than an attempt to force Resettlement.

"We don't have video evidence of Fleming or his followers starting the fire. We don't have his fingerprints at the scene. But what we do have is logic. Fleming wanted us to return to the surface so badly that he abandoned his elected position when things didn't go his way. If he was willing to do that, what else would he be willing to do? I think we all know the answer."

It was then Fleming's turn to speak.

"Once again, the Council is attempting to place their thumbs on the scales of justice. They've provided no evidence that I had anything to do with this crime. All their witnesses testified to was that the fire was arson. Perhaps the fire was started by someone attempting to frame me. Perhaps it was an accident. I don't know. But I can tell you that I had nothing to do with this. I didn't start the fire. I didn't order anyone to start the fire." He turned toward the judge. "I know that you were appointed by the Council and that you're an old friend of Councilman Stearns, but I ask that you put that aside and rule impartially. There is no evidence against me. Any ruling against me would be based purely on conjecture. I don't think our ancestors wanted New Haven to be the kind of place that held government-led witch hunts. I hope you agree."

Alex turned to CB while Fleming walked to his seat. "Think the judge will find him guilty?"

"I don't know. But it's going to be bad either way. I'm going to put the team on lockdown in the hangar, so they're ready to go at a moment's notice."

The judge deliberated for less than thirty minutes before

returning with a verdict. Daniel Fleming was guilty of treason.

The riots started in earnest less than an hour later.

———

TWO HOURS AFTER THE VERDICT, the team got notice to meet in the briefing room. CB, Alex, and the rest the team were already in the hangar, as were Brian and the general, but they had to wait for Director Bowen and Councilman Stearns to make their way through the tumult in the city.

As they waited, Firefly made his feelings on the court ruling clear. "You've got a judge Stearns appointed himself. The Council doesn't present any real evidence. And yet they find him guilty? Why even have a trial?"

"Firefly, let's keep politics out of the briefing room," CB said.

"It's not politics, Captain. It's a police state. And we're working for them!"

"I made myself clear, Lieutenant. Any more talk about that in here and you'll be sitting this mission out."

Firefly was fuming, but he didn't say anything else on the matter.

Director Bowen and Councilman Stearns entered together. Bowen greeted the team and then went straight for the projector. A moment later, it displayed a picture of a mountain.

"This is NORAD," she said. "North American Aerospace Defense Command. It monitored for and protected against aerial attacks against the United States and its allies. It was equipped with the most modern technology available at the time of the infestation, and it's built into the side of a mountain. I believe this is our best chance of finding the parts we need."

"Chance?" General Craig said. "I thought the whole point of getting the NSA intel was so we'd know for sure."

"I know they had the equipment at one time. But there's always a chance it's been destroyed by vampires. I believe our odds are extremely good, though. This place is well fortified and relatively remote. Reason dictates it would have been one of the last strongholds of humanity."

"So, we run it like the Texas mission?" Alex asked. "Find the reactor control panel, dismantle it, and bring back the parts?"

"Mostly," Jessica said. "However, I believe it will be important for you to have someone who can sort through the parts and find the ones we actually need. It would be easy to leave something important behind. That's why I'm going with you."

CB and Alex exchanged a look. CB cleared his throat. "Uh, Director Bowen, while we certainly appreciate—"

"General Craig and Councilman Stearns have already approved my request. This isn't up for discussion, Captain. I know reactors better than anyone aboard *New Haven*, and the stakes are too high for me *not* to accompany you."

"All right, then," CB said. He didn't look happy.

"It'll take Horace and his team until tomorrow morning to get us close enough. Stay nearby. We'll leave as soon as we get word we're in position."

38

ALEX LED Director Bowen to R&D to get her outfitted for the mission. It felt like déjà vu; she'd taken Wesley on this same trip only a few days prior.

"Director Bowen, I'm going to recommend you carry a gun on this mission." Alex held up a hand to cut off the objection that she assumed was coming. "I'm not saying it has to be an assault rifle or anything, but you should carry a pistol, just in case."

Director Bowen's eyes widened. "Are you crazy? If I'm going to the surface, I'm taking the biggest gun I can carry."

"Oh. Okay, then."

"I have fired a gun before, Alex. I was a badge for five years before Engineering lured me away from the streets. By the way, if we're going to be risking our lives together on the surface, you'd better call me Jessica."

Alex looked at the older woman with new respect. This lady was full of surprises. "Sure thing, Jessica." The name felt strange coming from her lips.

They spent the next hour with Brian and his crew. First, they had Jessica fitted for the uniform. The woman was taller than Alex and broader than Owl, so they couldn't use any of their spares. Thankfully, Brian pulled out a silver mail suit that had belonged to a woman who'd been on the team ten years ago. The thing was a bit musty, but it was in perfect condition. Once they had that, it was easy to locate the deceased GMTer's other clothing too. They were a perfect fit.

Despite Jessica's insistence that she was no stranger to weaponry, Alex made her spend time on the range with a pistol and a rifle. She'd be carrying both, and Alex wanted her to at least get a feel for the weapons. Protecting Jessica during the mission would be one of the team's primary objectives. If everything went well, the Director of Engineering wouldn't have to fire a single shot. But things rarely went well lately, so, better safe than sorry.

They left R&D, Jessica still aglow from the shooting range. Alex was concerned the woman might like guns a little too much. Between her and Firefly, they'd be lucky if this NORAD place was still standing by the time they were finished.

Alex advised Jessica to go to bed as early as possible. The woman would probably have trouble sleeping, but even resting in bed would do her good.

After saying her goodbyes, Alex decided to go for a walk. She left the Ground Mission Team headquarters and walked the surrounding area. This neighborhood was mostly GMT support staff. The single ones, like Alex, stayed in small apartments just outside headquarters, but the married staff was allowed larger residences. Drew and his wife lived two streets over.

There wasn't enough support staff to fill the whole neighborhood, but most of the other residences were filled with other government employees. Badges, elected officials, and Engineering personnel all called this area home.

All in all, these weren't the type of people likely to engage in riots. The neighborhood had not been spared. It was quiet now—the rioters must have moved on to other locations—but the damage was done. Trash and broken glass were everywhere, and many of the walls sported fresh graffiti calling for the Council's replacement in less than polite terms.

Alex sighed as she walked. Everything had changed so quickly. Only a few weeks ago, this place had been a virtual paradise. There were certainly problems—bar fights, domestic disputes, theft—but a *New Haven* badge was more likely to spend their shift writing tickets for loitering than they were dealing with serious issues. In spite of their nearly strife-free existence, the people had wanted change. And Alex had been among them, her voice raised just as loud as any of theirs. She'd even been willing to go against her team to help Fleming. It all seemed so silly now.

It wasn't that people shouldn't strive for change, it was just the lack of perspective. The rest of humanity had been violently wiped from the face of the Earth, and here they sat, living their lives in a city in the clouds.

Now their entire existence was in jeopardy. And still the people held trials and argued about the results.

All that buzzed around the front of her mind as she walked, but something else, something raw and painful, lingered beneath. Simmons was gone. He was gone forever, and she hadn't even begun the grieving process. There hadn't been time, and it didn't look like there would be anytime soon.

The pain she felt at his loss was like a gaping wound, always present and roaring with pain at the slightest provocation. Somehow, she'd have to push past it to do this one last job. Then she'd be able to take the time she needed.

She walked home slowly, meandering through the streets. Sleep would not come easily, and she was in no rush to get back to her bed.

———

THE NEXT MORNING, Alex headed down to the hangar, full of nervous energy before her first mission as the team's leader. She'd slept fitfully, and what sleep she had gotten was filled with nightmares of teammates dying under her watch. She'd woken with one thought fully formed in her mind: today, she needed to lead her team into the most secure facility on the surface of the Earth, protect Director Bowen, and bring back the equipment necessary to save humanity.

No pressure.

Jessica was already in the locker room, fully dressed in her silver mail and fatigues when Alex arrived.

"Morning, Director Bowen."

"Jessica," the director reminded her.

"Right. You sleep okay?"

Jessica smiled. "Like a baby." She looked like she had, too.

Firefly moseyed in and nodded a greeting. "I hear that you're in charge of this shindig, Alex."

"Looks that way," she said.

"You gonna let me blow something up? I'm in a blow-something-up kinda mood."

"Must be a weekday," Alex said.

The team gathered in the hangar outside the away ship ten minutes later. CB was waiting for them, his arm in its ridiculous cast. "Can I get everybody together for a minute?"

He stuck his head in the open cargo door of the away ship. "That means you too, Owl."

They all stood in front of CB. It was Alex, Firefly, Drew, Wesley, Owl, and Jessica. It struck Alex that this team was quite different from the one that she had headed down to Texas with only a few days before.

"I wish like hell I was going with you," CB said. "I guess you probably know that, but it's worth saying anyway. I talked to each of you one on one, but I'll repeat it for the group. Alex is one hundred percent in charge down there. Listen to her like you listen to me. What she says goes. You hear?"

"Yes, sir," came the reply.

Alex felt her cheeks grow red. She suddenly felt like the kid who'd been put in charge while the teacher left the room. If she wasn't able to lead the team without a stern talk from CB first, she wasn't much of a leader, was she?

"You'll be following Director Bowen—Jessica—into the facility. She has a detailed map and can get you in and out without our usual wandering around. As you saw yesterday, this place is built into the side of a mountain. Owl's a little concerned about finding a place to set the ship down. If all goes well, the landing and departure will be the toughest parts of the mission. Any questions?"

There were none.

"Good. I don't have to tell you how important this mission is. I'll be thinking of you the whole time you're gone, but you're the most capable people I've ever met. I wouldn't want this job in anyone else's hands."

The team stood staring at CB. This, Alex realized, was her moment to take charge.

"Thanks, CB," she said. Then she turned to the team. "Let's roll, people."

The team was beginning to board the away ship when the monitor on the wall of the hangar appeared.

"They're gonna announce Fleming's sentence," Drew said. "We got time to watch this, Captain?"

CB turned to Alex. "Your call."

She deliberated for a moment. This wouldn't be a long broadcast, and they were already ahead of schedule. "We've got time."

"Good morning, people of *New Haven*," Stearns said. "My apologies for the early morning broadcast. With the civil unrest we experienced last night, the Council didn't want to draw this out any longer than was necessary. We've reached a decision on how to sentence Daniel Fleming. After the sentence is announced, I'd like to discuss some steps the Council is taking to address the concerns of the Resettlement supporters and begin to explore the possibilities of Resettling in safe and incremental ways."

He paused for a moment, as if giving the people around the city time to take that in. "The now former councilman was convicted of treason, our highest crime. He put every man, woman, and child in this city in mortal danger, a danger we are not out of yet. The Council took the seriousness of the crime, his lack of remorse, and his continued contribution to stoking the fires of civil unrest into consideration in this sentencing decision."

"That's why the Council has—"

White light flashed across the screen, then it was replaced with static.

"What the hell?" Firefly took a step forward, his eyes on the screen.

"This is a joke, right?" Drew said. "It's gotta be a joke."

"I don't think so," Alex muttered.

CB dashed across the room and grabbed the radio off the wall. "Everybody hang tight."

It took CB three minutes to get anyone on the radio. The team milled around, their eyes fixed on the static-filled screen, hoping Councilman Stearns would come back and explain the strange outage.

Alex saw CB was talking to someone on the radio now. She wandered over, hoping to catch a bit of the conversation.

CB's face went pale. He looked up at Alex. "Get them on the ship. You need to go. Now."

Alex's voice sounded distant in her ears when she spoke. "What's happening?"

"There was a bomb. Someone set off a bomb in the Council building. The Council's dead."

39

THE TEAM WAS BARELY STRAPPED into their seats before CB opened the hangar door and Owl piloted the away ship into the open air outside of *New Haven*.

"What the hell just happened?" Drew said. "Somebody just blew up the Council? Are we talking about terrorists here?"

"More like a coup," Jessica said softly.

The words hung heavy in the air, no one saying anything, not wanting to acknowledge the truth of her statement.

Alex read the faces of her teammates, trying to take in their emotional states. This was bad, really and truly, but they didn't have time to dwell on it now. Very shortly, they'd be down on the surface in dangerous territory, on a mission they could not afford to fail.

Drew had a manic, crazed look in his eyes. Jessica wore a grim expression as if she were quietly resigned to the situation. Firefly and Wesley—despite their opposing political positions—had nearly identical devastated looks on their faces, like they'd just been punched in the stomach.

"We have to go back," Wesley said. He spoke quietly, but urgently. His voice was louder when he spoke again. "The badges will be fighting for their lives back there. We have to go back and help them."

No one replied.

It made sense that Wesley would be the most viscerally upset by these events. Until two days ago, he'd been in the thick of the political turmoil. He'd experienced the protests and the riots personally. He'd lived what the others had watched play out from a distance.

"I'm serious," he said. "We're supposed to help the people of *New Haven*. Owl, turn around!"

"Wesley." Alex looked him dead in the eyes. "We're not going back. Not until we've completed our mission."

"They're overthrowing our government!"

"We don't know that." In truth, they probably did, but now wasn't the time for semantics. "We still have a job to do. If we fail here, the government won't matter. We're trying to save the human race. The problems in the city will still be there when we get back."

"Problems?" Wesley let out a manic laugh. "That seems to be downplaying what just happened."

Alex touched her radio. "Owl, what's our flight time?"

The response came through her earpiece. "*New Haven* wasn't quite in the ideal position yet, but we were getting close. We should reach NORAD in about an hour."

"Roger that." Alex turned back to Wesley. "That means you have one hour to pull yourself together. You want to freak out, complain about how *New Haven* is going to hell, whatever, you do it now. But I need to know that the moment we touch down, you'll be ready to take care of business. Can you do that?"

A flurry of emotions flickered through the young man's eyes—anger, fear, disbelief—and then he simply nodded.

"Good." She looked up and down the line at the others. "That goes for the rest of you too. We don't have the luxury of taking time to process what's going on up there, just like we didn't have time to properly grieve for Simmons. There's too much at stake."

"We're pros, Alex," Drew said. "You know we'll bring our best."

"Firefly?"

His eyes were on the floor. He looked utterly devastated. Alex didn't know if that was because the side he'd backed had committed such a terrible crime, or if he was just shocked at this turn of events. He met Alex's eyes only briefly as he muttered his response. "I'll be fine."

Alex turned to Jessica. Out of all of them, she'd known the Council best on a personal level. As a director, she spent time with them on a nearly daily basis. Yet, somehow, she seemed the most together of all of them.

"It's simple crisis management," the director said. "We deal with the most urgent problem first. That's fixing the reactor. Then we can deal with the next most urgent, which appears to be an overthrow of our government."

Alex almost laughed. Jessica Bowen was one strange woman, but Alex couldn't help liking her.

"Good," Alex said. "Get your heads right. We'll be there soon."

———

FORTY-FIVE MINUTES LATER, Owl's voice came through Alex's earpiece.

"Alex, could you join me in the cockpit, please?"

Alex was almost too surprised to answer. In the two years she'd been on the team and the dozens of missions she'd been part of, there was only one time she remembered CB going up to the cockpit during a flight. That was just after the vampires got Simmons, when he had to force Owl to leave. Owl liked to be alone when she flew, Alex knew. The cockpit was a sacred space to her, one she didn't want anyone else invading. The fact that she was asking Alex to join her up there couldn't be a good thing.

"Affirmative," Alex said. "Be right there."

The flight had been quiet for the last forty-five minutes, each member of the team dealing with the events back on *New Haven* in their own way and in their own head. For Alex, distance from *New Haven* brought clarity. Down on the surface, the potential for death was always mere moments away. It simply didn't allow you to worry about anything outside of survival. The closer they got to their destination, the more confident Alex grew that the team would be able to focus on the mission when the time came.

She made her way up to the cockpit and found Owl gripping the controls with both hands, her eyes focused on the sky ahead. They were passing through a dense sea of clouds.

"Sit down and strap in," Owl said.

Alex sank into the copilot's seat. "I hope you're not going to ask me to drive."

"No," Owl said. She spoke slowly, carefully, as if each word was an unnecessary distraction from her flying. "I don't think these conditions are ideal for a first-time flyer."

"So, what's going on?"

"Storms," Owl said.

At that moment, the ship dropped out of the clouds and into a different kind of whiteness. Snow pelted the windshield, splattering in large, wet flakes.

"NORAD is built into the side of a mountain," Owl said. "It would be a difficult landing in the best of conditions, and these are definitely not the best of conditions."

The ship hit a bit of turbulence, and Alex's stomach dropped. "What are you saying?"

Owl reached out and adjusted a knob on the control panel. "I'm going to get us as close as possible to the north entrance, but there's a chance we'll have to do a bit of walking."

"Okay. Get us as close as you can."

Alex glanced at her watch. It was nine thirty. With Jessica along, dismantling the reactor control panel should go much more quickly than it had in Texas. But that didn't take into account the time that it would take to get to the reactor, possibly fighting their way through a blizzard to get there. Add in a hike up a snowy mountainside, and they'd be in a serious time crunch to make it back before sundown.

Owl touched her radio and spoke into her microphone. "Ladies and gentlemen, please make sure you're strapped in."

Alex waited for her to say more, but she didn't. "That wasn't the most reassuring message."

"Yeah, well, I'm not feeling all that assured." She leaned on the controls, causing the nose of the ship to angle downward. "Let's see what the Rocky Mountains have to offer, shall we?"

The jagged peaks of the mountains ahead appeared through the snow a few moments later. The visibility was terrible, but Owl kept one eye on the radar display that showed the topography below.

She tapped the screen on a spot between two mountains. "There. That mountain pass is our best angle. If we slip through there, I should be able to put us just outside NORAD."

That gap looked narrow, but Alex wasn't about to question Owl's piloting abilities now. "Let's do it."

Owl angled them down more sharply, and the ship dipped and bounced through the choppy air.

"Can I ask you something?" Alex said. "Why'd you call me up here?"

"Well, you're in charge of this mission, right? I figure if I crash and kill us, they'll blame the highest-ranking person they find in the cockpit."

Alex could only see snow through the windshield now, but she could tell from the monitor that they were about to enter the narrow mountain pass.

"Here we go," Owl said. She banked right, and the shipped slipped into the pass. "Ha! Nailed it!"

Alex squinted through the snow. There was something on the ground. Three dark spots in the sea of white. The familiar mechanical rattle of distant gunfire split the air.

"Shit!" Owl yelled. She gripped the controls. "We're hit."

Alex looked frantically through the windshield, gazing futilely down at the large spitting guns. Those things had to be fifty caliber.

Drew's voice sounded in her earpiece. "What's going on up there?"

The gunfire sounded again, and this time the ship spun widely through the air.

"We lost a wing!" Owl said. "We're going down!"

Outside the windshield, the world spun. They twisted wildly in a sea of snow and vague shapes beyond.

Alex braced herself for the impact she knew was

coming. A thousand thoughts raced through her head at once. *New Haven*. CB. Simmons. The reactor they'd never repair.

The ship hit the ground, and all thought was smashed from her mind as the world went black.

40

ALEX OPENED HER EYES, and her head swam with pain. She had no idea how long she'd been out; it could have been seconds or hours.

She slowly raised her head and looked out the windshield. The nose of the ship was buried in snow. A dull throbbing in her forehead confirmed what had happened. She must have hit her head on the control panel. It didn't appear to be bleeding. That was something.

With a start, she realized she had no idea about the condition of her team. She swung her head toward Owl and instantly regretted it as a wave of pain and nausea swept over her.

She must not have been out long after the crash, because Owl was still clutching the controls and gazing out at the snow beyond the cracked windshield.

"I know no one aboard the ship will fully appreciate this," Owl said, "but that was an amazing landing. If I may say so."

"I'm still alive, so I'll take your word for it." Alex touched the radio in her vest. "Team, what's your status?"

Drew's voice came back a moment later. "We're...we're okay, Alex. Only person hurt is Wesley. He took a bullet to the leg."

Alex and Owl exchanged puzzled glances. It took Alex a moment to realize he was talking about the fifty-caliber guns that had shot at the ship. If Wesley took one of those bullets in the leg...it wouldn't be good.

She unstrapped herself and stood up, the pain in her head receding as it was replaced by concern for her teammate.

Owl started to stand, too, but Alex put a hand on her shoulder. "Stay here and try to get hold of CB. Let him know what happened."

"Okay." There was a beat, then she said, "What *did* happen, Alex? Who the hell could have possibly been shooting at us?"

Alex wasn't ready to confront that question. Not yet. "Just tell him we need an evac."

"Roger that."

Alex marched through the ship, her mind reeling with the possibilities at hand, the sheer number of choices they would now face. The responsibility of leadership threatened to crush her.

When she got to the passenger hold, Firefly was bent over Wesley, putting pressure on the wound. The young man was startlingly pale. He leaned back, his eyes fixed on some unknown spot on the ceiling.

The passenger hold was lined with bullet holes. It was a wonder more of them hadn't been hit.

"How is he?" she asked.

"He'll live," Firefly said. "He'll have one hell of a cool-looking scar to show the ladies, though."

Alex caught Drew's eye, and the man gave his head the

slightest of shakes. The situation was worse than Firefly wanted to let on in front of Wesley.

Firefly adjusted the cloth pressed against the wound, and Alex tried not to visibly wince as she got a look at the hole in the kid's leg. Best case scenario, that leg would have to come off. But they were out in the middle of nowhere, where a wound bleeding like that would likely result in a more permanent diagnosis.

"What's the plan?" Drew said.

It took Alex a moment to realize he was talking to her. It seemed like there should be someone else in charge, someone more responsible. Maybe now that the situation was life and death, Director Bowen would pull rank and start giving orders. That didn't appear to be happening. Jessica was staring at Wesley's wound with as much horror as anyone.

Who was Alex kidding? CB had been clear as to who was to have field command. And this mission had always been life and death, even before the shooting started.

She took a deep breath and tried to sound confident when she spoke. "Owl's raising CB in the radio. While she works on that, we're going to prepare to move out."

For the first time since she'd entered, Wesley spoke. "We're going to leave the ship?" He sounded genuinely perplexed.

"This changes nothing," Jessica said. Apparently, she'd gotten over her shock and recovered her usual cool demeanor. "*New Haven* still has a reactor that needs fixing."

Alex nodded. "Additionally, someone just fired at us."

Wesley laughed weakly. "I hadn't noticed."

"Whoever it was might want to track us down and finish the job. I'd prefer we're not here if they do. We'll take the rover and head for NORAD. We can get the parts and have them ready by the time CB's rescue ship arrives."

She could tell Drew wanted to say something, but he was biting his tongue for now.

Alex touched her radio. "Owl, you talk to CB?"

"Not yet. The comm was damaged in the crash."

"Wonderful," Firefly muttered.

"I think I can fix it, but I need a couple minutes."

"I'm not sure we have a couple minutes," Alex said. "Work fast. In the meantime, Drew and I will get the rover ready."

There was a pause, then Owl said, "Whatever you do, do not break my rover. I already lost one child today."

"You got it, Owl," Drew said. "We'll be hopping it off snow banks if you need us."

Wesley laughed weakly. "No offense, guys, but I'm starting to think joining the GMT was a mistake."

Drew clapped him lightly on the arm. "Wes, my man, welcome to the club."

———

Fifteen minutes later, they had the rover ready to go. Drew, Jessica, and Alex stood beside it, dressed in their winter gear. Firefly was back on the ship, tending to Wesley.

Alex wished they'd thought to bring a bigger vehicle. The snow had to be two feet deep, and walking over a mile to NORAD's north entrance in these conditions was going to be a treacherous journey. The rover could plow through the snow, leaving a trail that would make walking a bit easier for the rest of them. Her plan was to load Wesley onto the back. Owl would drive. The rest of them would have to walk.

Alex scanned the horizon for what must have been the

hundredth time since they'd stepped out the cargo door. There had yet to be a sign of whoever had shot at them. She was doing her best not to think too hard about the possibilities. Either vampires had learned to use guns or there were humans down here. She wasn't sure which option was more ludicrous. Yet here they were, standing next to a downed aircraft, one wing hanging off by a few strips of mangled steel, the whole thing riddled with bullet holes.

The best move was to focus on what she could control, actions she could take. Whoever it was that had attacked them, they'd find the GMT was much more difficult to take down when they were holding their weapons and able to fight back.

Alex walked through the cargo hold and made her way back to the passenger area. Wesley had his injured leg up on the seat now, and he still looked deathly pale.

"Hanging in there, Wesley?"

"Yes, ma'am," he said. His voice sounded stronger than when last she'd heard him speak. That had to be a good sign, right?

Owl's voice spoke in her earpiece. "I think I got it, Alex."

"Fantastic."

She headed for the cockpit, where she found Owl wrist deep in the partially dismantled control board. She held the comm radio in her exposed hand, and she held it out to Alex. "You want to do the honors?"

Alex took the radio and held it to her lips. "CB, it's Alex."

She lowered the radio and waited, knowing CB wouldn't venture far from the comm room while his team was in the field. She was about to try raising him again when his voice met her welcoming ears.

"I'm here. What's going on?" The concern was clear in

CB's voice. He knew she wouldn't be calling unless something had happened.

Alex paused, not sure where to begin. "We got shot down just outside NORAD."

———

CB WASN'T sure he'd heard correctly. "Come again, Alex."

"We got shot down, sir."

She proceeded to tell him about the guns near NORAD, Wesley getting shot, and the plane going down. CB squeezed his eyes shut as he listened. The first GMT mission he'd missed in over a dozen years, and this happens. It was impossible not to blame himself, even if purely out of superstition.

When she finished, CB took a moment to organize his thoughts. "Okay, Alex, here's what you need to do. The ship is your best position. You go wandering around in the snow, you'll be easy pickings for whoever's out there. The ship's defensible, even if it's damaged. Brian and I will scramble the backup ship. It'll only take us a few hours to get to you. Until then, stay on the ship and shoot anything that approaches."

Alex's reply was immediate. "That's a negative, sir."

CB blinked hard, once again not sure he'd heard correctly. "Excuse me?"

"We won't be following that course of action, sir."

He exchanged a glance with Brian, who was leaning in close to listen. "Have you lost your mind, Lieutenant? I just gave you an order."

"Sir, all due respect, but I'm down here and you aren't. We still have a chance of completing our mission. Jessica says NORAD is one of the most secure facilities on the planet. If we can get inside, we'll be in a much better position than this highly compromised ship, waiting for our enemies to attack."

CB was standing now, pacing back and forth as he listened. He'd never felt so powerless. "I've been doing this a long time, Alex. I was right about the vampires at night, wasn't I? You need to trust me."

"No, sir. You need to trust me."

His mouth fell open, and he waited, too shocked to respond.

"Captain, you made me the leader. Let me lead."

Three things flashed through Captain Brickman's mind at that moment. He imagined how he'd feel if his command on the surface was overridden by an officer safely aboard *New Haven*. He remembered the way Alex had talked to Wesley, supporting him on his first mission. And he remembered being thrown against the wall by that vampire outside the data center in the NSA, being down on the ground and sure he was facing his death until Alex had arrived and saved him. She'd saved them all. Could she do it again?

"Lieutenant Goddard, you have field command of the Ground Mission Team. How you proceed is your call. Just keep your radio on. Brian and I are coming."

"Thank you, sir. We'd better get moving. Ground Mission Team out."

CB turned to Brian. "Let's get the backup ship prepped."

Brian nodded. "On it, Captain." He headed toward the door, then paused. "I can't fly that thing. Can you?"

"Just barely."

"Good enough." Brian started through the door, but then stopped. He backed up slowly.

A group of ten men entered the comm room. CB had never seen any of them before.

"Captain Brickman, could you please come with us? Councilman Fleming would like to speak with you."

"It takes ten of you to ask me that?" CB growled.

"Captain, let's not make this difficult."

CB sighed. "Honestly guys, I don't have time for this bullshit. I don't know what you guys are doing, but I'm working on saving *New Haven*."

The man who'd been speaking took a big step forward. He was standing right next to Brian now. "My apologies if I wasn't clear. This meeting with Councilman Fleming is not optional."

CB flickered his gaze to Brian. He wasn't sure a lab geek like him would catch the meaning, but he didn't have time to discuss it. "Once again, I'll have to decline."

"I was hoping you'd say that," the man said.

He was looking at CB, so he didn't see Brian's telegraphed punch coming. The punch connected with the man's jaw, and he spun like a top.

CB had time for one thought—*God bless that nerd*—before the real fight began.

41

ALEX, Jessica, Drew, and Firefly trudged through snow that came up past their knees. Every step was an immense effort. They'd been going for hours, yet through the heavy snowfall, it was difficult to tell if they were making any progress at all.

She began to wonder if she'd made the right call. Maybe they should have stayed on the ship as CB had ordered. At least they'd be conserving energy. The way they were going, even if they did manage to make it to NORAD, they'd be so worn out by the time they got there that a single vampire would probably be able to pick off the whole team.

Jessica moved next to Alex. To the Director of Engineering's credit, she was keeping up with her hardened soldier companions.

"I'm worried," Jessica said. The wind was howling loudly, but Alex somehow heard the words clearly over the din.

"Why's that?" Alex said. "Other than the obvious."

"We're going too slow. At this pace, I'm not sure we'll

make it to the entrance and be able to get the parts out before sundown."

The same thought had crossed Alex's mind. More than that, it had been gnawing at her for the last twenty minutes. "It's hardly worth worrying about now. Let's keep moving. I think we're making better time than it feels like we are."

The words sounded hollow, even to her own ears.

Drew's voice was strained when he spoke. "CB said he was on his way, right? Maybe by the time we get in there and gather the parts, they'll be waiting outside the door for us."

"Let's hope so," Alex said. She just hoped those guns didn't shoot down the backup ship too. She should have told CB not to come until they figured out what was going on down here. Like he would have listened, anyway.

Up ahead, the mountain rose dramatically, with a twenty-foot path cutting between two walls of snow.

Owl called to them from the seat of the rover. "That canyon takes us straight to the north entrance. It must have been a road."

Alex didn't much like the idea of putting her team in such a vulnerable position. If someone were waiting for the perfect opportunity to attack, that canyon would be it. But what choice did she have? The snow was coming down even harder now, and the parts they needed were down that path.

She drew her pistol. The gloves she wore were thin, and she was still able to operate the weapon easily, but it felt different somehow. There was a barrier, and she didn't feel the usual comfortable sensation of skin against metal. "I want weapons at the ready. If something does attack, get against one wall and stay low."

There was a flurry of metallic clinks as everyone prepared their weapons. Then they made their way into the canyon.

Up close, Alex realized the walls were quite a bit higher than she'd thought. The occasional glimpse of the top she saw through the snow let her estimate them about around two hundred feet. Her only comfort was that the visibility of anyone at the top would be just as poor. She doubted they'd be able to target the team from so high above. Although they could lob down a mess of grenades. No need for accuracy when sheer force would do.

The team stayed silent as they moved through the canyon. The wind moved strangely in the pass, and it played tricks on Alex's ears. Sometimes, she could swear she heard voices in the distance. A little while later, she thought she heard the howl of vampires. But that was impossible. There couldn't be any vampires out. Not with the sun.

Alex suddenly gasped, realizing her mistake.

She turned to Drew. "The snow. It's blocking out the sun."

Drew's eyes widened under his winter hat.

The howls came again, closer this time.

But why would vampires risk coming out in the daytime when the snowstorm could break at any moment? It was almost suicide. As feral as vampires were, they seemed to instinctively avoid situations where the sun might appear. Unless...

She spun toward the rover where Wesley lay on the back, the bandage on his leg stained red.

The vampires...they smelled the blood.

The howls were almost on top of them now. The way was clear both ahead and behind. Which left one direction from which the vampires could attack.

"They're above us," Alex shouted. "Keep moving, eyes on the sky."

They moved on, making it another fifteen feet. Then Firefly pointed upward. "There!"

Alex squinted through the snow. After a moment, she saw it. A quickly growing black shape descending on them, its arms outstretched. It was gliding down at them.

Behind her, Jessica gasped.

"It's okay, stay close to Drew," Alex said. Drew's shotgun would be the best protection if a vampire got past the rest of them.

She raised her pistol, but Firefly already had his rifle in position. He let loose a spray of automatic fire, and the creature tumbled from the sky.

Alex trudged toward the spot where it fell, struggling through the snow, pistol in one hand, sword in the other. The vampire began to stand, its body crisscrossed with bullet holes.

Jessica stifled a scream.

Alex reminded herself this was the first vampire that the woman had ever seen. Alex hadn't been much better the first time she'd encountered one up close. She swung her sword and removed the creature's head in one stroke.

"We got three more!" Drew yelled.

Alex put her pistol away and shifted her sword to a two-hand grip. She wasn't likely to take out many by shooting at them with her pistol, but when they landed, she could take care of them very quickly.

The three shapes in the sky glided on the web-like wings that stretched between their arms and bodies. They circled in a lazy spiral for a moment, then, as one, angled downward and shot toward the ground.

Drew fired vainly into the sky, but they were moving too quickly.

"Shit," Alex said. "They're heading for the rover!" She took off, running through the snow to defend Wesley.

The three vampires hit the ground smoothly, landing on their feet, and started running without pausing. They moved on top of the snow, hopping lightly from foot to foot, leaving only a small indentation behind.

In contrast, Alex trudged behind them, each step a struggle. The sword wasn't going to work. She grabbed her pistol, drew, and fired in one smooth motion, hitting the vampire in front of her in the back of the head. Owl and Wesley took out the other two.

Another howl, this one from behind them. Alex spun, eyes searching the path, but saw nothing but white. She took a deep breath. What was it CB had said to her after Buenos Aires? The GMT didn't need heroes, it needed leaders. She was in charge of this mission. It was time to start acting like it.

"Owl, keep the rover moving forward no matter what. Firefly, lock your eyes on the sky. You see one of those bastards, you put as many holes in it as you can before it hits the ground, you hear?"

"Yes, ma'am."

"Jessica, you stay as close to the rover as possible. One gets close, shoot it, but make sure you have a clear shot. Don't shoot if you might hit any good guys. Drew, you watch behind us. Your job is to protect Jessica and Wesley."

"Alex," Firefly said, "we got five incoming."

"Then light 'em up!" Alex said. She felt a strange sense of clarity. They could get through this. She could lead them through this.

Firefly opened fire.

Behind them, two dark shapes appeared in the sea of white.

"Drew," she said.

"I got 'em."

Alex fought her way forward to where Firefly was walking near the rover. She waited until the vampires landed. All five had at least a couple of holes in them, but they were all still moving. As they touched the ground, she began firing. Her shots were true, and she took out three of them in the time it took Firefly to finish the other two.

Two shotgun blasts from behind her told Alex that Drew had done his job.

Up ahead, she saw a shape, mostly buried in the snow, clawing its way out.

"My God, they're under us too?" Jessica asked in a shaky voice.

The vampire pulled itself from the snow and charged. Alex put a bullet in its head from twenty feet away.

She turned to check on the team behind her. Three vampires were descending toward the rear of the rover; the lowest was almost on top of Jessica. Alex started to shout to warn them, but Drew was already on it. He leaped to Jessica's side, pointed his gun skyward, and took off the lowest vampire's head.

The other two landed on either side of Drew and Jessica, only a few feet away. Alex could tell from her vantage point that it would be impossible to take out both before the vampires reached them. Drew would have to kill the one closest to him and hope Jessica could handle the one in front of her.

But Drew didn't do that. He dove sideways, putting his body between Jessica and the other vampire. The creature leaped at him, but he shot it out of the air with a shotgun blast to the chest.

The other vampire charged at Drew's back. Alex raised her pistol, knowing a vampire-killing shot from this distance was nearly impossible with this weapon. But what choice did she have but to try?

Before she could fire, a quick burst of shots cut the air, catching the vampire in the chest and dropping it to the ground. She spun toward the source of the attack.

Wesley was sitting up in the back of the rover, his assault rifle still pointed toward the fallen vampire.

"Whoa," Drew said. "It'll take more than a fifty-caliber to stop our boy Wes!"

Alex looked ahead of them. Behind them. Above. It was clear for now. Up ahead, she could just make out the end of the canyon.

She made her way back to Jessica and touched the woman's arm. "You okay?"

"Yes."

But Alex could see she wasn't. How could she be after what she'd just witnessed? She spent most of her days looking at engineering diagrams, and now she was forced to survive a vampire attack in a blizzard.

Jessica nodded toward Drew. "Thanks. I wouldn't have made it if you didn't have my back."

Drew grinned. "It's kinda what I do. Now, if you want to see something really impressive, ask—"

Snow blasted into the air behind him as a vampire leaped from below the powder where it had been hidden.

Jessica screamed, and Alex went for her gun.

The creature grabbed Drew by the top of the head, sinking its claws into his skull. It landed on the wall ten feet up and started climbing, Drew still dangling from its right hand.

Drew let out a moan. He was still clutching his shotgun, and he raised it slowly, angling it toward the vampire.

The creature growled. It twisted its wrist hard, and there was an audible snap as Drew's neck broke. His arms went slack, and the shotgun fell, landing in the snow below. The vampire climbed, quickly disappearing into the driving snow, taking Drew's limp body with it.

"No!" Jessica yelled hoarsely.

Alex's mouth hung open in disbelief.

Firefly ran to the wall and vainly tried climbing its snowy surface. He made it five feet before slipping back to the ground, but he immediately tried again.

"If we backtrack, we may be able to get up there," Owl said. She spoke quickly, frantically.

"He's dead." Alex hated the words even as she said them, but she knew they were true. "He's dead, and we have to keep going."

Everyone knew she was right.

They made it through the rest of the canyon in silence. The snow was slowing now, and as they exited the canyon, they saw the entrance to NORAD in the distance.

————

CB THREW himself against the locked door of the cell again and cried out in pain as his shoulder struck the steel door.

"Captain, you have to stop," Brian said.

CB spun toward him, his face a mask of rage. "They're killing my team!" He turned back to the door. "You hear that? You're killing them!"

Back in the hangar, it had taken six men to bring CB down. He was certain he could have taken the lot of them if it hadn't been for the broken arm. Still, he'd gotten his licks in and taken his licks in return. His left eye was already so swollen he could only see a thin slit of the world beyond it.

"I understand," Brian said. "I'm just as angry as you are."

CB laughed. "Kid, you got a funny way of showing it."

Brian looked up sharply, and his eyes were filled with tears. "I'd bash my body against that door until I was bloody if I thought it would make any difference. If I thought it could save them, I'd kill Fleming and every one of his followers."

CB was surprised to find he believed him.

"But the truth is, I'm locked in a cell," Brian continued. "I can either wear myself out pointlessly raging, or I can use this time to think. To plan."

CB hated to admit it, but the kid was right. He sat down on the empty bench on his side of the room with a sigh. "All right, so what have you been thinking?"

Brian leaned forward and spoke in a low voice. "Fleming's smart. And he's patient. Whatever he wants from us, he'll reveal it in his own time. We have to come to grips with the fact that it might be a day or two before he's ready to have that conversation."

CB grimaced. "And what happens to the team while we're rotting in this cell?"

"Unfortunately, we don't have any control over that. But you trained them better than anyone else could. You gave them a chance."

"Against vampires after dark? All the training in the world won't matter."

"Maybe they won't have to face the vampires. They're at NORAD, right? If they can get inside, secure a few rooms, they might just have a chance."

It was possible. For all CB knew, NORAD could be crawling with vampires just like the NSA. And yet, there was a chance it wasn't. Thank God Alex hadn't listened to him. If they'd stayed on the ship, they would have been easy targets after sundown.

He didn't know if they could survive the night, but they had a chance. And if anyone could do it, it was Alex.

42

THEY MADE their way toward the north entrance of the NORAD facility. Jessica had shown them pictures during their briefing, but seeing it in person was different. Alex could see it in the distance, marked by a fence stretching in either direction. In the center there was a tunnel that stuck out of the mountainside, blocked by a massive concrete door.

The snowfall stopped over the next ten minutes, and the sun beat down on them, making the snow sparkle. In other circumstances, it would have been beautiful. Alex briefly considered how she was one of the few humans alive who'd seen snow on the surface of Earth, but she bitterly pushed the thought away. She'd gladly trade the sight of snow for not having to see two friends slaughtered by vampires. The evil she'd seen greatly outweighed the good.

The sun was dropping quickly now, but they were going to make it. The landscape ahead rose in a thirty-foot ridge, but once they got over that, it was a straight shot down to the entrance.

Alex glanced over at Jessica. Her jaw was set and her

eyes were locked on the entrance ahead. Alex realized the woman was trying very hard not to cry.

"Hey," Alex said. "It's okay to be upset."

Jessica didn't take her eyes off the concrete door. "Not right now, it isn't. There's too much riding on us."

Alex thought about arguing, but she couldn't think of how to combat that logic. She walked to the rover instead.

Wesley was staring up at the sky, but his eyes looked clearer now. His bandage was still seeping blood, but he was alive, which meant the flow had to have subsided somewhat.

"We're going to get you inside soon," Alex said. "Then we'll let you stay still for a while."

"That would be great," Wesley said in a strained voice. "I'm pretty sure Owl is purposely driving over as many bumps as possible."

"Ha!" Owl said. "I'd like to see anyone else give this smooth of a ride through two feet of snow." She nodded toward the door. "We have a clear shot from here. No bad guys. Mind if we speed ahead and wait for you at the door?"

"Fine with me," Alex said.

The rover whined as it sped up, plowing through the snow a bit faster, and it started up the ridge. Alex and the team walked in the trail of displaced snow it left in its wake.

As the rover crested the ridge, Alex saw something sticking out of the snow at the top of the hill. She squinted toward it. Was that...an arm?

But that was impossible. The sun was still shining on them. A vampire wouldn't risk an attack now with the sun shining, blood or no. Unless it wasn't waiting to attack. Maybe it was already dead.

"Owl, wait!" Alex called.

But it was too late.

The rover went over the top, and the thunderous sound of fifty-caliber guns roared through the air.

Owl dove from the rover as bullets tore through the vehicle. She rolled toward the back.

Alex and the rest of the team sprinted for the rover. They were still blocked from the guns by the ridge.

Owl crouched behind the rover and reached up, grabbing Wesley and pulling him backward off the vehicle. He cried out in pain as he hit the ground. Owl dragged him back over the crest of the hill, out of the line of fire.

The rover tumbled down the other side of the hill, and the gunfire stopped.

Alex reached Owl and Wesley and dropped to the ground alongside them. "You okay?"

Wesley groaned. "Not really. But not worse than before."

"I'm fine," Owl said. "We got lucky."

Alex silently cursed herself. Why'd she let them go on ahead? It was only dumb luck that they weren't both dead.

"Stay here." She rose up into a crouch and carefully made her way up the top of the hill. Peering over, she saw a line of fifty-caliber guns along the fence. They'd been blocked by the ridge before, so she hadn't been able to see them.

These must have been the same guns that shot down the away ship.

How were they going to get past those guns? And who was firing them?

She let her eyes wander, taking in the scene, hoping some advantage would reveal itself.

The other side of the hill was blocked from the wind at Alex's back, and the snow was much more shallow. She could even see the shape of the ground beneath. It was oddly formed. Strangely lumpy.

Something about that ground wasn't right.

She spotted another arm protruding from the snow. And, ten feet away, a leg. And another, fifteen feet beyond that.

With horror, Alex realized what she was standing on. This wasn't a hill. It was a pile of bodies.

———

"I THINK the guns are on auto sensors," Alex told the team.

The team was still coping with the news that they were standing on a pile of bodies. Firefly, in particular, seemed uncomfortable. He shifted nervously from foot to foot, his eyes on the ground beneath his feet.

"The way I figure it," she continued, "vampires wander up toward the fence from time to time. The guns take them out. Over time, the bodies have piled up."

"Damn," Owl said. "So, no one was shooting at the ship?"

"Not purposely."

Alex glanced at the horizon. The door that had seemed so close only ten minutes before seemed further now that they knew there were fifty-caliber guns set to destroy anything that moved between them and it.

"We've gotta find a way past the guns," Alex said.

"Firefly," Wesley said, his voice a weak groan.

Firefly leaned down toward him. "What is it, bud? You need something?"

"Yeah, I need you to take out those guns. You've got those exploding rounds, right, moron?"

Firefly's eyes lit up. "Yeah. I do!" He looked at Alex questioningly.

"Do it," she said.

Firefly and Alex crept to the crest of the ridge while Jessica and Owl stayed down with Wesley.

Firefly loaded the exploding rounds into his rifle. They laid on their stomachs and peered down at the guns.

"You think this will work?" Alex asked.

"One way to find out." He took aim and fired. The base of the turret exploded, and the gun leaned sickly to the right.

"That one's out of commission," Alex said.

Firefly took out the other four weapons in five shots. The one he missed hit the fence and blasted a massive hole in it. "Whoops," he said.

Alex gazed down at the guns. They certainly looked like they wouldn't function, but there was only one way to know for sure. She started to stand, but Firefly put a hand on her shoulder.

"Let me go." He nodded back at the rover. "They need you a hell of a lot more than they need me."

She started to object, but she knew he was right. They needed a leader. "Okay."

Firefly stood tall and walked down the hill, striding over the mountain of bodies like he was on a Sunday-afternoon stroll through the Hub. He reached the bottom of the hill without a gun so much as twitching. Grinning up at Alex, he said, "I guess it worked."

Alex headed back down to Owl, Wesley, and Jessica.

"How we gonna get him there?" Owl asked, nodding at Wesley.

Alex stripped off her jacket and set it on the ground. Then she grabbed Wesley under the arms and put him on top of it. Wrapping the jacket sleeves under his arms, she took one and handed the other to Owl.

Jessica glanced at the horizon where the sun was now touching the land. "It's gonna be close."

"Then we'd better get started."

They dragged Wesley up the hill, Alex pulling one jacket arm and Owl pulling the other. By the time they crested the ridge and started down the other side, the sun was half sunk beyond the horizon.

"Jessica, run ahead," Alex said. "See about getting that door open."

Jessica nodded, then dashed through the shallower snow on the other side of the hill.

Alex, Owl, and Wesley quickly followed. Going downhill was much faster than going up, and they were soon at the bottom.

Hope sprang in Alex's chest as they crossed the last twenty yards to the concrete door. It was close, but they were going to make it.

"Alex," Jessica said. "Something's wrong."

The Director of Engineering was crouched in front of the door. She had her tablet out and was looking at it.

Alex noticed something else odd. The key pad on the concrete door was lit up. "It still has power?"

"Not just that," Jessica said. "The records we have from the NSA have codes for this entrance. None of them are working."

Alex went cold, and it wasn't just from the chill of the wind. "What does that mean?"

"Means someone changed them at some point. Could have been years ago. Maybe during the infection, when the NSA stopped updating their—"

"Does it mean we can't open the door?" Alex said.

"Yes," Jessica said. "I can't open it."

Alex's knees suddenly went weak. They'd been so close.

The parts they needed were right on the other side of that door. It seemed cruel, after everything they'd been through, to be stopped now, when they were so close.

The sun dipped below the horizon. Night had fallen.

Almost immediately, the howling began.

"Why?" Firefly asked in a husky voice. "Why did this happen when we were almost there?"

"Ours is not to question why," Alex muttered.

"Just to be prepared to die," Owl and Firefly finished, their voices hollow.

Alex drew her sword. "Weapons at the ready. Backs to the wall. They'll be able to smell us. It won't be long until they arrive."

Owl and Firefly wordlessly drew their weapons. Jessica stayed where she was, frantically punching numbers into the key pad.

The howls were louder now, coming from every direction.

Alex squeezed her eyes shut and took a deep breath through her nose to steady herself. If she had to die, this was the way she wanted to do it. She wanted to go out like her heroes. Like Drew. Like Simmons.

And she wasn't going out alone. Maybe night vampires were impossibly strong and impossibly fast, but she was taking at least one of those bastards with her.

The howls were so loud they made the ground shake. Any moment now, the vampires would crest that ridge and fall on them like rain.

She turned and looked her comrades in the eyes one at a time. Owl. Firefly. Wesley. Jessica.

"It was an honor to have served with you," she said.

She gripped her sword with both hands and waited, eyes

on the ridge top. This was how it should end. It was how she was always meant to end.

A loud grating sound came from behind her. She spun and then gasped at what she saw.

The concrete door was opening.

"My God, Jessica," Alex whispered. "You did it."

Jessica looked up at her, eyes wide. "That wasn't me."

The door swung open three feet. A man's face appeared in the gap. He was quickly joined by two others.

"Get in here," the man said. "Now!"

43

"GET INSIDE," Alex said to her team, echoing the tall man in the doorway.

The nearby howling shook the ground as Alex and Owl dragged Wesley through the open door. Firefly and Jessica quickly followed.

As soon as they were past the threshold, the tall man in the center said, "Shut the door."

The other two men did as he said. As the door swung closed, Alex saw it had a one-foot steel core inside the concrete on either side of it.

The door shut with a boom. They were safely inside.

For a few long moments, no one spoke. The two groups regarded each other in stunned silence. Alex wasn't sure who was more shocked, her and her team, or these soldiers. A rapid-fire pounding on the door woke them from their introspection. It sounded like a succession of cannonballs was hitting it.

"I can't believe you took out our artillery," the man on the left said. He was the shortest of the three, with close-cropped black hair and glasses. "You led them right to us."

"That's enough, Griffin," the tall one said. He had black hair, too, but his was longer, falling nearly to his shoulders. Not only was he the tallest person in the room, but he was also the broadest. His muscular frame stretched his army-green tee shirt. He pointed to Wesley. "Help me. Let's get them inside."

Alex had thought they *were* inside, but looking down the tunnel, she saw another massive door, this one made completely of steel.

Two of the men, Griffin and the one with the beard, picked up Wesley in a fireman's carry and carefully walked him down the hall. Wesley looked at Alex, wide-eyed. Clearly, he didn't like being carried by these strangers. Alex didn't blame him.

The tall man beckoned them onward. As they walked, he said, "I'm sorry for our confusion. We didn't think there was anybody left out there. Where on Earth did you come from?"

Alex considered how to answer the question. They didn't know anything about these people other than they were heavily armed. If they learned about *New Haven*, they might decide living in the clouds was preferable to living under a mountain and try to take it for their own. She decided to deflect. "We didn't know anyone else was here, either. How many of you are there?"

"Quite a good many," the man said. He stopped and held out his hand. "I'm Jaden."

She shook it. "Alex." She introduced the rest of her team, and Jaden introduced Griffin and Daniel, the bearded man.

They reached the door at the end of the hallway, and Jaden pulled it open. It swung so easily that Alex was surprised to see it was four feet thick and solid steel, perfectly balanced on its hinges.

Jaden paused at the open entrance. "Sorry, but we need to know a little more about you, before we go inside. We're in charge of defending the city, and it would be irresponsible to take you in there without a little more information."

The city? How many people lived under this mountain?

"I understand," Alex said. "We'd do the same."

"You didn't answer my question before. Where'd you come from?"

Alex's mind raced, trying to compose a hybrid of truth and lies that would be enough to get them through that door.

But Jessica spoke before Alex could. "We're from another city. The last city, we thought."

Jaden chuckled. "Same here."

"We don't know anything about you," she continued, "so you'll have to forgive our reluctance to reveal too much about our location until we get to know you better."

Jaden nodded thoughtfully. "I can understand that. I hope we can earn your trust at the same time you're earning ours."

Alex was impressed. Apparently, Jessica had recovered from what she'd seen outside and was back to being the no-nonsense director from *New Haven*. The more Alex got to know the woman, the more she respected her.

"Perhaps you can," Jessica said. "We need your help."

Daniel scoffed. "You don't want to tell us where you're from, but you want our help?"

Jaden held up a hand. "Let's hear them out."

This time Alex spoke. "We came here because our nuclear reactor is damaged. We figured this place would be abandoned and we could get the parts we need from the reactor's control panel here."

Jaden stroked his stubbly chin. "Hmm. We may be able to help you there."

"Jaden, we don't know anything about them," Daniel said in a gruff whisper.

"We know they're human. And they're in trouble. A city without power won't last long. If there's something we can do to help, we're going to do it. Let's go inside."

Alex had the sudden urge to throw her arms around the man's neck and hug him, but she didn't think that would be very professional.

They stepped through the door and entered the city.

It was a wide, brightly lit hallway, not all that different from something they might find in the interior of *New Haven*. A woman walked by and waved at Jaden as she passed. She looked oddly at Alex and the team, but she didn't stop to ask any questions.

"Welcome to Agartha," Jaden said.

Owl laughed.

"What?" Alex said.

"Agartha is a mythological city at the center of the Earth," Owl said.

"The impossible city," Jaden said with a nod. "Let it never be said that we don't have a sense of humor."

Wesley groaned softly. His eyes were unfocused as he stared into the distance. Alex realized he hadn't spoken since before the concrete door opened.

"Jaden, we gotta get this guy to medical," Griffin said.

"Yes. Take him there, and I'll show his friends the reactor control panel."

Firefly looked at Alex. "If they take him to medical, I'm going with them."

Alex didn't like the idea of splitting up, but she wasn't

going to send Wesley off with these people by himself. She nodded.

Firefly followed Griffin and Daniel down the hallway. Jaden headed the opposite direction, Jessica, Owl, and Alex by his side.

They walked through the corridors in silence, Alex not wanting to give up any more information than she needed to. She knew she'd probably have to reveal more about *New Haven* at some point. Would they really give up priceless reactor control panel components without knowing exactly where they were going?

Jaden stayed silent, too, as they walked. Maybe he didn't want to give up too much information, either.

They passed a handful of people. Most of them nodded a greeting to Jaden and looked warily at the visitors without speaking. Alex realized Jaden was probably taking them around the perimeter of the city, where they wouldn't see too much, or come into contact with too many residents.

They reached an unmarked door in an unmarked hallway, and Jaden led them inside and to the reactor control panel. A round man with glasses sat in front of it. He looked up in surprise as they entered.

"Give us a minute, Hank?" Jaden said.

The man nodded and scurried out of the room, his eyes never leaving the strange women.

The control panel was smaller than the one they'd dismantled in Texas. In fact, it looked about the same size as the one on *New Haven*.

Jessica hurried through the room, stopping here and there to inspect parts of the control panel. "This is it," she said in hushed excitement. "These are exactly the parts we need."

"Excellent," Jaden said.

"You'll let us take them?" Alex asked.

"If it means saving lives. Our system is completely redundant, so we can live without the parts."

Jessica looked up sharply. "This is the backup system?"

Jaden nodded.

Alex stepped forward and gently rested her hand on the control panel. Everything they'd been through had been to get to this moment. Simmons and Drew had given their lives to make this happen. Now, finally, their deaths were not in vain. She turned to Jessica. "You're sure these parts will work?"

Jessica didn't take her eyes off the control panel. "It's the same era as ours. Same make, even. Yes, the parts will work."

Alex's eyes filled with tears. She couldn't wait to tell CB. They'd done it. Though it had come at a terrible price, they'd accomplished their mission. *New Haven* was saved.

EPILOGUE

CB SAT in the interrogation room, the arm that was not in a cast, cuffed to the D-hook on the table.

Despite Brian's speculation to the contrary, they'd only waited in the cell for a little over an hour before five guards, each holding a baton at the ready, came for CB. They refused to answer any questions, just telling him that he was needed elsewhere. Then they'd stuck him in the interrogation room where he'd been waiting for the past fifteen minutes.

In the intervening time, CB had calmed down slightly. In the unlikely event that Alex, Drew, Firefly, Owl, Wesley, and Jessica were alive, he was their only chance of rescue. They needed him to be smart, to be cold and logical. The fury still burned in his chest with a fiery heat, but he'd managed to contain it. He promised himself he'd unleash it on those responsible for this madness eventually, but he knew that opportunity was probably a long way off.

The door to the room opened, and Councilman Fleming walked in, flanked by two guards carrying rifles. He wasn't wearing the smug smile CB had expected.

Instead, he looked tired. His face was lined with concern. He sank into the seat across from CB and got right to the point.

"I need your help, Captain."

CB raised an eyebrow at that. He had no idea how to respond. He'd expected Fleming to be holding all the cards, that the councilman would make him beg and swear loyalty for the opportunity to save his team. Instead, Fleming was handing him a poker chip and inviting him to play an honest hand. CB didn't trust himself to speak, so he just waited.

"First," Fleming said, "I need you to know that I didn't want any of this. I know you were close to Councilman Stearns and General Craig. Now Stearns is dead, and Craig is locked up awaiting trial, a fairer one than mine, I assure you."

CB struggled to keep the emotion off his face.

"I take no pleasure in any of the deaths today any more than I would the death of an elderly relative, whose time has simply come. It was a sad necessity, one I worked hard to avoid."

CB couldn't let that comment stand. He leaned forward. "They didn't pass away peacefully in the night. They were murdered. You and your people murdered them."

Fleming nodded sadly. "I certainly understand your perspective, and I'm not going to try to convince you to change your mind. I'm hoping we can still work together."

CB just waited.

"The guards tell me you've been screaming about your team. That they're on a mission and need to be rescued."

"That's right."

"I'm told they headed down to the United States. It'll be dark there now. My understanding is that you're strongly against Resettlement. That you say vampires at night would tear through any human settlement in a matter of hours."

Who had told him that, CB wondered? "That's right."

"Then how is it you believe your team might still be alive?"

"They were headed for NORAD. Jessica Bowen says there's a chance the facility would have held up against the infestation. If they got inside, it's possible they could survive the night."

"I see." Fleming regarded CB for a long moment before speaking again. "I'd like you to put together a team for a rescue mission. You'll have the full support of the government. Any people, any equipment, whatever you want. I'll personally guarantee you use of any of the considerable tools at my disposal."

CB suppressed the hope that was rising within him. There was a catch. There had to be a catch.

"All I need from you," Fleming said, "is your word that you'll continue to lead the GMT after the mission, whether you manage to rescue your team members or not. The GMT's mission will be changing slightly. We'll no longer be asking you to make trips to the surface to retrieve equipment. Instead, we'll be sending you down to prepare the surface for Resettlement."

There it was. The catch. To save his team, he was going to have to sell out his city.

"What do you say, Captain?"

CB considered for only a moment before responding. "I'm in."

———

JADEN LED them out of the reactor control room and up a

winding set of stairs. Alex had a momentary flashback to the stairs in Texas. Jaden bounded up the steps, clearly unconcerned about any potential danger.

Alex exchanged a glance with Owl. She looked as worried as Alex was. The wave of happiness she'd felt at seeing the control panel had quickly subsided, leaving a gnawing sense of concern in its wake. Why were these people so forthcoming and so generous with their equipment? Was it possible they were simply so happy to see other humans that they blindly trusted them? And could people that naive have survived on the surface this long?

Six levels up, Jaden led them through the door and toward an area with a sign that read *Observation Room*.

"I want to show you something," he said, and he darted through the door.

Alex followed, moving cautiously, her hand hovering inches from her pistol.

What she saw when she entered the room was so surprising that she momentarily forgot her concerns.

The room was long and thin, and one long wall was covered in large video monitors.

"Behold the city of Agartha," Jaden said.

The video monitors showed crowded hallways of people bustling to and fro. It showed a large, open area of green, tree and flowers growing under an artificial light, children playing in the grass. It showed a vast cafeteria lined with countless tables, most of them filled with people eating their dinner off trays.

The lone man watching the monitors started to stand, but Jaden held up a hand. "It's okay, Anthony. They're friends."

The man sat back down, but he kept a wary eye on the strangers.

Alex realized the screens didn't just show the interior of the city. Night vision cameras showed vampires climbing the door at the north entrance, futilely pounding on the concrete. Three other monitors showed similar concrete doors. These were clear of vampires. Must be protected by more of those automated guns, Alex assumed.

"What is this place?" she muttered.

"I told you," Jaden said. "It's Agartha. It was an old military installation, and it was one of the last human strongholds during the third wave of the infestation. Those who survived, remained here. Over time, we grew the facility into something more."

She looked at the monitor showing a child playing in the grass among the trees. "I can see that."

"The city's self-sustaining now. We're about ten thousand humans strong."

One-fourth the size of *New Haven*. And all living in this hidden city inside a mountain.

Owl scanned the monitors. "Do you ever leave? Go out into the world for supplies?"

"Not often," Jaden said. "Like I said, we're pretty self-sustaining here."

Alex stared at the people eating, either unaware or unconcerned that they were being watched. How would *New Haven* react to the existence of this place? How would this place react to the existence of *New Haven*? Would they be allies or enemies?

"How'd you do it?" Alex asked. "How'd Agartha survive when everyone else died?"

"I could ask you the same question," he said with a smile. "But I won't. I can see you're not ready to talk about it."

She wasn't going to argue with that. As long as he was

willing to continue giving information while demanding none in return, she was willing to go with it.

"As for us," he said, "this place provided most of the protection. It was built to withstand nuclear war, but it held up just as well against the creatures out there. And when additional protection is needed, they have *us*."

"Us?" Alex asked. Something about the way he emphasized the word was strange. Like *us* was apart from the rest of the city.

"The defenders of Agartha. There are one hundred of us. We take care of the people on the rare occasion something gets past our defenses. And, to Owl's point, we venture out into the world when we have to, gathering supplies by night."

"By night?" Alex asked. There was a sinking feeling in her stomach.

Jaden smiled. "Haven't you figured it out yet? We're vampires. The defenders of Agartha are the last one hundred true vampires, and we're going to save humanity."

DEAR READERS

Thanks so much for reading THE SAVAGE EARTH. We hope you had as much fun with Alex and the team as we did.

Alex and the GMT survived their first sunset on the surface and got the parts they need to save *New Haven*. Now the real challenge begins.

Fleming has control of *New Haven*, CB has agreed to help him, and Alex has just discovered the existence of a city filled with vampires.

Find out what happens next in THE SAVAGE NIGHT. Get your copy at:

http://mybook.to/TheSavageNight

Happy reading,
PT and Jonathan

Made in United States
North Haven, CT
22 September 2022

24451488R00200